"B-girls," said Mendoza . . . "You always get a certain amount of that, any city, Skid Row or environs, any time. The conniving bartenders, and the Mickey Finns, and the suckers rolled for what's on them. But it's getting aggravated lately. And sooner or later——¿cuanto apuestas?——one of the suckers will get an overdose and the whole thing will land in Homicide's lap."

Lt. Luis Mendoza gives up his Kipling for a night-time rendezvous with the sex-sellers who deal in a new commodity——instant death.

"If by now you don't know just how good a crime reporter Dell Shannon is, you don't belong in the mystery league."

—Dorothy B. Hughes

RAIN
WITH
VIOLENCE

DELL SHANNON

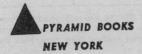

PYRAMID BOOKS
NEW YORK

RAIN WITH VIOLENCE

A PYRAMID BOOK

Published by arrangement with William Morrow and Company, Inc.

William Morrow edition published 1967

Pyramid edition published February 1971

Printed in the United States of America

PYRAMID BOOKS are published by Pyramid Publications
A Division of The Walter Reade Organization, Inc.
444 Madison Avenue, New York, New York 10022, U.S.A.

For every inch that is not fool is rogue.
> —William Drummond,
> *Absalom and Achitophel*

He who deals with blockheads will have much need of brains.
> —old Spanish proverb

Chapter 1

THEY met where they'd met a few times before, at a little coffee shop called Jean's on Sunset Boulevard not far from Highland. It was clean and quiet: decorated in very pseudo Olde Englishe, it didn't attract the casual male trade, and didn't mind customers sitting over pots of tea and sandwiches. Not that the older girl, Dorothy Swanson, who arrived first, meant to order tea; after four years in California, she'd discovered that Americans simply don't know how to make it properly.

She took a booth at the back of the little dim place and ordered coffee, waiting for the other girl. She'd about had California, she thought; like the many other English girls working here, mostly as children's nurses, she'd found the money good, but after you got used to the different atmosphere and the climate, well, there were other things than sunshine, after all. She got homesick sometimes for Winscombe and the quiet Cotswold hills. She sipped coffee and thought she might just tell Mrs. Spain that this temporary job she'd just taken would be her last here: she was going home.

Then the other girl slipped into the booth across the table from her and said, "I missed the twelve o'clock bus, am I late? I *am* sorry, Dot. Dot, I want to *ask* you—" she paused as the waitress came up, and ordered coffee and a bacon and tomato sandwich. "Dot—"

The older girl asked, "How's the job going?" She was feeling exasperated about Carole Leslie, about her own (quite unnecessary, reason told her) feeling of responsibility for the other girl and her naïveté. And nobody, Dorothy reminded herself ruefully, to blame but herself. If Carole hadn't gone to school with Dorothy's younger sister, and inevitably heard about the wonderful time Dot was having in America—if her mother, a friend of Dot's mother, hadn't written asking her to "keep an eye on Carole"—if she hadn't been raised to have some responsibility—Well, there it was.

"Oh, I'm getting fed up with it." Carole had very blonde hair cut short in a halo effect, and a peaches-and-cream skin, and very blue eyes, and was currently addicted to shocking-pink nail varnish and lipstick, of which Dorothy disapproved. Carole was nineteen. "I want to tell you— But what about your new one?" It was an obvious effort at surface politeness. "You said it was only temp'rary—"

"Their regular's off," said the older girl absently. "It's only for a couple of months. The twins are sweet—"

"Oh, twins, how darling. How old?"

"Nearly two—a boy and a girl." The waitress came back with Carole's sandwich and Dorothy ordered one to match. "But, Carole, I want to hear about yours. These Newhouses—the last time you said—"

"Um," said Carole through a bite of her sandwich. "I've got to *tell* you, Dot, I think there's something funny going on. *Queer,* I mean. I don't like it—I mean, any of it, not just the queerness but the job. I thought it'd be a *change* anyway—you know, after those horrible Miller children on the first job Mrs. Spain got for me—but even then it sounded a little funny—companion-maid—because she must be at least thirty-five. I told you. I mean, for a while it was all right, she's quite pretty and likes to talk about clothes and lipstick

8

and so on, just like anybody, but after a while she's just horribly boring. I must have heard about everything that's happened to her since she was *born,* and she says the most awful things about her husband and he's really a very nice man—he reminds me a little of Daddy, actually—and how she inherited all the money so unexpectedly from this old uncle she hardly remembered—I told you that. And I can't say it's hard *work,* there isn't really anything for me to do, getting her lunch and mostly just listening to her—she doesn't even knit or anything—but, Dot, I—I think there's something *funny.*" Carole put down her sandwich, her forehead wrinkling.

"How d'you mean?" The little Carole had told her a couple of weeks ago, Dorothy had thought it sounded strange, too. A queer sort of job. Possibly Mrs. Spain at the agency had thought so too.

"Well, not just all that I've been talking about. Even funnier. It's not as if I *tried* to listen to what they're saying, honestly, you know I wouldn't. But she'd asked me to make coffee and I was just bringing it in and couldn't help hearing—the other one, the brother, he comes around a lot, and— Oh, well, not a *lot,* I s'pose he's got a job too, but oftener than seems— Or he's ringing her up. Days, when Mr. Newhouse is at work. She said she used to keep after Mr. Newhouse to quit his job and go traveling with her, now she's got all the money, but he won't."

"Money can go as easy as it comes," said Dorothy.

"I s'pose. Anyway, it wasn't as if I tried to listen, Dot, I couldn't help hearing—just as I was bringing the coffee in, last Saturday afternoon it was, he was there, and he was saying, 'We could have fun together, Evelyn, if you were shut of that slowpoke,' and she said back, 'And you've got reasons to want to get shut of him permanently, haven't you?'—sort of thoughtful she was—and he said, kind of quick, 'We'll be in it together,' and then they stopped talking when I came

9

in. It just sounded funny, Dot. D'you suppose they're going to go off together and she'll divorce Mr. Newhouse?"

It sounded a little peculiar to the older girl too. "I don't know—but you don't like the job much, do you?"

"There's not enough to do. And she's paying me two hundred dollars a month, nearly seventy *pounds*—but it's so boring, Dot, I'd rather even have some horrible children to take care of again. I like Mr. Newhouse but he's only there evenings and sometimes he goes off to his chess club. That's another thing, Tuesday nights he goes out and the other one—the brother—he comes then to see *her,* the last three weeks anyway, and they shut the door to the lounge and—"

"I should think you'd better just leave when this month's up, and see Mrs. Spain," said Dorothy. "It sounds as if something's up, not very nice, anyway."

"That's what I thought."

"Where'd you go on Sunday?"

"Oh—to the beach. With Randy."

"Randy Bearley? That boy from the garage? I don't think he's a very good type, Carole. I—" The other girl hesitated. Sometimes Carole could be stubborn, and the more you said—

"Randy's all right." Carole sipped coffee. "Shall we go see a film or something? I don't know what's on—"

"Actually I've got some shopping to do." Dorothy looked at her watch. Two o'clock already, and on Thursdays she was supposed to be back by five-thirty or so, not that the new woman seemed very strict—nice she was, and ever so pretty, too, with red hair—but there was Mum's birthday present to shop for and if it hadn't been for feeling a little responsible for Carole, she'd never have wasted this time meeting her for lunch. She got out her coin purse, looking at the bill. "If you want to come along—"

"Um," said Carole cheerfully through the last of

her sandwich. "Love to, dear. All these wonderful shops." She beamed at Dorothy, wiping her mouth carefully and instantly rummaging in her bag for lipstick. "And I think you're right, it's a funny sort of place and I'll just leave it. Mrs. Spain says there's heaps of jobs, and I've got a little money saved. There was something else I heard him say that sounded queer—the brother—I couldn't make out what it meant, but anyway he doesn't think much of Mr. Newhouse either, and what I say, it doesn't look right, him coming, you know, and I tell you, Dot, I don't sort of feel *comfortable* about it."

"I don't blame you," said Dorothy. At least Carole still knew what respectability meant; she could be a little fool some ways, and in the six months she'd been here, Dorothy had worried a bit over a couple of the boys she'd taken up with, but she seemed to have some sense anyway, about this. And Dorothy would rather have gone shopping for Mum's birthday present by herself, without the other girl's aimless chatter to distract her; and after all Carole had to learn to stand on her own feet and judge people for herself, but she could hardly tell her so right out. That Randy, a low type if she had eyes for one—but good looking, and Carole *was* only nineteen, and she did feel a bit responsible, Carole coming from practically the next village. She put her coin purse away and brought out a note pad.

"You haven't got the address," she said. "Where I am now. And the telephone. You'd better. And look, dear, if anything else funny happens or—well, anything that bothers you, you just call me." She wrote down the address and phone number, pushed the torn-off scrap of paper across the table.

Carole was carefully blotting shocking-pink lipstick on a corner of paper napkin. "Oh, it'll be all right. I'll just say I'm leaving when the month's up—she can't tie me up, after all, but thanks, Dot."

The exact change left on the little tray, with a careful twenty-five-cent tip, they slid out of the booth and started for the door. When the waitress came to clear the table, she pursed her lips sourly at the tip, and swept the little débris off—crumpled paper napkins, crumby plates, used cups—onto her large tray. Into the big refuse barrel in the kitchen, along with the paper napkins, went a little torn-off piece of paper bearing a line of writing in a slanted backhand—

Mrs. Mendoza, 311 Rayo Grande Ave.,
Hollywood—377-4684

" 'But a fool must follow his natural bent, Even as you and I,' " said Mendoza, settling into his desk chair with a grunt. "These louts. These *punks*. Or am I just getting bad tempered as age creeps up on me?"

"Most of 'em," said Detective Grace in his soft voice, "wouldn't be where they are if they weren't fools."

"Oh, granted," said Mendoza, shutting his eyes. "Only I sometimes get very tired of dealing with them, Jase."

Higgins said nothing, just lit a cigarette and blew out smoke with a long sigh. They had just had a session with one of the fools. The louts they had perennially to deal with, incapable—or unwilling—thinking of five minutes ahead, who went through life doing what comes naturally and reacting with pained surprise or indignation when natural retribution caught up with them. This one, a William Roudybush by name, had a long pedigree of little offenses—D. and D., purse snatching, petty theft—and had just, quite inadvertently, got into the big time because he'd got into a brawl in a bar down on First Street and knocked the other participant down against the bar, effectively cracking his skull.

It would be brought in involuntary manslaughter

and he'd get maybe seven years, but they'd had to do some work on it all the same.

"Well, hell, I was drunk," he'd said. "I didn't go to kill nobody. I was drunk, thass all. I dint even know the guy. You ain't gonna do anything to me just for that, are you?"

Sometimes Mendoza got tired dealing with all the louts. But there they were, and it was the job to be done.

So far, this November—thank God, a November which had remembered that it was supposed to be an autumn month, and had brought gray skies and cool temperatures and a grudging half inch of rain to Southern California—so far, L.A.P.D. Homicide had had its share of louts. A hopped-up kid hunting money to support the habit shooting a liquor-store clerk. A couple of gang rumbles, with two teenagers knifed to death, over the other side of the Southern Pacific yards. An elderly woman beaten to death in the course of a robbery—they hadn't any leads on that at all and it looked dead: would probably get filed away in Pending. They had had a straightforward suicide by gas over on Fourth Street, with the note left, and then the fellow who strangled his wife because she'd been chasing around—Palisser was still busy on the paperwork on that, and Piggott and Glasser were out poking around trying to turn up whoever had (probably also inadvertently) fatally fractured the skull of the druggist on San Pedro Street while ransacking the place for narcotics.

Sergeant Lake looked in the door and asked, "Like some coffee? There was a new call while you were busy with the punk—Art went out on it."

Mendoza muttered, "*¿Pues y que?*" but Higgins asked with faint curiosity what it sounded like.

Lake shrugged. "Woman dead, all I can tell you. Pomeroy Avenue, over the other side of the San Berdu freeway." The phone rang out on his desk in the ante-room and he departed.

Mendoza yawned, and Lake came back and said, "It's Art, Lieutenant. On the phone." Mendoza picked up the outside phone.

"So what've you got?"

"Rape and murder, looks like," said Hackett in his ear. "I want the full team, Luis. It's sort of confused. Kid went to the neighbors and said there was a bad man came and hurt Mommy, Mommy fell down and the bad man hit her and the kid was scared and ran away. You know kids and time—no telling. Neighbor—a Mrs. Farber—went up to the house to see. And called us. All I've got so far, Mommy is Mrs. May Gerner, husband's a bartender somewhere, three kids from seven down, and the internes say she was probably raped and strangled. Looks that way, anyway. At least she's dead. Bainbridge will say how. Internes say, very provisionally, about an hour dead."

"No rest for the wicked," said Mendoza. He glanced out the window. Five-forty of a November day, and dark, yes, but an hour ago, only the deepening-toward-dusk of fall in Southern California. Pomeroy Avenue—one of the shabby old residential streets of downtown L.A., hardly a slum, even if the streets were old and tired down there—and the old houses cheek-by-jowl, forty foot lots: an assault, rape and murder that time and place? Well, it happened, unlikely as it seemed. "All right, we'll get on it. I'll come and have a look." He told Sergeant Lake to rout out the lab men, and got up. "We might as well all go. Fill out the day nicely."

Palliser came in and laid a report in triplicate on the desk. "That finishes that one off. Don't tell me—" as Mendoza took up his hat—"we've got a new one at this time of day."

"What else?" Higgins yawned. "What does time matter to the punks?"

Palliser looked apprehensive. "You want me?" he asked fearfully.

Mendoza grinned at him. "I'll let you off this time. Go home, *novio*." Palliser had a bride of two months waiting at home on Tamarind Avenue. "You did some overtime last night. . . . Damn, by the time we get there—I suppose I'd better call Alison." Sergeant Lake was already dialing, and held out the phone to him as Higgins resettled his tie and Grace reached for his own hat. *"Hermosa?* Me. I'll be—"

"Late," said Alison. "Yes. They are keeping you busy, aren't they? All right. I'll expect you when I see you."

"Everything serene? How's the nursemaid working out, satisfactory?"

"Oh, yes," said Alison. "Quite all right, though *not* like Máiri."

"Naturalmente." Their paragon, Máiri MacTaggart, was only temporarily lost to them: her sister had broken her hip and Máiri was dutifully departed to nurse her —("It'll not be long, mind you, if I know Janet she'll be on the mend in no time, it takes more than that to down the likes of us permanent, *achara*—but the two of us being sole alone, you can see it's my plain duty, and these things are sent to try us—I'm wondering now, there was this woman Janet spoke about, an agency like for foreign girls working here, English mostly and though it goes against the grain to say it, *achara,* English being English as we both well know, still some of them a sight better trained and willing to work—and it's only temporary if I know Janet—")

"I won't be late. I don't think," said Mendoza.

"Which I have heard before. It's only creamed chipped beef and saffron rice," said Alison. "And odds and ends. It'll keep. Go look at your latest corpse."

They went and looked at it. For a few minutes, before Mendoza said the internes could take it away for expert examination elsewhere, by the irascible Dr. Bainbridge. It wasn't the most unsavory corpse they had ever looked at, but no corpse is ever very pleasant. It was a young woman, who had been a rather pretty young woman, a lot of curly dark hair and a pert turned-up nose and a nice figure, dead and bloody on the floor of her own living room. A room neat and clean, in an old but proudly maintained house.

The neighbor, Mrs. Farber, from two houses down the street, was voluble, as the lab men Marx and Horder filed by there on the front porch with their little bags.

"It just don't seem possible—houses so close here and all—and I never heard a thing, of course there was kids out playing on the street, kind of noisy, but even so— And the Weavers next door, they both work and they wouldn't—but there's Mrs. Pitts right next door, you'd think somebody would have— A nice girl she was, pretty strict with the children, a good wife 'n' mother like they say—kids always nice and polite, they're nice people. I mean, you can tell—we don't know Mr. Gerner so good, naturally he's at work and not around, but Mrs. Gerner, she was *nice*—Just don't seem possible she's *dead*. Like *that*. *Killed*. I mean, a lot of people around and all, that time of an afternoon." She was a thin middle-aged woman in a faded blue cotton house dress, and in the chill breeze of evening she clutched a torn sweater round her shoulders, shivering. "I didn't think nothing at all, little Bobby Gerner coming over—he's the same age as our Kenny, I oughta say, maybe, I take care of my daughter's two, she works and her husband's in the service—Kenny's just turned five, and him and Bobby play together—only when I come out to bring the baby in, he says about this bad man hurting his mommy, and I thought —well, you know how kids make things up, but I— Beg pardon? Oh, my, I couldn't say at all when I first saw Bobby in the yard—maybe four-thirty, a

16

little later—I don't know. It was only when he said that—and I thought I'd just better *see*—and I went up here to the Gerners', and the door was open and that poor soul just laying there, all the blood—"

Sergeant George Higgins looked at May Gerner, before they took her away, with an unexpected little secret pang. May Gerner, lying there spread-eagled for the lab men to run their chalk-marks around, and the autopsy surgeon later to lay his knife into so methodically, reminded him remotely of Mary Dwyer. Mary Dwyer, widow of that good cop Bert Dwyer whom he had liked. Mary Dwyer who probably wouldn't have the most remote intention of marrying another cop, however desperately (and secretly) he might love her —and in a kind of different way the kids Stevie and Laura, and even the little Scottie, Brucie. This May Gerner had the same matt-white skin as Mary, and the unexpectedly gray eyes, and Higgins had seen a lot of corpses but hers was a very pathetic corpse, lying there on the worn beige carpet with the bag of groceries dropped and scattered all around her at random.

He cleared his throat and said, "She'd just got home from the market. Or she'd have put all this away— stuff to go in the refrigerator, the freezer."

Mendoza grunted. "Yes. Somebody on the block must have noticed her coming and going, to pinpoint the time."

"Mrs. Farber can't say," contributed Hackett, shifting his bulk from one foot to the other. "She was in the kitchen before she went to bring the baby in, didn't see Mrs. Gerner walk past. She does say she's pretty sure Mrs. Gerner usually shopped at the nearest market up on Marengo. Most people around here do. We'll ask the other neighbors—and at the market."

"Yes," said Mendoza. And Bainbridge would say, but it looked like the rape-murder. She'd had on a blue cotton dress, the expectable underwear: that was scattered around her, the torn nylon panties, the half-slip,

17

the dress itself ripped down the button-front. She lay half on her side, head twisted, legs spread, and all around her was the blood and the spilled groceries, a package of frozen peas, frozen veal cutlets, instant mashed potatoes, cereal, sugar, a carton of Marlboro cigarettes, a half-gallon of milk, margarine, a quart-bottle of orange juice, a cellophane-wrapped package of lamb chops, a jar of mayonnaise— "What about the husband?"

"Mrs. Farber doesn't know where he works, just that he usually gets home about six. She thinks." Higgins was by then out asking questions of the other neighbors.

"Helpful," said Mendoza. "He should be arriving any minute. Nice for him."

"Somebody must have noticed something," said Hackett, "in a neighborhood like this. As Mrs. Farber says, people all around. And kids playing on the street."

"Don't count on it, Arturo," said Mendoza. "The crude ones are so often the tough ones."

"Oh, don't I know it," said Hackett resignedly, smoothing his sandy hair.

Just, probably, another of the louts. Doing what came naturally. Whether they'd ever catch up with him—

Carole Leslie came into the big, expensive apartment on Sunset Plaza at six-fifty. She had a key. There were voices in the living room; she couldn't help hearing what they said. The door didn't make much noise, and the place was deeply carpeted.

"But, Harry, if anybody ever found out—"

"Nobody'll find out. Nobody'll know. That's just *it*. It's your money, after all. We'll be rid of him and that's that, see. Who's going to know? Like he's a drag on both of us, no? And who's to miss him? Who does he know, who gives a damn about him? And then—"

"But, Harry—"

"It's no sweat," he said boastfully, optimistically.

"But if anybody——" Her petulant voice rose.

"It'll be O.K. You just do like I say."

It sounded awfully funny, Carole thought. The way she'd said to Dot. What did he *mean?* Mr. Newhouse? That one hanging around. And Mr. Newhouse nice, really, if he was sort of ordinary and dull. If there was anything—well, not quite right—she didn't want to be mixed up with it. Maybe she ought to leave right away, but it'd mean half this month's salary——

Chapter 2

THE HUSBAND, Bill Gerner, arrived about a quarter past six, simultaneously with the oldest boy, Ray, who'd been playing at a friend's down the block. The husband's reaction was normal—surprise, grief, indignation— and by all that showed so far the husband didn't come into this; but they'd check him out anyway. One of the neighbors took the children in—they heard for the first time about then that the baby, safe and serene in a Taylor Tot, had been found beside the body and taken away by Mrs. Farber—and now there was just a lot of normal routine to do on it.

At six-forty the night men, Detective Bob Schenke and Sergeant Nick Galeano, arrived, so Mendoza and Grace went home. Higgins elected to hang around awhile; as a bachelor he hadn't anyone waiting for him.

Mendoza drove up to Rayo Grande Avenue in Hollywood, and was pounced on by Sheba before he took his hat off. He said automatically, *"Monstruoso,"* and kissed Alison. "I said I wouldn't be late. Just a new corpse at the end of the day."

"I waited, but another ten minutes and I'd have been having dinner over a book. They are keeping you busy, *amante*. It won't take a minute to get everything on the table. You want a drink?" Alison headed briskly for the kitchen.

"Nada. Where are the offspring?" He wandered after her.

"Having their baths, thank goodness. Yes, Dorothy's fine, I guess, but I just wish she wasn't so—so—well, English," said Alison. "Yes ma'am and no ma'am. She's good with the twins, though—no nonsense—and at least she's talking English to them all the while. And she likes the cats. You might bring the asparagus." Alison departed for the dining room with the big casserole held before her.

He was hungry; he hadn't taken time for a decent lunch. Replete, he held out his cup for more coffee and groped for cigarettes. "I do get so tired of the louts," he said, thumbing his gold lighter. "It gets monotonous."

"What was the new case?"

"A couple of new ones. No shop-talk. Monotonous, *Dios.* The louts," said Mendoza sleepily, "of both sexes, come to think. I ran into Percy Andrews this morning, down in Robbery—had to see Goldberg on that liquor store shooting, he thinks it may be one of his old pros turned violent. Which remains to be seen. Technically it—this other bit—does belong to Vice, so it's Percy's own little problem, but the way things are going I wouldn't doubt that Fate may hand it over to me before long. Knockout drops being so damned uncertain."

"Knockout drops—"

"B-girls," said Mendoza, sliding down comfortably in his chair and emitting a long stream of smoke. "You always get a certain amount of that, any city, Skid Row or environs, any time. The conniving bartenders, and the Mickey Finns, and the suckers rolled for what's on them. But it's getting aggravated lately, Percy says. Twenty and thirty a night by what they can guess, down on Main—San Pedro. A lot of 'em don't lay a complaint—they feel like fools, which they are, of course—but some do, they've had the innocent young servicemen passing through and such—and the squad-cars have picked some of 'em out of alleys. Percy thinks it could be a regular ring operating. And sooner or later—¿cuanto apuestas?—one of the suckers will get an overdose or turn out to have a weak heart and the whole thing will land in Homicide's lap."

"No bets," said Alison with a smile. "It could happen, all right."

Presently she carried the dishes out to the kitchen and Mendoza settled down in the living room with *Puck of Pook's Hill*. Like everyone else holding membership in that rather exclusive coterie of fanatical Kiplingphiles, he had discovered that Kipling can be reread practically ad infinitum and always present some new and admirable facet.

Apparently the temporary nursemaid was worth her salary, however English; there wasn't a peep out of the twins. Bast, that settled middle-aged matron, was dozing on the credenza; Nefertite and Sheba were sound asleep with their arms around each other on the sectional, and El Señor appeared from nowhere to occupy Mendoza's lap.

Alison shook her head at *Puck of Pook's Hill*—she would never understand Mendoza's sudden madness in regard to Kipling—and went off to write letters.

Higgins stayed on down on Pomeroy Avenue to lend a hand to Schenke and Galeano. By seven-thirty they were building up some more of the story, talking to neighbors, to the husband. Gerner worked at the Black and White Bar and Grill up on Olympic Boulevard: he was half-owner, with a partner. Normally he'd have gone back for a spell of duty from eight to midnight, and Higgins amiably offered to go and break the news to his partner.

The partner, Hadley Willetts, was upset: he'd known May Gerner, the two couples were old friends. He was so upset that he closed the bar and grill and said he was going right over to stay with Bill: a terrible thing,

22

these damn punks on the loose and respectable citizens killed and robbed right and left, and sure he knew the cops tried, but there just weren't enough of them, a city this size. A *terrible* thing, as nice a woman as ever—

Higgins upset him some more by asking questions about Gerner, and Willetts said this and that about suspicious damn cops, but in the end—what with the evidence at the scene and what the neighbors said— Higgins was satisfied that Gerner was clear; he'd been on duty at the bar from one, when it opened, to five-thirty, visible all the time.

The rest of the story they'd got from the various people on the block was fairly clear. Several people had noticed May Gerner walking up Pomeroy Avenue, and one woman over on Lord Street had talked with her, that afternoon. Mrs. Jean White, who lived on Lord Street, had known her, and May Gerner had stopped to chat. She'd had little Bobby with her, and the baby in the Taylor Tot. Mrs. White hadn't noticed her coming back; but it had been about three o'clock when she passed, on her way to the market, and she'd said she had just a few things to pick up, so she wouldn't have been long at the market. They could reason, maybe three-thirty when she started home.

The market people were vague. It was a big market, and a fairly busy one. One cashier remembered her being there, but couldn't say what time except "the middle of the afternoon."

Mrs. White and everybody else they talked to, shocked and indignant, said it was a quiet street and nothing so terrible as this had ever happened before. Everybody was surprised that nobody had heard May scream, because she must have had a chance to do that.

"Though it could be," said Jean White to Higgins thoughtfully, "that even if she did, the racket that city crew made covered it up. They've been out there for three or four days, just at the intersection of Lord and Pomeroy, I don't know whether it's the sewer or the gas or what, but they're using those pneumatic drills and you know what they sound like. . . . No, I don't really remember hearing the drills about that time, but it's off and on every few minutes—hardly hear yourself think—and it just could be—"

That, of course, was quite possible.

"The way I see it going," said Galeano when they foregathered back at the Gerner porch about eight o'clock, "is, he must have followed her into the house. Maybe been waiting for her—maybe he'd spotted her before, or for all we know he could have followed her from the market. Gerner says she wouldn't have left the house unlocked, and it's a fact the back door was locked and bolted. So she unlocks the front door, and it takes her a minute or so to maneuver the Taylor Tot in—we've all seen women shopping with babies, she'd have had the bag of groceries balanced on the back of the Taylor Tot—God, what a silly name—and in the living room she'd have put down her purse, and started to pick up the groceries to carry them out to the kitchen. That's when he grabbed her—from behind most likely. After walking in behind her. But why nobody noticed—"

"Maybe natural," said Higgins. "Look what we heard. This woman out in the back yard, that one fixing a casserole for dinner, some more out to market themselves. The kids wouldn't take any notice of a grown-up. And what you got out of Bobby—" he sighed.

"Yeah," said Galeano, and sighed too. As the least likely of three tough homicide cops to scare a five-year-old, soft-spoken Galeano had tackled Bobby, under Gerner's vigilant eye. Bobby, confused and scared already by all the commotion and adult emotion around, told a fairly coherent story as far as it went. He said—with repetition, prodding, and a few translations of his five-year-old English—that he'd run in the house ahead of Mommy when she unlocked the door, and gone to his room to get his real cowboy gun she wouldn't let him take to the store, and then he heard Mommy yell so he came back and there was a bad man hitting Mommy and he was scared so he ran out the front door again and went down to Kenny's house and when Kenny's grandma came out he told her about the bad man.

How did you ask a five-year-old to describe the bad man?

Maybe the lab would turn up something. Latent prints or something. Time would tell.

There wasn't any more to do on it tonight, for them. See what the lab work showed.

Schenke and Galeano went back to headquarters, and Higgins went home to his bachelor apartment on Bronson Avenue.

When Mendoza came into the office on Friday morning, to find Sergeant Rory Farrell sitting in for Lake—it being Lake's day off—Galeano was hanging around waiting for him. Higgins, Hackett and Landers came in on Mendoza's heels, and Galeano said, "You'd better all hear—you might be working this one for a while, all the deadly routine. I never *saw* such a thing. Such a *thing*. Those poor damn women—" he shook his head. "A mere typed report couldn't cover it, reason I stayed."

"*Another* new one?" said Hackett. "What?"

"God," said Galeano. "We got the call just after midnight. Albion Street—just below the park there—shabby little street, well, what else have we got down here mostly, but also mostly the respectable citizens. It was the man next door called us, but most of the neighbors had heard the row and came out. God. You wouldn't believe it. It's an old house, once pretty well built, and I know a little about doors and locks—a good solid door, inch and a half thick, and a good lock even if it was old, *and* a bolt. A regular steel bolt. He must be a Samson, I'm telling you. He kicked it in— the whole damn door—the bolt's wrenched right off its hinges—you can see the prints of his heels on the door, for God's sake. And these two poor damned old women—sisters living alone, both widows, one eighty, one eighty-three—both beaten to death. Two frail little old women, and it looked—" Galeano swallowed—"as if he'd just picked 'em up and torn them apart. Almost literally. With his bare hands. Well, we didn't come across a weapon, but the doctor'll say about that. And besides that, it's maybe a little offbeat other ways."

Mendoza took the overnight report with a grimace. "Thanks so much. Why offbeat? Another of the violent louts."

Galeano yawned. "That far I'll go with you. And maybe hopped up. But why should anybody pick that house, the two inoffensive old ladies? And the fact is that there's nothing missing from the house. That we could spot. None of the neighbors knew them very well, and couldn't say. But I've got eyes, and I've been a cop some time. We found over ten G's in cold cash in paper bags in the closet, and what looks like a small fortune in diamonds. Untouched."

"*¡Vaya por Dios!*" said Mendoza mildly.

"Now that *is* a little offbeat," said Detective Grace's gentle voice behind him..

"Say it again. Have fun, boys," and Galeano took himself off.

Mendoza read the report, Higgins and Hackett starting out for Albion Street and Grace for Pomeroy Avenue. Piggott and Glasser came in with the latest report on their pokings around on the dead druggist, which amounted to nothing.

"And never will," said Piggott disgustedly. "The lab turned up nothing. It might have been any junkie in L.A. It'll go in Pending eventually, why not now?"

Mendoza constitutionally disapproved of throwing

cases in Pending. But he admitted they'd done about all they could on this one. That kind did come along. Landers came in, handed over the last triplicate report on the suicide, and—having been off the day before—was briefed on what had come up since. "Either a feast or a famine," he said philosophically. "Which one shall I go work?"

"You may as well come along with me," said Mendoza, "and hear about Samson." As they went out Sergeant Farrell was answering the phone and beckoning Piggott urgently. There was usually something going on in the Homicide office of any big-city police force, if it was only the vagrant dead of *vino* or a heart attack.

Albion Street was only about four blocks long. It was a street of old houses, a narrow street, not any shabbier than many down here. The house which murder had visited last night was in the middle of the block: there was a mobile lab truck parked in front of it now, and Hackett's scarlet Barracuda was parked across the street. As Mendoza pulled the Ferrari up behind it, they saw Higgins' big burly shouldered figure down the block on a front porch, and Hackett ringing the doorbell at a house on this side of the street.

There was a man sitting in an ancient rocking chair on the front porch of the house next to that where the lab truck stood. He regarded Mendoza and Landers with interest as they came across the street, and hopped up spryly to accost them.

"You detectives—more detectives? How-do. I'm Mick Frawley. I guess I knew Mis' Prothero and Mis' Turner as well as anybody did along here. Kept themselves kind of private, know what I mean, and that's O.K. by me, live and let live like they say, but like I was always telling 'em, not so young as they were and accidents can happen to anybody and there might come a time you appreciate your neighbors. Don't do no harm to be friendly, ain't that so? Those two poor old ladies living alone, on the pension I guess, what else—"

Which was interesting, of course. Mick Frawley as open as day; so, the nearest neighbor quite unaware of the hoarded cash and diamonds. Mendoza regarded Mr. Frawley with interest too. A scrawny, wrinkled little man with cheerful blue eyes and an inquisitive long nose: a shabby little man in an old pair of tan chino pants and a white shirt without a tie.

"—And Lordy God, whoever'd have thought they'd end *such* a way? And how in hell's name you'd ever find the guy did it I don't know, but then I ain't a detective. Retired plumber. I talked to another one last night—one of the detectives came. Eyetalian feller, very nice feller. These drunks," said Mr. Frawley, and clicked his tongue disparagingly. "And I ain't saying I don't like a glass or two of beer or maybe a little nip of whiskey, no harm, but these lushes pouring it down till they don't know January from Tuesday, well, what can you expect? Not that I believe in prohibition and that. Human nature like they say. But some of 'em, you know better 'n me, I suppose, it turns 'em what they call berserk. It was one like that, I told the Eyetalian feller."

"Why did you—" Mendoza began, and was overridden by Mr. Frawley, who was enjoying himself. What Mr. Frawley had to say would be in Schenke's report, anyway, but in somewhat less colorful terms.

"On account I saw him and heard him, didn't I? Waked me up out of a sound sleep—Lordy God, what a racket—this is sort of a quiet street, general rule, backwater like they say—suits me, but before I lost my wife God-rest-her-soul a matter o' twelve years back, she was forever sayin' it'd run down and we oughta move, but I lived here thirty-four years and it suits me O.K.—nothing fancy, so what's wrong with that, I got my house all paid for and I don't owe a dime to nobody. Anyway, there's this terrible racket—shouting and banging and all—and I wake up, and go look out the window. See, my bedroom window's on the same side as Mis' Prothero's house next door—it belonged to her, Mis' Turner just came to live there when her husband passed on—and right away I think, some drunks, only it was only one—at least I only *seen* one man," said Mr. Frawley with scrupulous objectivity. "On the front porch next door. Mis' Prothero's house. And I—pardon? oh, I told the ones last night as much as I could 'bout that, what I saw of him, a biggish feller he was, what I could see, I never saw him close—but he was kicking at the front door there and pounding with his hands, and yelling at the top of his voice—and *that* was the funniest part of it all—drunk as a skunk, any fool could tell that—and yelling something about wanting to see a Frankie Colson or Holton or some such name—"

It was, when Mendoza looked, all in Schenke's report. Something a trifle offbeat you could say. Frankie Colson or Holton. Dalton? Folsom? Jolson? Poulson? Mr. Frawley shook his head and couldn't say. Nobody with a name anything like that lived around here, he said, and he ought to know. There were some Ralstons down the block, but he didn't think that was the name the drunk had shouted. And he'd slipped on his shoes and gone to the living room and called the police, a drunk annoying two old ladies like that, and then he'd got dressed decent and started over there—couple of other neighbors had been waked up too and Jay Burnson across the street came out—but that drunk, he'd been fast and mean, and just those few minutes, there was the two old ladies laying there—"Make you sick," said Mr. Frawley. "What he'd done to 'em. And no reason—These drunks."

And all the hoarded cash and the diamonds untouched. Nobody knowing?

Mendoza left Landers there to lend a hand to Hackett and Higgins, and found a public phone a block away and called the office. "What was the new one?" he asked.

"Matt went out on it—fellow dropped dead in a restaurant on Seventh. Looked like a heart attack."

More paper work. The routine kept coming along. Mendoza drove over to Pomeroy Avenue. He ought to get Bainbridge's autopsy report on May Gerner sometime this afternoon, he reflected.

He spotted Detective Jason Grace's new car—new to him—parked at the corner of Lord Street, as he turned the corner: the electric-blue Elva *(she goes,* he thought) looking even more insolent and Roman-nosed than usual, in this neighborhood. Ostensibly hunting for cheap transportation, the ordinarily conservative and practical Grace had been seized with midsummer madness on beholding the Elva. . . . Hadn't somebody, thought Mendoza vaguely, said that to twentieth-century man the status automobile replaced as a symbol the blood horse of another time? Very likely.

He parked the Ferrari (the only reason Mendoza drove a Ferrari was that he believed in buying the very best on the market and driving it until it died of senility—prestige had nothing whatever to do with it) and stood looking up the block. There was a dirty white Chevy Corvair sitting in front of the Gerner house. Grace came out of the house four doors down and stopped to light a cigarette. Tossing away the match, he saw Mendoza and jaywalked across the street to join him.

"I kind of think," he said, "I'd like to talk to the kid Bobby again. Slow and gentle. He just might remember more about the bad man than Nick got out of him." He drew strongly on his cigarette. "Kids," he said. "Sometimes they're smarter than grown-ups think."

"And if anybody could sweet-talk it out of him, you're the boy," said Mendoza.

Grace's coffee-colored face, with its neat moustache as precise as Mendoza's, split in a brief grin. "Flattering me again. I could try. Kids I don't know so much about. . . . His sister's there."

"Gerner's?"

"Mmh. Seems she took the kids, last night, and now she wants to pack some clothes for 'em. Seeing as the lab boys had been over the house, when she showed I said it was O.K. for her to go in. Suppose I should have checked with you."

"*Non importa.* Did you get anything from her?"

"I don't think she liked me much," said Grace amusedly. "Said she was in a hurry, she was paying a baby-sitter. She lives in Monterey Park, I got the address. . . . I just think," said Grace, "it being very damn all from the neighbors aside from the little we got, it wouldn't do any harm to—er—press the kid some more. Not that I know much about kids." He was silent, and dropped his cigarette and stepped on it. "We'd like a couple of our own, Virginia's seeing this doctor—married four years and she's never—" He shrugged.

"You might have a try at Bobby," said Mendoza. "No harm."

He left Grace there lighting another cigarette, and went across to the Gerner house to see the husband's sister. It was a little waste of time. Mrs. Sally McElroy was a brisk, dark, brusque young woman, busily packing children's clothes and toys into a battered suitcase, and she couldn't—or wouldn't—tell him anything.

Her sister-in-law had never mentioned any men annoying her or making passes. She'd had no enemies—ridiculous, absurd. Just an ordinary young woman, now dead at twenty-eight, and three young children for somebody to look after, their father couldn't do everything, had to hold down a job, after all. These criminals just let out of jail, give them six months or something and let them out—on account of those court decisions, she did read the right columnists after all—oh, it wasn't the police's fault, she realized, but after all in broad daylight—

The spilled groceries were gone, picked up by someone, tidied away.

The house bore out what everyone had said about May Gerner. Good wife and mother. Victim of another of the punks.

Just hope the lab came up with something useful.

And ditto on the other one.

Mendoza flipped a hand at Grace just getting into the Elva, and drove back to the office.

Piggott was hunched over the typewriter on his desk in the big communal sergeants' office, pecking out a report. "Nothing much," he said gloomily. "Heart attack, for pretty sure. ID on him—a Harvey Wallace, shoe salesman for Gallen Kamp. I tried to contact his wife, no luck."

The routine. It did go on, in the big city, day to day.

Mendoza sat down at his desk and lit a cigarette. It was ten-fifteen.

And Sergeant Farrell looked in and said, "New one, Lieutenant. Manager of a hotel on Main—you might say, a very fifth-rate hotel, I seem to remember there was a Vice raid on it not too far back—no questions asked, you get me, that kind of hotel. The El Centro. Maid just found a body in one of the rooms. A woman. Manager very nervous but who else would he call? I've sent an ambulance."

"*¡Porvida!*" said Mendoza. "The citizenry is keeping us busy. So, I'll go and look at it."

Chapter 3

THE HOTEL had been there a long time. Like other buildings down here which had been new when Los Angeles was almost new, it had started life quite high in the social scale and been going steadily downhill since. In this year of grace, it hardly qualified to be called fifth-rate: most of its trade would consist of the casual prostitutes, and those of both sexes on the way down.

The narrow lobby was dirty and uncarpeted; there was an unpainted, chipped counter across one side of it. A patrol car was parked along the yellow-painted curb in front and one of the uniformed men was standing at the counter, eyeing the despondent-looking cadaverous man behind it. He snapped to attention as Mendoza came in.

"Barrett, sir. My partner's upstairs with the body—Gomez. We got the call first. This is Mr. Shadwell."

Shadwell eyed Mendoza's dapper gray herring-bone, gold links, black Homburg and neat hairline moustache sourly. "So hello," he said gloomily. "Lieutenant, Sergeant, whatever."

"Lieutenant. I'll see what we've got here and then I'll want to talk to you," said Mendoza. "Where is it?"

"Room four-oh-eight, sir," said the patrolman.

There was no elevator; Mendoza climbed old, narrow, high-riser stairs uncarpeted. Four-oh-eight was in the middle of the lefthand corridor; the other uniformed man was on guard beside the door. Mendoza introduced himself. "Yes, sir. Pretty obvious homicide, sir, we called in right away. We didn't touch anything but the maid that found her opened the door, probably messed up any prints on the knob."

"We so seldom get it that easy," said Mendoza, and shoved the unlatched door open and went in.

The woman lay at the foot of the bed, sprawled untidily on the thin dusty once-flowered rug. Her lips gaped darkly, the tip of a bloated-looking tongue thrust out, and her bulging eyes stared at Mendoza over one shoulder as she lay twisted on one side. She was naked except for one high-heeled black patent-leather pump. Its mate lay a little way off, and various other clothing was scattered about the room—a black rayon dress and half-slip on the one rickety straight chair, a black brassiere on the bed, black lace panties on the floor, a green wool coat with a dyed rabbit collar also on the bed, a black patent-leather tote bag sitting on the floor beside the chair.

The bed, with an ancient gray-white chenille spread on it, looked undisturbed.

There wasn't much else in the room. Just a room, no bath connecting: that would be down the hall. There was the double bed, the bedstead ancient brass, the mattress old and shapeless, the chair, the ancient carpet too small for the room, and a shaky painted bureau with a spotted mirror over it. But there might, Mendoza knew, be a good deal more here than the layman would expect; turn the lab men loose with their microscopes and vacuum cleaners, you never knew what they'd find.

On the other hand, in a hotel like this, it was probably years since the room had had a thorough cleaning; certainly it hadn't been shining clean when the woman walked into it, and whatever turned up, how to prove it wasn't connected with another temporary tenant?

He sighed, looking at the woman. Hard to tell now,

but she'd once been at least pretty. Around thirty-five? A little too plump, the flesh soft and unhealthy-white. Bleached blonde needing a touch-up. Nails blood-red, polish chipped. Toenails blood-red too.

He told Gomez to stay where he was and went down-stairs again. He used the phone on the counter to call the office, told Sergeant Farrell to call the lab, and asked who was in. Glasser was there and that was it. "Chase him down here," said Mendoza, and put the phone down and faced the gloomy Shadwell. "So, when did she check in, what name have you got for her, did she have any visitors?"

"I don't know," said Shadwell.

"What do you mean, you don't know? Don't you have a register?"

"I—no," said Shadwell. "Look, we get a lot—well, just overnight, it's too much trouble keeping—Look, it was cash, I just—uh—give him a key. And—"

"He? There was a man with her?" Shadwell nodded. "And you don't keep a register. All right, when was this?"

"Uh—about, well, maybe like ten-thirty last night."

"Do you know the woman?" Shadwell was silent. "Come on, come on," said Mendoza. "We can continue this down at headquarters if you want it the tough way." After a long moment Shadwell reluctantly nodded, once. "You know her. Who is she?"

"I never said I know her. I'd—seen her before, is all. I think her name's Shirley something. I didn't *know* her."

"Had she been to the hotel before? Well?"

"Oh, for Godsakes," burst out Shadwell, "you god-damned fuzz got to be so damn moral alla time, God-sakes, this ain't the Sheraton West, mister, we get all sorts and three bucks is three bucks and it ain't exactly the policy of this place getting nosy about customers, what the hell—Now listen, I'm answering you, ain't I? Give me time. Just, I don't hafta like you cops lookin'

35

down your damn noses. All right, all right, she had. Been here before. All right. Am I supposed to say, naughty, naughty, sister, you was here a couple nights back with another guy so you can't bring this one in? Well, am I? Three bucks is—"

"Three bucks," said Mendoza. "Yes. She'd been here with other men. How often?"

"Mister, I ain't no goddam computer," said Shadwell. "I don't know. I never counted. Just, sometimes. She'd come 'n' go—like some others."

"All right." The ambulance had just arrived, the internes coming in, and Mendoza gestured for Barrett to take them upstairs. "She came in with a man about ten-thirty last night and he paid you for the room. Tell me what he looked like. Had you ever seen him before?"

"I had not," said Shadwell in a hurry. "No. I don't know. I ain't much good at describing people. It was only a minute, I didn't look at him close. Why the hell would I? I couldn't say at all."

"Now, you must remember something about him," said Mendoza with conscious patience. "Was he short or tall, fat or thin, About what age?"

"Uh—kind of tall. Kind of big. Bigger 'n' you, anyway."

"Age?"

"I don't know—I didn't pay any notice. Not so old, I guess. Or he wouldn't—Uh. I couldn't say about coloring. He had a hat on."

"What kind of hat?"

"I couldn't say," said Shadwell. "I didn't notice. Jesus God, a thing like this got to happen! A body! What Mr. Norman's gonna say—"

That was about all they got out of him. Glasser came with the lab team arriving just after him, and while the lab boys took possession of the room Glasser and Mendoza pressed on at Shadwell, and at the sullen maid—but she didn't know anything, just that she'd found the body. People supposed to be out of the rooms by nine o'clock, and she was just checking they were. She didn't remember when that room had last been cleaned—understandably: it could have been during her innocent childhood, and she was in her forties. Shadwell either didn't honestly know more than he'd say, or had some reason for shutting up, and Mendoza was inclined to think he really didn't know. In this hotel, probably the handing over of a key to a casual prostitute and her current game, for the three bucks, happened a dozen times a night and who was taking any notice of the man or girl? And with the cops now aware of that, Shadwell and the hotel were in enough trouble; if he knew anything helpful, he'd be all too eager to come out with it.

It was discouraging, considering that whoever the woman had had in tow last night had probably killed her.

Mendoza went upstairs again. The lab men had printed the patent leather tote bag and its contents, and let him have it. It contained a lot of odds and ends, dirty powder puffs, half-used lipsticks, two loose-powder compacts, dime-store variety, a package of Kleenex, a handkerchief with a big S on one corner, a full pack of Salem cigarettes, and an old letter in an envelope.

The envelope was addressed to Miss Shirley Corrigan at an address in Hollywood, Berendo Street; the postmark was Wilmington, Delaware, and the date was five years back. Mendoza cocked his head at it. He put everything back in the bag, pocketed the letter, and went back downstairs. "Was her name Shirley Corrigan?" he asked Shadwell.

"I never heard her last name. Shirley, that's right, I guess."

"So," said Mendoza to Glasser on the sidewalk outside, "suppose you start to make the round of bars around here. Say six blocks around, for a start. Ask if she was ever in, if they know her, who she was with. You know."

"Yeah," said Glasser, "I know. The legwork. All to find out who took off a no-good little tramp, and what loss is Shirley to our fair city, anyway? Oh, I know, I know, don't say it—"

"Next time," said Mendoza, "he might pick on a respectable upright citizen, Henry. Go look. I'll try to send you some help."

He went back to headquarters and met Landers just coming in. Landers' perennially boyish face wore a slightly smug look. "Don't tell me you've turned up a lead on Samson?" asked Mendoza.

"Not exactly a lead. We've seen most of the neighbors around there who heard the row." They got into the elevator together and Mendoza pushed the button. "Nobody seems to have actually seen Samson except that Frawley and a man from across the street, Jay Burnson. Apparently by the time Frawley had got his clothes on and come out, Samson had already broken into the house. Burnson claims he saw him run out and down the driveway of the Prothero house. Just a glimpse, he says, as he was coming across the street." The elevator landed and they started down the hall. "So I had a little brainwave and started to track him. It was sort of easy. Hackett came along—"

"One thing that struck me," said Mendoza, "he must have done what he did do very damn quick, Tom. Here's Frawley waking up to see him pounding on the front door of the Prothero house, and Frawley calls us —taking what, maybe a minute on that—and then gets dressed, call it three or four minutes, and goes out and next door—another minute at the outside—and by then Samson's already beaten two women to death and is running away."

"Yes, well," said Landers, "I can't contribute anything helpful there, but when we came to look, he'd left a trail all through the back yards up to the corner. That's how he went. Maybe he saw people coming out, and had enough sense to go that way—maybe he wasn't thinking. Frawley says he was berserk drunk. Anyway he went through back yards there, and we found three very nice footprints." He looked complacent.

"*¡Es hermoso sin pero!*" said Mendoza. "You don't tell me. How nice."

"I thought you'd like it. Looks like about a size eleven, left heel run over, and he walks—or runs—straddle-legged, judging by the angle of one print. The woman in the corner house had just washed her car in the drive that afternoon, a dirt driveway, and it being nice and cool the dirt was still wet."

"I like it, I like it," said Mendoza. "I trust you've taken steps to get the nice casts?"

"Oh, yes. Hackett called the lab and Scarne came out. He was still working on them when I left."

"Mmh. I am now wondering," said Mendoza, making a steeple of his laced fingers, "whether—yes, Frawley said he was drunk—very drunk— At least it's worth a try." He picked up the inside phone and said, "Rory, get me Traffic."

"But you haven't heard the rest of it," said Landers. "We found this fellow over on Avenue Eighteen—that's the cross street that—"

"Crosses Albion Avenue, yes. So?"

"And he says this drunk—or somebody, but considering the time it's almost got to be Samson—came crashing through his yard last night, about a quarter of one—fellow's a ham radio operator and he was still up—and he went out and chased him off, the drunk had got tangled up in the gate into the yard, and he cussed him out and saw him stagger off down the street. He didn't hear about the murder until this morning. But that's got to be Samson, doesn't it? And this fellow saw him close, well, in the dark, but closer than Frawley or Burnson. And he says—"

Traffic answered and Mendoza asked for Captain Fletcher. Could a check be run, please, on any and all D. and D.'s picked up by patrol cars last night between 12:30 and 1:30, roughly in the vicinity squared by Avenues Sixteen to Nineteen, Spring Street and Main?

"—That the drunk was a Negro, a big fellow, with a Deep South accent," said Landers.

Possibly, Mendoza added to Fletcher, a Negro with a Deep South accent. Thanks very much.

"They'll run a check. It just occurred to me, if he was as drunk as all that—"

"So maybe we break this one fast after all," said Landers.

"Take no bets," said Mendoza sardonically, "We've got the plaster casts, but that's a long way from having the shoes—or the man who wore them."

He dispatched Landers to go and help Glasser canvas the bars for any trace of Shirley, and put in a request to Records: did they have any pedigree for Shirley? Probably soliciting, if they had.

He sat back and did a little ruminating on the several cases they had on hand. They were all pretty much up in the air still: but give it twenty-four hours, the lab might come up with something useful on all three. The lab frequently did. On the anonymous ones like all these three cases, the lab was sometimes the best detective. But on any kind of case, the human factor was operative in crime as in any other facet of human life, sometimes it was the little hunch, the vague smell, the feeling up a good cop's spine, that did the trick.

After a while he got up and went out again, drove up North Broadway to Federico's for lunch, and met Higgins and Hackett just going in.

Hackett regarded the menu darkly and ordered the low-calorie plate. He'd forgotten about his diet for a while after getting out of the hospital last year, but Angel's gourmet cooking had inevitably caught up with him and these days he was back to counting calories. "I warned you about that girl a month after you married her, Art," said Mendoza, grinning.

"What can I do, I love her," said Hackett gloomily. He drank black coffee and made a face.

Higgins beckoned the waiter back and said on second thought he'd have a Scotch and water. Hackett cast him a sympathetic glance; if they hadn't been so busy in Homicide, doubtless somebody would by now be making book on George Higgins' chances with Mary Dwyer. On the one hand, having had one cop-husband shot, Mary Dwyer might not be so eager to take on another cop, but on the other hand George Higgins was quite a man if not exactly a movie star for looks, and, Higgins not being much of an actor any other way, probably Mary Dwyer was well aware of how he felt about her; and he was a career cop who might end up some day as Captain at ten thousand a year. In his leisure moments, which were few and far between, L.A.P.D. Homicide was agog with curiosity as to Higgins and Mary Dwyer; but nobody, of course, ever mentioned it to Higgins.

Mendoza told them about Shirley and they both groaned. "I can guess all the legwork we'll be doing on that," said Hackett. "A cheap chippie—"

"I think," said Mendoza, regarding his steak sandwich, "you'll spend the afternoon down in Records, Arturo, instead of pounding pavements. Looking for anybody with a pedigree of rape and or assault, and at M.O.'s of same. On May Gerner."

"Oh. Yes. But we don't know she was raped—"

"It's nearly a foregone conclusion. Or, in the polite language of the true-detective magazines, molested, anyway. Go and look. We should have the autopsy report this afternoon."

Landers, not being inclined to trust any of the kitchens of the sleazy places down here, hadn't had any lunch up to one-thirty, and was figuring on taking some time out after talking to his tenth bartender and going uptown for a decent meal. But the tenth bartender—he and Glasser had divided the bars between them, and there were plenty down here too, but at least they were all open by noon, unlike the more elite bars—delayed him.

"Sure, she was in here. Shirley. Corrigan, you say? Dunno as I ever heard her last name. Blonde, dyed, in her thirties—yeah, that's her. Nope, I dunno where she lives, but she hangs around. Like a lot of these dames. Now look," said the bartender earnestly. He was a big burly man about fifty, with curly gray hair and a cynical mouth. "Now look," and he fixed Landers with a hard black glare. "This ain't a fancy part of town and I don't get fancy customers. I don't like the lushes coming in, dirty up the place, *and* I don't let the B-girls operate if I know it. Just had a pair of fuzz in here about that and I told 'em straight. B-girls, no. I don't keep the knockout drops under the bar, am I crazy? A liquor license costs something in this state, and one fall, you don't get it back. But I ask you, as one honest man to another, this female—these females —come in, I know good 'n' well they're on the make, what can I do about it? They don't do nothing in here, see. Sure, give the fellow the eye, he buys 'em a drink, so how am I gonna know they don't know each other from before? And so does that make me a procurer or somethin'? I'm runnin' a business, that's all. I can't stop 'em coming in, they don't cause any disturbance."

"Well, I see that," said Landers diplomatically, his stomach rumbling.

"You sure you won't take a beer or nothing? On the house."

"No, thanks. This Shirley, was she in here last night?"

"Yeah. Yeah, she was. You after her for something, good riddance, one less to bug me. But what can I *do?*

42

Yeah—early, about seven, seven-thirty. She didn't pick up nobody though, she was already with a guy."

"Oh. What did he look like?"

"How'd I know? I just noticed she was with a guy. She was drinking old-fashioneds—she could sure pour it down. No, I didn't know him, never seen him before that I recall. I guess he was a kind of young guy— far as I remember—not so tall as you but some heavier." The bartender shrugged. "All I could say."

And of course that was about three hours before Shirley had gone to the hotel. She could have been with somebody else by then. Landers thanked the bartender and went out to the gray squalor of First Street and Alameda. His car was in a lot up toward Second; he turned that way, and coming past another bar in the middle of the block was accosted by name.

"Hey, Tom, what's Homicide on down here?"

"Lew," said Landers. "When did I run into you last? You looking for women or gambling-dens?" Detective Lew Reising was attached to Vice; they'd been through the Academy together.

"Joe Pierce," said Reising, indicating his partner. Landers shook hands. "Women. B-girls. We've been having a spate of 'em rolling the suckers. We were just thinking about lunch, you had any?"

They went up to Federico's in Landers' car, and exchanged the shoptalk. . . . "The hell of it is, of course," said Reising, "they don't all come and tell us about it. Naturally. But by the complaints we have got, the lieutenant thinks there could be a regular organiza- tion behind it. We got another this morning, reason Joe and I are asking around—kind of a thankless job. Poor devil of a sailor—three months in, just turned nineteen —not dry behind the ears. Feeling the devil of a guy, uniform and all—I saw him, nice young guy, and if he's so much as kissed anything female—talk about innocent. He's from a little farm town in Kansas, first time away from home. He lands here with two days

43

on hand before he's got to report to the naval base at 'Frisco, and not knowing the town—and trying to live up to the Navy's reputation, you get me—he hits a bar on Alameda, up from the Union Station. Tells us a real pretty girl got friendly with him, said her name was Sue, and next thing he knows, he wakes up in the Georgia Street Emergency. Wallet gone with about ninety bucks in it. Auggh!" said Reising. "There's too much of it, organized or not. And how many bartenders in this neck of the woods look the other way?"

Landers felt a little depressed; and inevitably, cops might tend to be pessimists, seeing so much of the seedy side of things. "Too many people on the make," he said. "That's for sure, Lew. Too many people just thinking, what's in it for me. Sometimes you get discouraged about people."

"Brother, you have said it," said Reising.

Detective Jason Grace had been frustrated over in Monterey Park by Bobby Gerner's aunt, who told him firmly that Bobby was taking his nap and couldn't be waked up. Detective Grace, who was a perspicacious man, did not wholly put down Mrs. McElroy's attitude to any prejudice for a Negro police officer, but certainly that entered in if only partly. He acknowledged it philosophically; people had foibles. He even had some himself.

He came into the Homicide office at three-thirty and told his tale to Mendoza. "I just thought if you'd give me a little moral support," he said mildly. "We might just get something a little useful from Bobby. I'd like to try anyway."

"*Así, así*, said Mendoza, who was perusing Dr. Bainbridge's autopsy report on May Gerner. "Yes. She was raped, by the way. We're looking through Records for anybody who's got that kind of pedigree. All right, Jase, I'll back you up and we'll see."

"Even a five-year-old—when he actually saw the man—well, I don't know much about kids, but—"

Jason Grace, however, had a kind of instinct about people, as Mendoza well knew. The empathy for people. Sweet-talking Jase. A valuable addition to Homicide—and then Mendoza remembered, of course, that Grace had come to Homicide as a replacement for Bert Dwyer, also a very good cop.

But they were frustrated again. Bill Gerner and the children had apparently moved in with Gerner's sister Mrs. McElroy, in a new tract house in Monterey Park. There was a neighbor acting as baby-sitter—the kids, two to seven years old, in the big back yard—Gerner and the McElroys off making funeral arrangements, pending the coroner's release of the body. And the neighbor was a strong-minded woman who knew a citizen's rights.

"I don't really think I could let you question the child when Mr. Gerner isn't here—I mean, I don't want to obstruct the police, but this has been a terrible shock to the boy, and I really don't think I can let you talk to him alone. If you can come back when his father is here—I'm quite sure Mr. Gerner wouldn't want me to—"

"So, tomorrow," said Mendoza resignedly.

"Listen," said Grace, "a five-year-old—twenty-four hours is like a year to them. Any more delay getting at him, and he'll have forgotten anything he does remember."

"Tomorrow," said Mendoza, "is also a day."

Chapter 4

ABOUT THREE o'clock on Friday afternoon Piggott finally found Mrs. Harvey Wallace at home. He asked her politely to expect a visit from a police officer, drove up to Catalina Street in Hollywood, and broke the news to her that her husband had dropped dead over his breakfast downtown that morning. This kind of thing is also part of the thankless job, of course.

Mrs. Wallace promptly went into hysterics, as tactful as Piggott had tried to be, and in the end he had to enlist the help of a sympathetic neighbor who gave him the address of the Wallaces' married son. He appeared almost immediately with his wife, who took charge of the widow, and manfully accompanied Piggott down to the morgue to identify the body formally.

It seemed that Wallace had had a known heart condition and had been under the care of a doctor, so an autopsy wouldn't be necessary.

Piggott didn't enjoy breaking bad news to people, but at least for a while he'd been dealing with the upright citizens, which was a change. He was sorry for the Wallaces, but he figured that the Lord had had some reason for snatching the man away so hurriedly. By the time he'd driven Wallace Junior home it was a quarter to six and a waste of time to go back to head-quarters; he headed for home. It was choir practice night; he'd only recently joined the choir and rather enjoyed it. Driving along Hollywood Boulevard, stopping for the lights, he saw the headlines—BATTLE

RAGES, ELDERLY WOMEN BEATEN, HOUSE-WIFE RAPE-MURDER, HOARD OF DOPE SEIZED, PORNOGRAPHY TRIAL, JUVENILE GANGS. He thought darkly that Wallace Senior had probably been spared the working out of the dire predictions in the seventh book of Daniel.

"Sodom and Gomorrah," muttered Piggott to himself. But then, quite aside from the fact that he was a confirmed fundamentalist Christian and a good cop, Piggott did tend to be something of a pessimist.

It was John Palliser's day off. He and Roberta spent it looking at houses. They didn't find anything remotely possible, what with the inflated price of real estate and Palliser's rather modest salary, but they weren't discouraged. They were reasonably young and in love, and both optimists by nature. They went out to dinner, and Palliser only fleetingly wondered what new mayhem and murder his colleagues downtown were coping with.

Tomorrow he'd find out.

Hackett and Higgins had gone down to Records after lunch and begun looking at the pedigrees of rapists. There were a lot of them, but they were being selective, looking only for those known to be still around recently; even of those there was quite a handful. And some of the others, who had done time longer ago, could still be around.

One they both liked was Tomás Obregon, Caucasian, five-ten, thirty-one two years back, dark eyes, dark hair, no marks, a hundred and fifty, U.S. citizen, who had been charged with rape-assault in 1963 and done two years of a three to five. He was still on parole. There was a recent address, Union Place.

He sounded very possible for May Gerner—he'd attacked a housewife in her own house before—so they went to look for him. At the Union Place address, a rooming house, they learned that he worked at a gas station on Wilshire, so they drove up there.

"If it is Tomás or if it isn't," said Higgins on the way, "what silly damn fools they are, Art. Once in a while I read one of these detective yarns, and that's what's wrong with them."

"What?" said Hackett, watching the light.

"They've got the crooks acting so smart, and they just damn well aren't. Not as much sense as a four-year-old, the way some of them act, just plain fools. Get away with a job once, so ever after they go at it the same way—whatever lay they're on. Why else do we go looking at M.O.'s? Most of 'em can't think ten minutes ahead, to make any real plans."

"Doing what comes naturally," agreed Hackett.

"I tell you," said Higgins, "sometimes it gets me wondering whether we've made any progress since we left the caves."

"Well, Neanderthal man didn't have a police department," said Hackett.

"There is that."

They found Tomás Obregon at the gas station, and Tomás was indignant and annoyed at being questioned by fuzz. "I ain't done nothing," he said. "I been in no trouble since I got out. Honest."

They couldn't, of course, take his word for it. They wanted to know where he'd been from three to five yesterday afternoon. "I was right here, Goddamn it. Where'd I be, a workday? You can ask Mr. Evans, he's the owner, he was here too."

They asked Evans, who seemed to be a good type, and Evans said that was right. Tomás had been right there all day, and the mechanic could say so too.

At least that was definite. They crossed Tomás off. But there were others to look up. They had a list of a dozen men they wanted to talk to, out of Records.

"You know something, Art," said Higgins as they got back into the Barracuda.

"Mmh?"

They'd known each other for a long time—they'd

been through the Academy together sixteen years back —and worked together in Homicide a long time. "It's just," said Higgins uneasily, "damn it, I feel sort of *shy* with her. Damn silly as it sounds, Mary. I can't, you know, sort of bring myself to— Diffident, that's the word. Me. I know it's—but, well, Mary's different, and I—"

If the ludicrousness of associating big, tough George Higgins with the word *diffident* struck Hackett as funny, he didn't say so. In fact, he saw Higgins' difficulty. He and George were a lot alike, only Angel hadn't happened to be the widow of a fellow police officer.

"I see what you mean," he said seriously.

"And I don't know what the hell to do about it," said Higgins miserably.

Hackett couldn't advise him. He had been considerably aided and abetted in his courtship of Angel by Alison Mendoza, but he didn't suppose that even Alison could help George. Though it mightn't do any harm to ask her advice. . . .

Mendoza got Dr. Bainbridge on the phone at four-thirty. "This autopsy report. On Gerner. You didn't mention any scrapings from her nails, etcetera. Nothing in that line? She didn't fight him?"

"Gerner—oh, no. No," said Bainbridge. "My guess'd be that he knocked her unconscious almost at once."

"She had time to scream—once, at least."

"All right, all right," said Bainbridge. "I understood she was probably attacked first from behind. So she screamed, damn it. And then he knocked her out, because going by her fingernails—and most women instinctively use 'em in an—er—extremity—she didn't fight back. Ten nice manicured nails—shell pink polish, if you want every damn detail—all unbroken. And why the hell you're criticizing my reports—"

"I'm not, I'm not," said Mendoza hastily. "I just wondered."

"What I'm thinking about," Bainbridge went on grumbling, "is this other one. My good God, Luis, you'd better get that one fast. These poor damned old women. My God, I never saw anything like it, and I've seen a few corpses. The damage he did—my God. I'm on Prothero right now."

"Qué es?"

"Well, both of 'em frail—in the eighties, and old bones fracture easily. But even so—and this and that chronic, arthritis and a certain amount of degeneration of the heart muscle in Prothero—and the other one he apparently knocked out immediately, same like Gerner, she didn't fight back either. But, my God. I think he must have jumped on them after he got them down—ribs shattered, pelvis cracked, one arm fractured in three places—this is Turner—and a good many internal injuries. Prothero—she did fight him, some, as well as she could probably. What I've counted up so far on her, poor damned old soul, ribs cracked, pelvis broken, both legs broken, a fractured skull. And I don't think there was any weapon used. But there was hair and a little flesh under a couple of her nails."

"Ah," said Mendoza. "Interesting. Anything useful?"

"I don't pretend," said Bainbridge disdainfully, "to be as omniscient as your holy damn lab. I've sent the material to them. But I did have a look at it first, under the microscope. And this much I'll say—the lab will confirm it—there were six hairs under the nail of the right forefinger, and under magnification they look damn like typical Negroid hair. Quite distinct differences, you know, Caucasoid, Mongoloid, Negro."

"I know," said Mendoza. "Well, well." So the ham radio operator was right. Probably. "Thanks very much, doctor."

"Always glad to oblige," said Bainbridge, not sounding it.

Mendoza called Fletcher in Traffic, who said he'd been about to call him. A check had been run on the

D. and D.'s picked up last night, and there were none in that exact vicinity. A few just outside the area—Avenue Twenty-One, North Broadway, Spring: but none of those had been Negro.

Mendoza thanked him absently. Shelve that, he thought: far-fetched. The drunk hadn't been picked up. Or, if he had, he'd got farther away. Well, they had his footprints, which would help when and if they ever put the finger on him. What about this Frankie Colson or Holton or whatever? They really couldn't do anything on that angle. Just a funny angle.

At least, *Dios,* they hadn't had any new calls this afternoon. Tomorrow might be another story.

Sergeant Farrell came in and laid a manila folder on his desk. "Records just sent this up. Pedigree on that Shirley Corrigan."

"Oh, *gracias,*" said Mendoza, sitting up. If it was anything like complete it might contain some names of known associates and so on. Though he didn't really think any known associate had murdered Shirley. Shirley, who had been—like nine out of ten pros, big and little criminals, this or that type—just a plain damn fool. The first thing you warned little girls about was going with strangers, and a smart little girl took in the lesson. Shirley had taken up with a stranger just once too often.

As he opened the file, he thought of the letter in his pocket.

Hackett got home at six-fifty after battling traffic rather heavier than usual out to Highland Park. As he came in the back door, he took in the scene: his peaceful ordered household, as compared with the chaotic and rootless lives he dealt with every day. His brown-haired Angel stirring something on the stove, and beyond a glimpse into the dining room with the table set and waiting: Mark Christopher, aged three, peacefully bent over a coloring book and his darling Sheila, aged eleven months, ensconced in her high chair occupied with a squashable stuffed dog.

"Hi," said Angel. "Reasonably tough day?"

"Reasonably," said Hackett, kissing her.

"You've got time for a drink."

"I just want to relax." Mark scrambled up and made for him, demanding praise at the top of his voice for the drawing held up, Sheila began to howl. and the great silver Persian marched ostentatiously out, tail held high, looking annoyed. "What did I ever do to deserve all this?" asked Hackett with a mock groan.

"You're just lucky," said Angel.

And thinking of Higgins going home to the bachelor apartment—and despite the gourmet cooking which added the pounds the doctor frowned on—Hackett decided he was. Hostages to fortune be damned, at least somebody cared what happened to Art Hackett.

Higgins didn't go straight home. He stopped at the London Grill on Hollywood Boulevard and had a drink and dinner. Usually, in the interests of thrift, he ate at home; once in a while he indulged himself.

And whenever he wasn't with Mary, it was easy to tell himself to be a man, he wasn't exactly the poorest prospect for a husband there was, pull himself together and take the bull by the horns and ask her—but when he was with her, he just turned tongue-tied. Mary was the only one who'd ever been important.

He'd made some headway. But chiefly with the kids. And tomorrow was his day off and he was taking Stevie and Laura to Disneyland. He'd have to be damn careful, thought Higgins. She'd get mad if he spent too much money on them. All the rides and so on. And the kids wouldn't keep quiet about what they'd seen and done. But how could he be careful? Good kids, and they didn't have many treats—and when Laura looked at him that way, with her mother's gray eyes— Oh, hell, thought Higgins, he'd just have to play it by ear and see how it went. And if she got mad, so what? It was his money, damn it. And Bert had been a friend of his. He could tell her, in a sort of way, he was doing it for Bert—but it wouldn't be true.

Oh, hell, thought Higgins, I wish I knew how to talk to her—really.

Mendoza took Shirley Corrigan's record home with him. His household was serene—the cats all safely in before dark, fed and settled down in their chosen places: Alison in the kitchen dealing with dinner. It was a little strange not to find Máiri there, but she'd be back. He strolled into the nursery and was set on by a pair of excited twins. The rather prim-faced English nursemaid reprimanded them quietly.

"You really don't mind looking after these two little monsters?" asked Mendoza, smiling at her.

"Little *monsters*," said John Luis. "*Monstruoso,* Daddy?"

"*Monstruosos muy maisano!*" said Mendoza emphatically. Teresa Ann giggled.

"Oh, no, sir," said the girl in a neutral tone. "They're very sweet, sir."

Well, he saw what Alison meant. Over dinner he asked her, "You still satisfied with that girl? She seems—"

"Oh, she's very good really, Luis. Only *English.* And I hope Máiri doesn't have to be away too long. . . . Johnny called me Mummy today," said Alison inconsequentially. "They do pick up things so easily."

Mendoza laughed. "If that's the worst they pick up from her—"

"Well, I know it's a little thing, *amante,* but I don't like it. It makes me," said Alison, "think of Tutan-kahmen. All right, laugh. I just—"

"I will say," said Mendoza, "at least they're getting a wealth of experience. What with Máiri talking Gaelic at them, and I'm not at all convinced that either of them knows the difference between Spanish and English—"

"I suppose it's all to the good really," agreed Alison doubtfully. "By the way, those brochures came from those private schools. I want you to look at the one from the Stancliff School specially—"

"Dios me libre, woman, we've got at least three years before they'll be ready for—"

"Well, I just want you to look at it."

He'd look at it later. After dinner he looked over Shirley Corrigan's pedigree again. Shirley Corrigan, Caucasian, five-five, one hundred and thirty, no marks, hair blonde, eyes blue, born March 5, 1930. She'd been picked up first—here—in 1956, on a soliciting charge, and vagrancy. The usual suspended sentence. And again: soliciting, soliciting. 1957—1959—1960. Common drunkenness. Then something more serious: in 1961 she was charged as accomplice before-and-after to an armed robbery. *See Chaudrey, Robert,* said the pedigree. Mendoza had seen Chaudrey, Robert. That particular armed robbery had been his fourth in California, and he was still in Quentin on a five-to-fifteen. Shirley, lucky girl, had been acquitted.

1962, soliciting. A three-month term and fine. Then there was a hiatus. All those stiff new rules in, state supreme court, Federal Supreme Court, about the resorting law, and rules of obtaining evidence, and these days the ones like Shirley were largely going around unchallenged. You didn't get, these days or for some while—even when he'd been doing his stint down in Vice, not that he'd had much to do with the females, they'd sent him after the gamblers, Mendoza being halfway a pro card-sharp himself—you didn't get the old-style bawdy houses, the definite red-light district. You got a little of the organized bit, the pimps running a stable, and a lot more of just the casual lone women, the women who had drifted that far down and picked up the casual men in bars to take home or to the nearest accommodating hotel. Like the one where Shirley had got herself killed. It was even possible, he thought, that Shirley hadn't had a regular fixed residence. Some of them didn't. The few clothes they owned stashed day by day in a public locker somewhere. There had been nine single dollar bills in her purse. Yes, and the bed looking undisturbed—had he attacked her as soon as they were in the room?

He put the file down on the coffee table and, careful not to disturb El Señor coiled on his lap, brought out the ancient folded letter Shirley had carried in her handbag. It was much folded and refolded, as if it had been often read. He wondered why she had kept it; and understood why even as he wondered. It was a link. She had drifted far and downhill all the way: but the letter said, *I had a place, and people who cared.*

But evidently the awareness of that hadn't been enough to make her turn back on the path.

He unfolded the worn sheets of cheap paper and read the letter again. There was no heading or date, and the writing was round and careful, in green ink.

Dear Shirley,

I am writing to tell you Mom died three days ago. She didn't have much pain thank God and I want to tell you she said she forgave you for all the worry and all you made her. She asked me to write Shirley and this is the last address we had so I hope it gets to you all right. She prayed for you every day for you to live a better life and not get into any more trouble. She asked Father Sargent to pray for you and the sisters too and I have too Shirley. I wont say anything about the trouble you was in here that is water under the bridge and we know the baby would be raised right at St. Michaels' if not taken by some good family so that is all right. The doctor knew Mom was going so Father Sargent was here and she had the last rites and all. But she wanted me to write and tell you she forgave you and was praying you are living a good life like you wrote last year the last we heard. I hope the good job singing with that band worked out like you hoped, and you are doing good and maybe are going to church again. Frank and I are fine and we have three now, we named the baby for Mom, Patricia Ann, she was born in April. We are all fine, missing Mom, but Pa is pretty good only for the arthritis. Please Shirley will you write and say how you are doing, we think of you a lot and pray for you that youre alright. It would do Pa a lot of good to hear from you, you know you were always kind of his favorite.

Love,
Mary

Mendoza dropped the old letter on top of Shirley's pedigree out of Records. Symbolical, he thought sleepily. She had kept it: *I had a place.* But she had drifted down. Why? And echo answers why.

Had they better contact Wilmington, Delaware and trace Mary? Tell them what had happened to Shirley in the end? Or let it go and leave Mary thinking hopefully that Shirley was still somewhere in life, reformed and doing O.K.?

It was a question. Maybe the kindest thing to do.

And he thought, as inevitably as any devotee of Kipling, " 'For the sin ye do by two and two ye must pay for one by one——' "

Poor Shirley.

Carole Leslie was feeling bewildered. She'd meant to tell Mrs. Newhouse she was leaving, but not until the month was up; and here was Mrs. Newhouse apologizing for such short notice, they were going around the world, arrangements being made now, and giving up the apartment—and fifty dollars for such short notice—

Well, she'd meant to leave. That was all right. Carole was vaguely surprised that Mrs. Newhouse had managed to persuade Mr. Newhouse about traveling, but evidently she had.

Only it made a problem. Carole had only had two jobs here, the six months since she'd been here, with the Millers and Mrs. Newhouse. They were living-in jobs, and she'd given the Millers her month's notice and the agency had found the job with Mrs. Newhouse and she'd come straight here. She hadn't anywhere to go, to stay, and Mrs. Newhouse saying if she *could*, tonight, because of all the hurried arrangements—

"So that's all right, isn't it?" said Mrs. Newhouse brightly.

"Yes, ma'am," said Carole. Just for a minute she felt a little frightened, which was silly. She was nineteen and perfectly capable of taking care of herself.

"And we're leaving Sunday, so—"

It was funny. So sudden. But she wasn't thinking so much of that, right now, as of where she would go. Because Mrs. Spain's agency would be closed over the weekend, and before she got another job—

She was a bit fed up with the domestic jobs. The horrible children, and people like Evelyn Newhouse. Just like what everybody said Americans were. Jumped-up trash, Mum called it. Well, Mr. Newhouse was a nice man, but all the same—

Maybe she'd try to get a regular job. In a store or something. And an apartment of her own. Packing her clothes in the two worn suitcases—one Mum had had for her wedding trip—Carole thought about that. For the first time since she'd been here she felt suddenly, violently homesick, for the familiar Rowberrow village in the green valley, the known neighbors and streets she'd been so sick of, and Mum and Daddy and the obnoxious little brother.

That kind of job, in a shop or like that, would pay a lot more. She could have her own place. After all her letters home, how she was getting on so well, she wasn't going to run home like a scared rabbit just because she was suddenly out of a job. Mrs. Spain would—

She could call Dot, and—

It was only then she realized that she didn't know where Dot *was*. Dot's temporary job. Bother, thought

Carole, pushing down tiny panic. It was *silly*. She had money, she had lots of money, what she'd saved as well as the extra fifty dollars Mrs. Newhouse would give her. She could go to a hotel. And on Monday go to see Mrs. Spain, and get another job. There were heaps of jobs, a lot of English girls working here.

And Mrs. Spain, of course, would know where Dot was.

Bother Dot! thought Carole. Dot was just a bit too managing, just because of being four years older and knowing Carole's Mum and Dad and all. Carole Leslie could manage for herself, thank you.

Though it was a little funny that, all of a sudden, Mrs. Newhouse had talked Mr. Newhouse around. What he'd said to Carole just the other day—

Mrs. Newhouse insisted on giving her five dollars for the cab.

And it wasn't until she was safely installed at the Sunset Palms Motel on Sunset that Carole realized two things. She'd left her second-best coat at the apartment, the green corduroy car coat that had been one of the first American things she'd bought, and she still had the key to the apartment on Sunset Plaza.

Oh, well, she thought, tomorrow she'd go and give the key back, and get her coat. Travel arrangements and all—they couldn't be leaving *that* soon.

Chapter 5

ABOUT FIVE o'clock on Saturday morning it started to rain. By eight o'clock, when the day men came into headquarters, it was still coming down in a thin steady drizzle and it was clear to everybody that the first real rain of the winter had arrived. It so seldom does rain in Southern California that the natives are always pleased and surprised when it begins; but they very rapidly get tired of it, especially in the city. And once a real rain worked itself up to do a job on Southern California, only God knew when it would stop. It might rain all day and clear up tomorrow, or it might go on for a week.

Grace came in at eight-fifteen and, shedding his wet coat, went into Mendoza's office. "I want to go and see Bobby. Still."

Mendoza looked up. "Give them time to have breakfast, Jase. You're persistent, aren't you?"

"Earmark of a good detective."

"You have a hunch?" asked Mendoza seriously. He respected real hunches.

Grace hunched his shoulders. "Let's say a smidgin of a hunch, Lieutenant."

"O.K.," said Mendoza. "Just a minute while I finish looking at this." Hackett looked in and Mendoza beckoned him in; Landers followed. "Lab report on the Albion Street house." It had been waiting on his desk. "They give us this and that. Bears out the doctor—Samson jumped on the bodies, by the clothes. And—"

"My God," said Grace.

"Mmh. They found a broken bottle in the living room, and a little rye whiskey spilled on the rug there. The women were both W.C.T.U. members. Ergo, Samson dropped it. Old Overholt rye. Also a switchblade knife with a broken blade."

"Don't tell me, prints," said Hackett.

"Wait a minute, I hadn't— No, but they think they might bring some up. They're going to try with the oblique-light technique. We'll get a further report on that. Mmh, yes, Samson got his knife out, but was too drunk to use it—dropped it? Now, why? Two inoffensive old women." Mendoza rubbed his moustache the wrong way, which meant he was annoyed, and then carefully smoothed it in place again.

"Frankie Colson Holton whatever," said Landers. "Was he drunk enough to think the two old women were somebody he wanted to carve up? Two somebodies?"

"¡Ca!" said Mendoza. "The shoes are size eleven-B with a metal plate on the right heel. The other heel is run down a half-inch and there's a hole—never mind the dimensions—in the right sole."

"Typical derelict—Skid Row," said Hackett. "But how did he end up in that particular house beating the W.C.T.U. ladies?"

"Canvass the street for Colsons, Holtons," said Grace. "That's who he was looking for. And enemies should know their enemies."

"Oh, for God's sake," said Mendoza, "we've only got so many men!" There had been, this morning, an interview with Mick Frawley in the *Times,* mentioning that. And it might suggest this and that to them, but there wasn't anything practical they could do about it. "No prints in the house but those of the women." He put down the report. "So that's that. Let's all think about it and if anybody has any bright ideas—" He stood up.

Glasser and Higgins were off. Hackett and Landers started out to work more bars, trying to trace Shirley back on her last night; Piggott went out to wander up Albion Street seeking more positive sightings of Samson; and Mendoza and Grace started for Monterey Park. They took Grace's little Elva.

"Nice little girl," said Grace over the sudden roar of the racing motor.

"You realize," said Mendoza, nervously averting his eyes from the street ahead—he didn't like being driven—"that even if Bobby gives us anything, a judge is apt to look askance at evidence from a five-year-old?"

"It's a long way from a courtroom yet," said Grace tranquilly. "Sure. But any lead we get is a gain, no? And we might, getting a pointer where to look, find some other nicer evidence."

"Real hunch, Jase? The boy was questioned—as well as we could—then. He couldn't tell us much."

"And I don't doubt," said Grace in his soft voice, "that whoever talked to him was nice and kind. Sure. But maybe he didn't ask the right question, Lieutenant."

"A real hunch," Mendoza decided amusedly. "So all right, I'll play along."

At the McElroy house in Monterey Park, he let Grace stay well in the background while he gave Mrs. McElroy and Bill Gerner his smoothest line. They wouldn't frighten or upset the boy, just wanted to talk to him a few minutes, and Mr. Gerner was quite welcome to be present.

"Well, I don't see why not," said Gerner heavily. "I guess he's really too young for it all to mean much to him. I'll go bring him in the living room. You don't need to come—" as his sister got up. "You tend to the dishes." Unwillingly she went into the kitchen.

When Gerner brought the boy in, Mendoza sat back to listen interestedly while Grace took over. Bobby looked like a bright little boy; and Grace was the sweet-talker all right. He might not know much about kids, but instinct told him not to talk down to Bobby, adult to child. He sat Bobby beside him on the couch and gave him a warm smile. "You know we're looking for the bad man who hurt your mother, Bobby."

"Um." Bobby's eyes were busy on Grace's coffee-colored skin, white teeth, discreet-patterned tie.

"You saw him, didn't you?"

Bobby nodded gravely. "He hit Mommy and she fell down."

"Yes. What did he look like, you remember anything about him to tell? Was he a colored man, like me, Bobby?"

"Nope. He—he—he hadda blue shirt on. An' he hit Mommy and she yelled. He had hair over his mouth like Uncle Jim."

"Oh, he did?" said Grace comfortably. "A moustache, like I've got—and the Lieutenant there?"

"Uh-uh. A lot *more*. An' onna side o' his face, too, He was *dirty*," said Bobby emphatically.

"Mmh." Grace smiled at him again and uncertainly Bobby smiled back. One thing about kids, thought Mendoza, they instinctively recognized the artificial: and one of Jason Grace's greatest assets as a detective was that he was genuinely interested in people of all sorts, and that got through. "You ever see that bad man before, Bobby?"

And Bobby nodded. "Sure. He was workin' inna street where they tore up all the cement. I seen him there."

Grace glanced at Mendoza, Gerner said, surprised, "Oh, I don't think that could be, son. You just imagined that."

Grace stood up. "Well, thanks, Bobby."

"You aren't running away with the idea that's so, are you?" Gerner went to the door with them. "A kid his age—he wouldn't know, he only saw him a minute—that sounds crazy! A man in a city crew—"

"Might just be a resemblance," said Mendoza vaguely. "We won't put too much faith in it, Mr. Gerner."

"God," said Gerner. "I should've moved us out of there the minute I could afford it! I should've—but all I could think of was putting every damn cent back into the business! Drunks, bums wandering around down there—I should've—" He looked haggard.

They got into the Elva. "And I suppose that was the question you wanted to ask," said Mendoza. "My bright boy. And you will carefully refrain from asking. Why didn't anybody else have the sense to ask it?"

"Why, no," said Grace. "Why didn't anybody? I just wondered, that's all. Of course you do get the psychos who just all of a sudden get the urge and jump on the first female they see. But the way you had this thing figured out, he'd either followed her or waited for her, and that being so I thought it was a fifty-fifty chance he'd seen her before. And almost anywhere she went, she'd be taking the kids with her, so Bobby might have seem him."

"Such a bright boy. You don't think it was one of the street-department crew, do you?"

"Funnier things have happened," said Grace. He adjusted the windshield wipers; the rain was coming down a little harder now. "As I understand it, the city's got regular skilled men on hand all the while, but they hire the strong backs as needed, all casual like. I don't suppose they screen 'em for police pedigrees. And our boy may not have one anyway. Has to be a first time. I will say this, Lieutenant. If I round up the crew working on the sewer line along Pomeroy Avenue there a few days back, and find among 'em a white man with sideburns and a little bit heavier moustache than you and me, I'm going to want to ask him quite a few questions."

Mendoza grinned. "Let's hope we'd get some interesting answers. But you're going to have a time rounding 'em up. It's Saturday, and the city works a five-day week."

"I think I'll spend some time at it anyway," said Grace.

Mendoza got back to his office in time to take a call from Scarne up in the lab. Scarne was apologetic. They'd tried every which way, he said, and they weren't going to be able to get any prints off that switchblade knife. "And we're not doing you any good on that hotel room either," he added. "It adds up to nothing. There were a million prints there, good, bad and indifferent, but who's to say whose? We can isolate the corpse's, and any of the hotel staff, but I ask you, Lieutenant—joint like that, there's probably been a hundred temporary occupants since it was last dusted—the drifters, the easy females."

"I appreciate that," said Mendoza with a sigh.

"And there wasn't much of anything *there* but her clothes. I don't see much point in analyzing dust samples. And the clothes—*nil*. Cheap anonymous stuff. The only thing that had a label in it is the coat, and it's from The Broadway. Oh, and the shoes from Leed's."

"Well, it can't be helped," said Mendoza. "Thanks very much."

"Sorry," said Scarne. His pride was hurt; usually the lab could do better than that.

Palliser, coming in a little late, had been sent out on a freeway crash; routine, anybody dead. Homicide had to make a report. He came in as Mendoza put down the phone, and went into the communal sergeants' office to type up the report. The phone shrilled on Sergeant Lake's desk and a moment later he poked his head into Mendoza's office.

"New one," he said tersely. "That was the patrol car. Body found in an alley, by the manager of a movie house over on Los Angeles Street."

"*Caray,* am I having a hunch?" said Mendoza. "All right, Jimmy." He stood up, glancing out this eighth-floor window. The gray overcast hid the undulating Hollywood hills entirely, and it was still raining hard. He took up his hat and looked into the sergeants' office. "Come and lend some moral support, John—we've got a new corpse."

"What? November's usually quiet," said Palliser.

The movie house, which ran exclusively Mexican films, was seven blocks up from the Police Facilities Building. Mendoza parked the Ferrari illegally across the alley mouth behind the black-and-white patrol car. The ambulance wasn't there yet: no need to use sirens for a corpse. There weren't many people around at ten-thirty of a rainy morning—an old man huddled in a yellow raincoat on the corner opposite over a stack of newspapers was the only sign of life around. The old street lined with dirty old buildings—tan brick, stucco, red brick dirtied to black—looked tired and gray in the gray wet morning. The gutters ran with gray rain, carrying all the endless refuse of the city along with it, and the rain made a steady drumming, gurgling down the gutter pipes on the buildings, splashing on the pavement.

They walked up the alley.

The building which housed the theatre was along one side of the alley; on the other side there was a block of small shops, a bar, a pawnshop, a men's clothing store, a drugstore on the corner. The alley was also very dirty with flotsam and jetsam. Up there about twenty feet in was a little group of men: the two patrolmen in uniform, a stout man in dark civilian clothes with a large black umbrella, and of course the body. There was a door into the theatre there, a side door on the alley. It was open, on a narrow linoleum-covered hallway.

"—And my God, such a thing never happens to me before, and I don't know him from Adam, and my God, a body, I had to step over him to get in the door and I was shaking like a leaf. I didn't think L.A. had no gangsters like in Chicago, and even in Chicago I never came across no bodies I come to work in the morning, open up the place it should be ready when we start to sell tickets—"

Mendoza introduced himself and one of the uniformed men said, "This is Mr. Klein who called in, sir."

"You're a detective? Pleased to meet you." The umbrella gestured dangerously and Palliser dodged. "I couldn't see was he shot or stabbed or what, but I called in, all right. Such a thing. I only been here a year about, I didn't think L.A. had any gangsters like in—"

Mendoza looked at the body. It was a body, all right. Very obviously dead. "*¡Ay de mi! ¿Ya lo decia yo?*" he said. "Didn't I say it would happen?"

"What?" said Palliser.

The body was the body of a man, about thirty to thirty-five. Before he had become a body he hadn't been bad-looking—fairly regular features, sandy crew-cut hair—and he hadn't been badly dressed: a navy-blue suit in fair condition, a white shirt and dark tie now pulled loose and up around one shoulder. The rain had soaked his clothes and his upturned wide-eyed face, and he looked like a bum lying there—one of the winos dead drunk in a doorway over on Skid Row—but he hadn't been a bum. His suit jacket had been pulled back each side, across both arms, and the inside breast pocket was ripped open halfway down. Jacket pockets and trouser pockets had been pulled

66

inside out and beside the lefthand trouser pocket, dull-glittering in the rain, lay a single overlooked dime.

"Percy Andrews and his damn B-girls!" said Mendoza savagely. "Didn't I say sooner or later they'd give one of the suckers an overdose and land the whole damn mess in our lap? Because I'll give you fifty to one that's what it is, damn it. Look at him—all the earmarks!"

"Oh, I see what you mean," said Palliser.

"There's a bar down there—I'll give you a hundred to one," said Mendoza. "As if we haven't got enough to cope with! ¡Valgàme Dios! Is there any ID on him?" he asked the patrolmen abruptly.

"I haven't looked, sir—I thought—"

"So we look." Gingerly Mendoza squatted over the corpse. He felt like a cat about rain; he didn''t like it, and it was coming down with a steady drumming on the pavement now, a dreary noise. The single thing on the body was a worn leather wallet, dropped in the folds of the torn-apart jacket. There was no money in it, but several cards in the little plastic slots.

He'd been one James M. Seeley, of an address in Inglewood; there was a membership card in the Electrical Workers Union, Social Security card, driver's license, Automobile Club membership card, and a couple of snapshots of a dark-haired girl.

"¡Condenación!" said Mendoza, standing up. "As if we hadn't enough—"

"Shaking like a leaf I was—and I didn't think L.A. had any gangsters like in Chicago, not that I ever even in Chicago found a—"

After two, three o'clock, in the bars and hole-in-the-wall restaurants with liquor licenses, down here, the regular customers would be dropping in, and also the females. Up to that time Hackett and Landers, wandering around separately, had been talking mostly to the bartenders, but when they met for lunch at a slightly higher-class place up on Broadway, and compared notes, they hadn't turned up much.

Shirley Corrigan had been known, here and there. Fairly well in some places, barely in others. As one of the crowd. Landers had found a barkeep who could tell them that she'd once lived in a furnished room in the building across the street. And she'd held jobs, around. Waitress in a greasy spoon joint, and as a barmaid somewhere else. On the way down. That had been, vaguely, a year, two years ago.

They had heard that she had lived for a while, regular, with a guy named O'Leary, but that was sometime back and nobody could remember his first name, and he hadn't been seen around lately.

But they hadn't heard any more about anybody seeing her on Thursday night, with or without a man.

"Look," said Landers reflectively over his sandwich, "most of the ones like Shirley have got a room somewhere, no?"

Hackett agreed. "Unless they're really on their uppers."

"So let's say she did. Somewhere. But—"

"There wasn't a key in her bag."

"Well, no. There is that. But what I'm getting at," said Landers, "she went to that hotel with him. Whoever. The pickup—the john. So I say, *if* she had a room somewhere, it must have been a little way off so they picked the hotel as handier—if the john didn't have a car."

"Which says?"

"Read it," said Landers. "The john's eager, he doesn't want to waste time getting to her place. I say the last joint they hit has to be somewhere pretty damn near that hotel, Art. The john gets hot and bothered, let's go, honey, so they pick the nearest place."

"And you may have something there," said Hackett thoughtfully. "So we hit the nearest joints and see."

He ought to have figured that out for himself, he thought.

But to even things out, it was Hackett who came across the first really solid lead. It was at the fourth bar he'd tried after lunch, which made it almost three o'clock: a small bar and grill a block and a half from the hotel, called The A-B Grill. The glum-looking bartender listened to his questions, and without wasting words said, "Wasn't here Thursday night. Day off. Them two females over there you might ask. Birds of a feather."

Hackett swung and looked at the two females. They were the only two females in the place, along with four or five men at the bar. They were sitting at a table: one blonde, one dark; one consuming an old-fashioned, one a highball. He placed them instantly: the fun-girls who didn't know they were on the way down. They weren't nearly so far down as Shirley, probably both of them held jobs off and on, as waitresses, barmaids. They were on the make, but still being choosy. Probably neither of them had ever been dropped on by police—yet. They were approachable, and he approached them.

They eyed Hackett's wide shoulders and genial grin and giggled at him. They didn't even mind that he was a cop; they were wise girls, they knew that these days the cops couldn't bother even the pros much and they weren't pros. Besides, they had a kind of stake in the thing: somebody killing a girl like Shirley, any girl could be next.

One of them, the blonde, had known Shirley only vaguely, but the other one had something to tell him. Her name was Louise.

"Like I didn't *know* her like a pal, see, I knew who she was and I seen her around. Like that. In different places. Jeez, think about a girl getting murdered like that! Gives you the shakes. I wondered after if he was the one. Because it was that night. In here."

"You saw her here Thursday night? With a man?"

"Um-hum. You sure a big one, aren't you? I guess they like them big in the cops. Sure, I tell you about it, I don't mind, but you might buy me another drink, honey, will you?" Hackett raised a hand at the bartender. "Yes, I saw that Shirley that night, in here. I was with a new date, a nice sailor-boy from back east he was, Teddy was his name, a nice boy. He's shipped out now. Yesterday. I only happened to notice this Shirley on account—I don't want you to think I'm like sounding high-lady about her, honey—but she was sort of on the skids. Like with the fire-water. You know. Kind of lushy-like. I seen her with some guys, oh, brother, I'd hafta be real down and out to look at. You get me, she was taking what she could find. Just by what I seen—I mean, now 'n' then I'd see her here 'n' there, and that's what it sort of looked like. I know one night about a month back, Mike put her out o' the Swing Club, she was falling-down high and botherin' people. And once I seen her with a real crumbum, like off Skid Row. I mean—"

"This man on Thursday night," Hackett prompted her.

"Yeah, well, it was in here. Teddy and me wasn't here long but I noticed her—on account of the guy she was with. I thought to myself, she's met up with some good luck for a change. She was kind of old, you know, thirty-five at least, and not so good looking any more. But the fellow she had with her, he looked pretty good. Young, and he wasn't minding the bar bill. And another reason I remembered," said Louise, finishing her old-fashioned, "was his name."

"His *name?*" said Hackett.

"Yeah. A real kooky name. See, for the while Teddy and me was here—we went on to my sister's place pretty soon—we was sitting at the next table to them, and I heard her saying his name. I don't remember what they were *saying*—like about the music and all—

but she was kind of high already and giggling silly like, and she called him Julie. Real crazy."

"Julie?" said Hackett. "Julie?"

"That's right. Like a girl's name, you know."

"What did he look like?"

"Oh, sharp," said Louise. "Kind of. He was real blond, and not more'n twenty-five. Nice clothes, gray pants and a sports jacket, and a white shirt. They was both pretty high when I noticed 'em. . . . Well, honey, honest, I'm not a camera eye, I wasn't taking down statistics like on him, but he wasn't so big as you —maybe six foot give or take some, and blond like I say. And—"

And, thought Hackett, Shirley had called him Julie. "What time was that?" he asked.

"Now that I can tell you pretty good, honey. Because Teddy and me we landed at my sister's place just when she and Ed were starting to listen to a TV show, what a drag, some crime bit, and it comes on at ten, we went straight from here, so it must've been about nine-thirty when I noticed Shirley and the guy."

Jackpot, thought Hackett. Or at least a lot more than they'd known about him before. He thought he'd go back to the office and tell Mendoza about it.

Julie? A nickname? It wouldn't do any harm to look in Records. There was a small vague whisper at the back of his mind trying to tell him something about that—

Jason Grace was patient at the routine. Most of the city departments were shut down tight over the weekend, among them the one responsible for streets and public works, but he had been persistent. He had, however, made very little headway. Nobody had been at all cooperative. He would have to contact Mr. Conway on Monday when he'd be in his office—authorization would have to be made by Mr. Wayne—several numbers just hadn't answered, offices deserted on Saturday.

Grace sighed and relinquished the phone after his latest abortive call. Was it all that important, he wondered. His little brainstorm? A five-year-old kid's possibly vague recollection? Couldn't it wait over to Monday, when the city crew would presumably be available for inspection and questioning?

Probably. It was just, he was curious—to know if the little hunch would pay off.

He looked out the window. It was still raining. Harder now.

Carole had put off going back to the apartment, hoping it would stop raining. It hadn't; and she had to go and get her coat, and give back the key. She didn't know why she felt so reluctant, even a little nervous about it. A perfectly natural thing to do.

When she came to think about it—the whole thing —it was just that she was still feeling awfully surprised that Mrs. Newhouse had managed to persuade Mr. Newhouse into the trip around the world. By what he'd said to Carole, he never would have been. But there was Mrs. Newhouse saying—

And how they were leaving all in a hurry. On Sunday.

Carole finally went out, in the rain, about three-thirty. The steady downpour had surprised her; she hadn't thought they had rain like that in California. She took the bus up to the nearest stop, Holloway Drive, and walked up the hill to the big apartment house. She'd just hand the key back to Mrs. Newhouse and get her coat. If the Newhouses weren't there, well, she *had* the key and she could just nip in and get her coat and leave the key.

Nobody *was* there. She rang and waited, rang again.

After all, all she wanted was her coat. Nobody need know.

Carole got out the now illicit key, turned it in the lock, and opened the door.

"Hell and damnation!" said somebody beyond the door. She knew instantly who it was. The other one— the brother. Her horrified, uncomprehending glimpse into the lounge straight ahead of her—*all that blood*— took in the whole scene. *What*—

He said angrily, "What the hell are you doing here?" And then something hit her head and she was floating away, a million miles away—and all she had wanted was her car coat—

Chapter 6

MENDOZA WASN'T in the office when Hackett came in at four o'clock; nobody was there but Sergeant Lake, who was reading a paperback at his desk. But five minutes later, just as Hackett had got a form rolled in the typewriter and was about to start his report, Mendoza came in, fast and annoyed, with John Palliser at his heels. They looked, thought Hackett, like a tough gangster boss and his bodyguard.

"Percy and his *damn* B-girls!" said Mendoza, sweeping off his black Homburg. "I swear to God—it's not our business, damn it, it's a Vice matter—"

"Well, the man's dead," said Palliser soothingly. Hackett got up and went into Mendoza's office.

"Oh, granted, granted," said Mendoza irritably. "Undeniably the man's dead. But it all goes back to the B-girls rolling the suckers, probably with the connivance of the bartenders, and nobody intended to kill the fellow—so all right, technically it's a homicide—right in our laps, as I said—and we've got all the routine to do on it, and meanwhile we've got all these other killers running around loose, and very much more dangerous killers at that, and I just—"

"What's up, Luis?" asked Hackett.

"*¡Infierno!*" said Mendoza succintly, and told him about the body left in the alley. "Quite obviously left there. Stripped of valuables—so kind to leave his ID on him. So very obviously the sucker slipped the knock-out drops—a little too much, quite by mistake—and rolled for what he had on him. So we come in for all the damn routine. And I've already wasted the best part of a day for nothing." He snapped his lighter viciously.

"Well, it's Saturday," said Palisser. "We've been trying to find out something about him—who to notify and so on," he added to Hackett. "All they knew at the Inglewood address—it's an apartment—was that he works at an electrical service store there. On Western Avenue. It's closed. The owner's one Sherman Atwood, but his phone doesn't answer. We routed out all the bar owners and bartenders of the places for a block around where we found Seeley, and nobody remembers him at all. I wouldn't put it past a couple of them to be playing with the B-girls—"

"That Carlos Feliz," said Mendoza darkly.

"But of course, even if we could get search warrants, any evidence is long gone now. Had I better try Atwood again?"

"You can try calling Satan in hell," said Mendoza. "Ultimately he's the one who arranged the mess. B-girls!"

"Well, it *is* a homicide, Luis," said Hackett.

"I know it's a homicide, damn it," said Mendoza. "So we're landed with it. What annoys me, Art—and it annoys me like hell—is that it's a purely accidental homicide, the B-girls and conniving bartenders are scarcely homicidal maniacs, and a lot more important, we've got whoever strangled Shirley and May Gerner, and beat the two old women—all a damn sight more important and dangerous—and so now we've got to waste time on the B-girls. . . . Jimmy, try Andrews' office again. I've got to set up a meeting with him, see what he's got on the B-girls so far. *And* find out about that sailor—Jimmy, I briefed you on that, you get any-thing?"

75

"Just waiting to get a word in," said Lake cheerfully. "Lieutenant Andrews was still out but his office knew, of course. The sailor is Scott Robinson, he laid a complaint yesterday morning about getting rolled. He was in Georgia Street Emergency then. He's been released and was due to report at the naval base in San Francisco tomorrow but I told the Vice office we wanted to talk to him, and went through the red tape, and he's staying over till Monday. He's in the Grant Hotel on Seventh, Lieutenant."

Mendoza grunted. "Something. He can at least give us a description of the pretty little girl who was so friendly. My God—running around the bars looking for B-girls, when—"

"Well, I've got something for you on Shirley," said Hackett. All the way back to headquarters, thinking over what Louise had told him, he'd been conscious of something at the back of his mind—a very faint bell had rung, at something she'd told him, but he couldn't pin it down at all. "I came across this girl who'd known her—well, knew her by sight—and she saw her about nine-thirty Thursday night, with a man."

"That's a step further on," said Mendoza, stubbing out his half-smoked cigarette. "She give us any description?"

"Fair. About six feet, twenty-five, blond. And apparently in the money. She says both he and Shirley were middling high then. This is in a place about a block and a half from the hotel."

"*Bueno.* Could she—"

"And she heard Shirley call him Julie. Which seemed a little funny to me, and I thought it'd do no harm to look in Records. If it's a nickname—but an unusual name anyway and I just—"

Palisser said thoughtfully, "Julie. That's a funny one, all right. For some reason it rings a faint bell in—"

"Does it? You know, that—or something—did with me, too, but I can't for the life of me—"

"*¡Oigame!*" said Mendoza loudly. "*¿Cómo dice?* Wait a minute—Julie? J—"

"What's bitten you?" asked Hackett.

Mendoza flung open the top left-hand drawer of the desk. "*¡Porvida!* I know, damn it, not the best cop in the world has total recall of everything, but—" He brought up a single-sheet flyer from a little pile, scanned it rapidly, shut his eyes and said hollowly, "*Eso ya es llover sobre mojado.* Insult to injury, my God. What else are we going to get, I ask you. *Dios.* Now we've got the Feds to cope with—"

"What are you talking about?"

"Julie!" said Mendoza bitterly, and handed over the flyer and got out another cigarette. "Oh, hell. Jimmy, you'd better call the Feds. Tell them to send somebody over. Everything happens to me."

"Oh—*ow!*" said Hackett over the flyer. "Oh, what a—talk about bells ringing! I should be hearing a whole churchful of—"

"What is it?" asked Palliser. Hackett handed over the flyer. It had been circulated to all police departments in the nation six weeks ago, and it detailed the known recent activities, appearances and habits of one Julian John Kincaid, who had just had the dubious honor of being placed on the F.B.I.'s list of Ten Most Wanted criminals. Julian John Kincaid was described as a native of Louisville, Kentucky. He was six feet even, a hundred and sixty, blond, blue eyes, born December 30, 1940; knife scar on left forearm, appendectomy scar, tattoo on upper right forearm of a skull and crossbones, and he was known to his pals as Julie. He had a long string of minor arrests in Kentucky, Virginia, Iowa, and Nebraska, for drunkenness, common assault, varied violence. When he worked, he worked as a farm laborer, or in town he had been employed by several roofing companies. In December of 1966 he had perpetrated a rather wholesale massacre on a farm family named Jenkins, who had employed him for four months on their farm near Hagarsville, Arkansas, shooting the farmer, his wife, their four teen-age children, a visiting cousin, and wounding another cousin who witnessed the whole thing. No trace of him had been found at once, but it was to be assumed that Kincaid had also been responsible for the murder of Mr. and Mrs. Henry Raftery at their farm outside Clinton, Iowa, as laboratory tests had determined that the same gun—a Savage deer rifle—had been responsible for all nine murders. Kincaid was also suspected of the strangling death of a farm laborer in Nebraska, and was definitely known to have beaten several women after having (said the austere F.B.I.) paid them for their favors. In all known cases where Kincaid had perpetrated violence, he was known to have been drunk. But drunk or sober, he was to be considered armed and dangerous. Any information as to Kincaid's present whereabouts—

"Ouch!" said Palliser. "Julie. Oh, dear. And I saw that when it first—"

"And so did I," said Hackett dismally. "Oh, my God. If that was Kincaid—"

"It's a big country," said Mendoza sardonically, "but are there two walking around so much alike? Six feet, blond, about twenty-five—actually he's twenty-seven now—with the same nickname, and with a habit of leaving murderees behind him?"

"I've got the Feds, Lieutenant."

Mendoza picked up the outside phone. "Who's that?—oh, Hamblen. Mendoza here. You boys are looking for a fellow by the name of Kincaid. . . . That's right. . . . And I know it's very remiss of us, but he seems to have got away with another murder locally while we were looking the other way, and . . . Thursday night. A pushover down here . . . I've got no idea where he is now. I just thought you'd like to know. . . .

Well, you'd better come over and hear all we've got, but it doesn't amount to a damn. Yes, I know. Well, I can't help that. We're supposed to cooperate, but I can't give you what we haven't got. All right, half an hour." He put the phone down. "Everything happens to me—and why the hell it all has to come along at once—"

"I've got Lieutenant Andrews now," said Lake. "He says if you'll come down he'll give you everything Vice has got on the B-girls ring."

Mendoza snarled. "Call him back and tell him I've got the Feds on my neck now. And you, Arturo, will take this flyer with the pretty picture of Julian John Kincaid back to that bar, and ask Louise if this was the John Shirley was with—"

"She's probably home, or picked up a sucker of her own by now—"

"So you'll track her down," said Mendoza. "We'd better make sure where we can. *Dios,* what a—And *nothing* in on Gerner, or Samson, or—"

"Well, I suppose I'd better," said Hackett.

"And we haven't got anything on Seeley yet," said Palliser. "I'll try that number again."

"And if it was Kincaid—and I'd give fifty to one—Kincaid sampling the big city for a change—where is he now?" wondered Mendoza. That, of course, was the big question.

Palisser called Roberta at a quarter to six. "You'd better get used to it. I'll be late. We've got quite a lot coming up all at once—it happens that way sometimes. I don't know how late—"

"I'd better get used to it," agreed Roberta with a smile in her voice. Palisser felt better.

He'd finally got an answer from James Seeley's employer, Atwood. Atwood sounded very surprised and genuinely regretful, hearing about Seeley's untimely end. He said he didn't really know much about Seeley, who'd only worked for him for about six months, but he'd seemed a nice young fellow, and a steady worker—needed experience, but he was learning. Seeley hadn't been very talkative, but Atwood did know he had a brother here, a John G. Seeley in Long Beach. Probably the brother could tell the police more. And Atwood had surely never thought Seeley would be one for hanging around bars or anything like that, but maybe he'd got into some bad company.

That was a foregone conclusion, thought Palliser on the way to Long Beach; he called first, finding the phone number in the book, and John Seeley would be waiting for him. But, like Mendoza, Palliser wasn't very much concerned with James Seeley who had somehow got involved with the B-girls and been slipped the inadvertent overdose and rolled for his wallet. This Kincaid—my God, if one like that was in their territory —and how the hell to hunt for him?

On the other hand, of course, if it was Kincaid who had accounted for Shirley Corrigan—he didn't seem to be too smart, using his own name. Even part of it.

The Feds had been excited. They'd like to drop on Kincaid. Well, one like that—hair-trigger, apparently, whenever he got loaded.

Another one like their Samson? Well, it took some like that. And no leads on that one at all. As for whoever had raped May Gerner—Palliser had heard about Grace's little brain-storm and its rather funny results, but he didn't think much of it. But all that—especially Kincaid—was a good deal more immediate than James Seeley and the B-girls.

Like a conscientious detective, however, Palisser switched his mind off Kincaid when he saw John Seeley. Seeley didn't know about all the rest that was bugging Homicide; to him his young brother Jim was important.

He was a settled citizen about forty, an accountant with a substantial firm, he had a wife and two daughters, and he was broken up over Jim. He wanted to go downtown right away for the formal identification of the body, but Palliser convinced him tomorrow would do as well. He filled in a little for them: not that any of it was very important from their point of view, as offering a line on the girls. "You see, Sergeant, Jim always wanted to get off the farm. I've been doing pretty well, and he always wanted to come out here— but while Dad was still alive—Well, Jim planned it out, he'd taken this correspondence course in electrical work, always good with his hands—and I always thought that was why he never got married, to be tied down—though he was always kind of shy, the quiet type, you know. After Dad died he sold the farm—I was agreeable, half came to me of course—and came out here. What? Yes, he drove—he had Dad's car— and he'd come down to see us most Sundays. I thought he was doing fine. . . . A *bar,* down there—Jim wasn't a drinker!—but I guess I can see, Sergeant, if he— well, he was the quiet type, and he sure wasn't wise to all the big city ways, I can say that—and I know some of the friends he'd made, in the union and around, but maybe not all of them—"

"The car," said Palliser. "What is it?" They hadn't known Seeley had a car. The driver's license didn't necessarily mean ownership of a car. And unless the car was parked somewhere near where he'd lived—

"What? Oh, it's a Ford—1960 two-door Ford, white, I'm afraid I don't know the license. I can't get over it. *Jim.* Down there. A *bar.* I'd have expected Jim to have better sense. My God, I'm only glad Dad doesn't know—"

Higgins got home at ten o'clock, surprised he wasn't more tired. Of course he liked the kids, they didn't bother him at all, but nevertheless they still surprised him. The dismal gray rainy day—he'd called and said maybe they'd better put it off, but the kids wouldn't hear of it, and Mary said resignedly if he didn't mind she didn't. And of course they might run out of the rain, going inland toward Pomona.

They hadn't. It rained all day, never letting up, a steady downpour the way it did when it really got started here. And Stevie and Laura had a wonderful time. Some of the rides weren't running, of course, but the submarine one was, and some others, and all the inside things—and there wasn't a crowd, naturally. Higgins fed them at judicious intervals, and in a moment of inspiration made a slight detour on the way home and stopped at Knotts' Berry Farm and took them to see Independence Hall, and they'd never, they said, had a *better* time. The rain, they said, was *nice*.

He delivered them to Mary halfway soaked through, but they didn't seem to have any sniffles and reacted to the suggestion of cinnamon toast ecstatically.

And Mary had smiled and thanked him and hadn't said a word about spending too much money.

Higgins felt pleased with himself.

He wondered what, if anything, new had turned up downtown. He'd find out tomorrow.

About nine o'clock, when Schenke was completing a crossword puzzle and Galeano had finished reading Hackett's initial report of Kincaid, the night desk sergeant downstairs rang Homicide.

"I've got a guy here wants to talk to somebody up there. He says he's got some information on that murder of the two old women. A William Ellis. Shall I send him up?"

"Does he look like a nut?" asked Galeano. They sometimes got the nuts.

"Not specially. Ordinary citizen. Says he's a retired druggist."

"Well, send him up," said Galeano. It was still raining; it had been raining for some sixteen hours now, and once it passed the twelve-hour mark in Southern

California it was probably going to keep up for a good long while. Galeano supposed the farmers appreciated it, but it got damn tiresome in the city.

About ten minutes later a uniformed man who had escorted William Ellis up through the labyrinth of the big building delivered him to Homicide and Galeano got up to greet him. "Mr. Ellis? I'm Sergeant Galeano. You said you have some information for us?"

"Well, I don't know if it'll mean anything to you," said Ellis nervously, apologetically. "My wife said I should come. After I saw the *Times*. I didn't get round to reading it until this afternoon, and that terrible murder—those two poor women—we were naturally concerned, it happening nearby—a very quiet neighborhood usually, I should say that we live on Darwin Avenue—and when I saw in the *Times* what this Mr. Frawley said—well, I said to my wife— And she said I had better tell the police—we almost called the police at the time, but of course he went away when I told him—But when I thought about it—"

"Yes, sir?" said Galeano. They had to be patient with the citizenry. He got out his notebook.

Mendoza got home at eight-thirty, still feeling annoyed by the intrusive B-girls. Logically he had to admit that it was Homicide's business; but considering Kincaid, and the other dangerous X's around, he was annoyed at the necessity of using time and men to chase down the girls and the bartenders. He had an interview set up with the sailor at nine in the morning; he had all Percy Andrews' gleanings on the case so far, and meager they were. He had had a long session with the Feds over Kincaid, and the Feds were annoyed with him because he couldn't tell them where Kincaid had gone after strangling Shirley.

At least they were pretty sure it was Kincaid. Dismally, the Feds didn't have Kincaid's prints; nobody did; but Hackett had done some overtime tracking down Louise. Located, and shown the F.B.I. photograph—a slightly fuzzy blow-up of a snapshot—of Julian Kincaid, she had agreed that that was the guy who'd been with Shirley on Thursday night. They would now, with immense trouble and a lot of legwork, look up other patrons of that bar on Thursday night and ask. Also the bartender. Shadwell at the hotel had been uncertain; it might have been the guy.

And with one like Kincaid possibly still in their territory, the time to waste over Seeley.

"Talk about making bricks without straw!" he complained to Alison. "And what's the end of that? Involuntary manslaughter and a three-to-five. But we've got to look, damn it."

"I don't see how," said Alison. "There must be dozens—more—of those girls. And any bar down there—"

"Not any bar. No. Most bar owners are very chary of losing the license. But the hell of it is, the bartenders needn't know. They might suspect, and chase the girls out. Some of them don't even do that, it's business after all. Shut their eyes to it. I have no doubt," said Mendoza, "that that Feliz is one like that. *Pues si.* He could tell us this and that, and I think I'll lean on him a little. And the *hell* of it—so we get a search warrant for Feliz's place, one of the two nearest where Seeley's body was left—by the time we go and look, even if there was any cache of chloral hydrate—or anything else—it's gone. *Dios,* what a waste of time."

"Yes, I see that."

"I need a drink." He went out to the kitchen, inevitably pursued by El Señor, and poured a half-ounce of rye in a saucer for their alcoholic cat before coming back to the living room with his own full shot glass. "Kincaid—*¡Santa María!* Sampling the big city—he could be in New York by now. What that flyer didn't say, I now hear from the Feds, is that he got upwards of six grand in cash from the Jenkins—a home safe with a lock opened by a key—"

"*¡Parece mentira!*" said Alison.

"Oh, yes. Such a one to have loose, and I thought so when I first saw that flyer, but now I know he could be loose in my territory— We heard a little more about him. The low I.Q., and the kind who goes crazy with the load on, genuine head-doctor crazy. The Feds say. I don't buy all the jargon, but—" He shrugged. He was walking up and down the living room, drink in hand, and didn't notice Sheba poised on the coffee table.

"*¡Cuidado!*" said Alison, but Sheba took off as she spoke and landed neatly on Mendoza's left shoulder.

"*¡Demonio!*" said Mendoza, staggering to preserve his drink.

"Nyeouh," said Sheba, affectionately patting his moustache.

"Jargon!" said Mendoza, swallowing the rest of the rye and hauling Sheba down to lie on her back in his arms, where she smirked up at him enjoying the attention. "Poor orphan—farmed out to foster families—society to blame! So how many former orphans go around strewing corpses in their wake?"

"The head-doctors," said Alison. "But of course he could be on the other side of the country, Luis."

"And I hope to God he is," said Mendoza. "But on the other hand, if he is still here, I'd damn well like to—" The telephone rang in the hall and he lengthened stride to answer it. Alison went down to the nursery. . . .

"You got them off early, the lambs," she said to Dorothy. Johnny and Teresa were pinkly sweet in slumber; she bent over them fondly. Funny how Johnny looked so much like her own father, and Terry had Luis' deep widow's peak. Genes. "We'll have to start thinking about a birthday party next week—" She must call Angel. Angel would make one of her special cakes, and if Máiri could get away just for the afternoon—they were really too young to know what a birthday party was, but they must have one.

"Yes, ma'am," said Dorothy automatically.

Alison glanced at her. The nice young English nursemaid. So good with the twins, if not like their Máiri. The pretty fresh-complexioned face just a little more consciously fixed than usual: the impersonal servant. "You're—liking it here?" asked Alison. "Everything's all right, Dorothy?"

"Oh, yes, ma'am," said Dorothy sincerely.

Actually, Dot was a little worried. Just a little. She had decided she'd like to see Carole tomorrow, when they were both off, and find out if there had been any awkwardness with Mrs. Newhouse. What Carole had said about the woman, she might have been—difficult. The type that could be. That type took easy offense. She'd got the phone number from Carole a couple of weeks ago, and in her first free moment this afternoon had called. After several rings a woman's voice had answered her, and at her polite request to speak to Carole there'd been a little gasp, and then the woman had just said abruptly, "I'm sorry, she's left, she's not here," and hung up.

Left already? But where? There *had* been a row, thought Dot. And where had Carole gone?

Chapter 7

PATROLMEN WORK a three-shift day, and Patrolmen Gomez and Barrett came on duty and started their regular tour at eight o'clock on Sunday morning. It was still raining; it had gone on steadily all night and didn't show any signs of letting up. Gomez was driving. He cruised slowly down the wet, largely empty streets; visibility was poor in the gray morning. He turned down Third from Los Angeles Street, went down to Grand and turned left. There were a few people about, on their way to work, bundled up in coats and carrying umbrellas.

Suddenly Barrett said, "Hold it, Joe." Gomez put his foot on the brake. "Look at that damn fool lush. If he's been there all night, lucky he hasn't got pneumonia. We'd better——" He opened the passenger door.

The drunk was sprawled up against the building there, appropriately just outside a bar, under no cover at all. Gomez's first thought was, the citizens. Probably several people on foot had passed him since it was light, but they would have averted righteous eyes and given him a wide berth. Barrett got out, hunching his plastic-raincoated shoulders against the downpour, and went over to the sprawled figure. A minute later he came back, thrust his head in the door and said briefly, "Better alert Homicide. He's dead."

Gomez reached for the mike. "Not surprising, if he passed out there last night. A wonder he didn't drown."

"No," said Barrett seriously. "His head's bashed in, Joe. A real homicide."

"*Caray,*" said Gomez, and spoke into the mike.

The message, relayed up to Homicide, produced something like consternation. They were all there— Hackett, Higgins, Grace, Palliser and Landers—and Sergeant Lake, after commenting on the rain, had just told them that the boss had called and said he wouldn't be in until he'd seen this sailor, when Gomez's message came through. Body found in street outside the Sweet and Low Bar on Grand Avenue, male body.

"My good God in Heaven," said Hackett, "he'll have a *fit*. You know how he feels about this damn Vice thing anyway—and it is a hell of a nuisance, just now. And here's another one!"

"I suppose somebody'd better go and take care of it," said Higgins, looking up from the F.B.I. flyer on Kincaid. "Yeah, isn't it the truth. But the B-girls are getting kind of careless, killing two in two nights, Art. I wonder if it is."

"Oh, hell," said Hackett, "I'll go look at it. Well, that's what it looks like, doesn't it?—and the nerve of it—left right outside the bar—"

He told Lake to dispatch an ambulance, put on his hat and coat again, and went down to the lot for the Barracuda. Just past Fourth on Grand. The windshield wipers were little use against the hard downpour, it was like driving in fog, and it took him fifteen minutes to get there. He spotted the patrol car and pulled up behind it.

At least on a day like this the few citizens out weren't stopping to form a crowd.

"We thought it was a drunk at first," said Barrett, who was standing beside the body.

Hackett squatted and surveyed the body gloomily. Luis would go straight up in the air, he thought, and he couldn't blame him. With the intentional killers, the dangerous ones, running around, the time had to be wasted on the unintentional homicide. Though it did seem a little funny that the would-be robbers of drunks should be so unlucky twice.

The body was that of a man about forty-five, a spare man with thinning gray-brown hair, clean-shaven, nothing remarkable about him except a distinctively long, high-beaked nose. He was unobtrusively dressed in a cheap gray suit, white shirt and dark tie. He was reminiscent of the body of James Seeley in that his suit jacket had been thrown back and the breast pocket torn open, and both trouser pockets were turned inside out. Obviously, either rolled after he'd passed out, or deliberately doped so he could be rolled.

"If you'll look at his head—" said Barrett.

Hackett looked, and felt. An old gray felt hat was lying beside the body. It, and the body, and the clothes on the body, were sodden with rain. "Oh," said Hackett. "Well, fancy that." There was a soft depression at the back of the skull.

So maybe it wasn't the B-girls after all. Maybe he'd just fallen down and fractured his skull, and somebody had stumbled across him and taken advantage of it. Or, of course, maybe somebody had tried to roll him before he was quite out and he'd fought back. It was up in the air.

Hackett groped under the jacket, and in what remained of the breast pocket found a billfold. He ducked back through the rain to the protection of the patrol car, where Barrett had already taken refuge, and with the uniformed men watching impassively opened the wallet. It was very unlikely that there'd be any prints on it; it was rough simulated lizard.

There wasn't, course, any money in it, but there was a lot of identification. Garvin Trumbull. A birth certificate neatly folded, why the hell was he carrying his birth certificate around? Garvin Wesley Trumbull, born

June 28, 1921, in Chicago. A Social Security card. An out-of-date driver's license issued in Illinois. An L.A. library card. A folded form, carbon of the original, issued by the L.A. County General Hospital—he had been a patient there, apparently, from August to September, and as usual required to sign the form agreeing to pay minimum costs when possible. A torn-off piece of paper with the address of the downtown State Employment Agency written on it. Two carbon copies of letters Trumbull had written applying for jobs, the dates months past—apparently Trumbull had been a bookkeeper. A postcard from Phoenix, bearing the scrawled message, "Dear Garvin, How you doing over there, hope you found a job O.K., we are all fine, Len." There was, in the first plastic slot of the wallet, a card carefully filled out with his name and an address on Carondelet Street, but the space for "who to notify in case of emergency" was left blank. And there was a bankbook—that and the letters were tucked into the money compartment. It was a bankbook from the Bank of America, a savings account book, and it showed a balance of $52.75.

"Well, well," said Hackett. "Poor devil." The ambulance arrived. There was nothing to be gained by a minute examination by an eagle-eyed detective of the corpse *in situ*—any evidence left around would have been thoroughly eliminated by the downpour by now. Hackett told the internes to take the corpse, sent the patrol car on its way, and drove back to the office.

Everybody but Jason Grace groaned when he told them about Trumbull. True, a different M.O. so it hadn't necessarily been the string of B-girls, but it fell into the pattern, and a very anonymous kill it was, the kind they slaved over on all the routine and threw into Pending eventually. Last night, on that dark street deserted and lonely after midnight, who could even guess what had happened to Garvin Trumbull? The little unimportant man, drunk or sober? Drunk, robbed by the casual late pedestrian? Deliberately struck down for the little money in his pockets? How ever to find out?

"No next of kin indicated," said Palliser. "The city'll take his $52.75 to help bury him."

"Probably," said Hackett. "Damnation. Look, we've got things to do." There were the other known rapists out of Records to hunt up and question, on Gerner; and Seeley to backtrack (with luck, what Mendoza got from the sailor would give them some lead there, plus what Vice had already turned up before); there was just nowhere new to look on Samson, but now the possibility that Kincaid had been here had showed up, somebody would have to cover all those bars where Shirley was known, all over again, and show the picture and ask specifically about Kincaid. Hackett sighed. And in this rain. Californians are apt to take more than a reasonable amount of rain—a nice little hour-long shower—as a personal affront. "John, suppose you take a couple dozen of those flyers and cover all the bars. George and I can start after the rapists again—" He had heard about Grace's brain-storm and was reserving judgment on it; he knew a little more than Grace about the vagaries of childhood. "I suppose somebody'd better hang around in case the boss—"

"I think I'll be busy," said Grace dreamily from his desk. "Any of you take a look at this?"

"I saw it," said Higgins. "Does it say anything? Just more corroboration backing up the tale we heard from Frawley and Burson."

"I think it might say just a little bit more," said Grace mildly.

Hackett took the report from him and read it rapidly. It was signed by Galeano. A Mr. William Ellis had voluntarily come in at nine P.M. to offer information on the Prothero-Turner homicide. Mr. Ellis lived on Darwin Avenue, about three blocks away from the

Prothero house on Albion Street. He stated that on Thursday night when he and his wife were just retiring, at approximately eleven-thirty, somebody began pounding loudly on the front door. Ellis looked out a front window without opening the door and was alarmed to see on the front porch a very large male Negro, apparently very drunk. The Negro said he was looking for Fred Holt. He repeated the name several times, and Ellis was quite sure of it; by his talk, the Negro had a quarrel to settle with Holt. On being told there was no Fred Holt at that address, the Negro finally staggered off and down the street. It was not until Ellis had seen the interview with Mr. Frawley in the *Times* that he realized that his intruder might have something to do with the murder on Albion Street, and he had promptly come in to give his information.

"Interesting, but does it take us anywhere?" asked Hackett. "You have another brainstorm, Jase?"

"There's just something I want to check. Give me a couple of hours on it."

"O.K."

"Hey, are you leaving me to hold the baby and tell the boss about the new one?" asked Landers in alarm.

"We'll let Jimmy. You go along with John and distribute the flyers."

"Now look—" said Sergeant Lake.

"He'll go up like a rocket, but he can't eat you," said Hackett. "Come on, boys, let's get to work. The better the day the better the deed."

When Mendoza got to headquarters at ten-thirty he was feeling pleased and optimistic. What he'd got from the young sailor, Robinson, more or less reinforced some of what Percy Andrews' Vice boys had turned up on their poking around for the B-girls.

He had questioned the sailor in his room at the Grant Hotel, a good second-rate hotel, clean and plain. He wondered if he had ever—even at the age of five, say, what he could remember of Luis Rodolfo Vicente Mendoza, the ragged little Mex kid running the squalid streets down here—been as young as the sailor. He decided he never had been.

Young Robinson blushed at every third word, and was painfully naïve. "She seemed like a nice girl, sir," he said. "She'd only let me buy her Coca-Cola, she didn't drink the real thing. She wasn't fresh or anything." He still looked a little surprised about it. He was nineteen, with a very fresh, pink-cheeked complexion and very blue eyes and a round face under sandy hair.

"She said her name was Sue? Didn't give you a last name?" asked Mendoza.

"No, sir. I didn't think about it then, I guess I should've, but I—well," and he blushed, "I'd had, well, a drink of whiskey. Two, I guess. I never had any before, I'm not used to, well, drinking—Pa's strictly death on it—and I guess I wasn't thinking straight."

Mendoza reflected that Sue—and the probable male accomplice—had been unnecessarily hasty; if they'd just let nature take its course, probably the third or fourth drink would have put Robinson out without the need for knockout-drops. "Can you give me a description of her?"

"Well, I guess so. She was kind of little, only about five feet high maybe, and—you know," he blushed again, "an awful nice figure, but *little*. Thin. I don't mean scrawny or—but sort of cute. She had black hair cut kind of short but curly in front, and big brown eyes with long lashes, and I couldn't tell she had on much makeup but lipstick, bright red lipstick, and some nice perfume like—sort of like lilies, I thought. She seemed like a nice girl, sir. I couldn't rightly believe —but that other police officer said—"

"You didn't see her put anything in your drink?"

"Oh, no, sir!"

Mendoza glanced at his notes. "This was in Pete's

93

Grill on Alameda? Yes. Were you at a table or the bar?"

"Kind of a booth like, sir."

"And who was bringing the drinks, the bartender or a waiter?"

"I think it was the bartender, sir. I don't exactly remember too good, but I think—well, it was just a little place."

"Yes. Did you see the girl speak to anyone while she was with you?"

"I kind of recall she said thanks to the bartender when he brought the drinks—and she said hello to another girl who came in—a big blonde girl that was, dressed sort of flashy—she was with a man—"

"Remember what he looked like?"

"Gee, I don't guess I do—it was dark in there—he was kind of tall and thin—"

"That's very helpful," said Mendoza. It was. What Vice had turned up before, from the various complainants who had been rolled, was a description of four different women: and two of them, who had given the suckers various names, were described as a small dark girl about twenty with a very good figure, big brown eyes and bangs, and a voluptuous big blonde about twenty-eight. The other two were respectively ash blonde and auburn, somewhere in their mid-thirties. There was also mention of a tall thin man seen with one or the other of the girls.

"Well, I guess it was an experience," said the young sailor, "but I sure never suspected anything. She seemed so nice."

"So you'll think twice in the future," said Mendoza. "Not such a good idea to hang around cheap bars, sailor."

"Well, I guess not. But, well, gee—"

"*¡Diez millón demonios!*" he said to Sergeant Lake. "*Another* one?" But to Lake's secret surprise, he wasn't really exploding. "I will be damned—and the nerve of these punks—just left outside the bar? Details, *por favor.*"

"Well, Art didn't write up a report on it—yet. There's a lot to do—he and George are out chasing down the rapists, and it's Matt's day off, and Tom went out with Palliser to hand out those flyers and—All I can tell you is what Art said. And he left the guy's ID on your desk."

Mendoza heard what Lake could tell about the unfortunate Garvin Trumbull, and said thoughtfully, "Annoying. Even more anonymous than Seeley. Because —Yes." He went into his office, sat down and looked at Garvin Trumbull's well-filled if moneyless billfold.

Pay your money and take your choice. The different M.O. said very little. It could be that they'd been clumsy and Trumbull had noticed his drink being doctored. And so there'd have been a row—ask the patrons at that bar, and what a job to track them down —and somebody had bashed in his head. It could also be—Mendoza was as depressingly aware as Hackett had been—that Trumbull had either passed out drunk, or quite innocently fallen and banged his head, and subsequently been robbed by a passer-by. And it could be they'd never know much about it. The autopsy would tell them whether he'd been drunk, of course.

But at any rate, there was a distinct possibility that they could clean the B-girl thing up fast, with these descriptions. Quite definite descriptions; there shouldn't be too much difficulty locating the pocket Venus or the voluptuous blonde. Somebody was always ready to tell tales, and there was a lot of jealousy in that trade.

And it wouldn't do any harm to lean a little heavier on that bar owner Carlos Feliz.

These stupid little punks, the lazy mean little people, how very tired he did get of dealing with them. . . .

Meanwhile— He slid Garvin Trumbull's wallet into a manila envelope and went to the door. "Doesn't anybody remember any basic rules, Jimmy? There's no next of kin listed for Trumbull but there is an address. If possible we've got to get formal identification on him."

"Oh, sure. Art said he'd try at that address first while George got busy on the rapists again. One of them was following up Trumbull, anyway—and John said he had to be back by eleven, he had a date set up with Seeley's brother to make that formal ID at the morgue."

"Bueno. Just so I know everything's being taken care of," said Mendoza. "Where's Jase?"

"Oh, he had another little idea and went off somewhere. About that overnight report of Galeano's. It's on your desk."

"Nobody tells me anything." Mendoza went to find it. "Fred Holt. *Holt.* Now what does that say to me?" He ruminated.

"It seemed to say something to Jase. You'd better polish up your crystal ball, Lieutenant—he gets hunches too."

Mendoza laughed. "And sometimes hits the jackpot. A bright boy." And there were things he could be doing, but he sat down at his desk again and took the worn deck of cards from the top drawer. He always thought better with the cards in his hands.

Not so hard, probably, to drop on Sue and the blonde. They would probably talk. Little pros—stupid, stupid people, as ninety-nine percent of the pros always were—and they might give away the man. Or men. What they wanted, to make any charge of manslaughter stick, was some concrete evidence of one of the girls being with Seeley before he died. All these bodies— he wondered when Bainbridge would get round to sending up the autopsy report on Seeley.

He dealt himself a poker hand from a set-up deck, and was gratified to find his old skill for a crooked deal remained with him.

All precincts had been alerted about Kincaid. He had heard this and that about Kincaid from the Feds, and he thought now it was a fairly good chance (or bad) that Kincaid was still around here somewhere. Kincaid hadn't run after he'd committed the massacre back east; he'd been seen in neighboring towns four and five days afterward, before the wounded witness had recovered consciousness and named him. He hadn't run after his next murder in Iowa; he'd dawdled around in his victims' car for a week, the local officers not aware of his past history or guilt. He wasn't a very bright fellow, Kincaid. Were any of them? He could still be around. And he was a distinctive fellow, with that shock of blond hair.

See what turned up from all the bars. Somebody must have seen him, if he'd been here any length of time. Had he picked up other girls, when he wasn't drunk, before Shirley?

Poor Shirley.

Mendoza cut the deck and turned up the ace of diamonds. *Tuerto,* the one-eyed—best ace in the pack. He smiled at it. He shuffled, marking it, and cut the deck apparently at random, and turned it up again. Shuffled and cut, and turned it up a third time. He was one of three men in the country could do that little trick, and it needed practice. . . .

Well, a lot of tough routine still to be done on all these damned cases, but time and hard work would get the job wound up. With any luck.

"You like some coffee?" asked Sergeant Lake.

"*Sí.* And then I'd better go and do some work for a change."

Dot got off the bus still wondering what she'd say to Mrs. Newhouse.

The violence of the rainstorm didn't surprise her— quite like London at its worst—because she'd been

through three California winters. She wouldn't hav
come out, even on her day off, if it hadn't been fo
Carole: she'd have stayed on in the house on Ray
Grande Avenue and written to Mum. Not as if she ha
anything special to do. She'd dated some boys here
but nobody regular—and there'd always been a sor
of understanding between her and Reg Stanborough
she didn't mean to stay here forever and Red was do
ing fine in Winscombe at home, in the Austin agency
there.

One thing she'd just found out would make a fine in
teresting item to go in the letter to Mum. Mr. Mendoz
was in the police here. No, he had some title, Mrs
Mendoza had said—they weren't Constable and In
spector and so on like at home. Dot hadn't known be
fore, just that he went off in the morning like any mar
with a job. The police must pay awfully well, she
thought—it was an expensive house, beautiful furni
ture and all. And Mrs. Mendoza had the most smash
ing clothes, and jewelry. Of course, perhaps she wa
the one who had the money.

Like Mrs. Newhouse, Carole said. Dot was just a
little worried about Carole. Putting two and two to
gether, by what the woman—Mrs. Newhouse?—ha
said on the phone yesterday, when Carole said she wa
leaving there had been a little row, and evidentl
Carole had left right then. Only, where?

I'm silly to *bother,* thought Dot crossly, toiling up the
hill with her umbrella pulled by the sudden gusts o
wind. Carole might be a little idiot some ways but she
wasn't a complete fool—she said she had some money
saved—she'd have gone to a hotel until she could tell
the agency, or—

And just what was she to say to this Mrs. Newhouse?
Carole wouldn't have told Mrs. Newhouse where she
was going, especially if there'd been a row. Suddenly
seeing that clearly, Dot nearly turned back; but she'd

come this far, and she didn't *know* there'd been a row, Carole could have said something to the woman—

It was, when she came to the address, a large apartment building. Very modern, very posh, if only two-storyed. The apartment was 12-C. Dot went in, leaning her umbrella tidily against the wall in the foyer, and climbed silent carpeted stairs. She found 12-C at the rear of the second floor corridor, and feeling nervous pressed the bell.

Quite distinctly she heard a sudden exclamation in a woman's voice, from beyond the door—muffled, but audible—and then there was silence. She pressed the bell again and waited quite a long time, but there was no response. Dot was annoyed, and for no reason a little frightened. There was somebody in there, she was sure.

After she'd rung a fourth and fifth time, she turned away, frustrated. She didn't know what else she could do.

Carole, after all, had some sense—and it wasn't as if she were penniless. She was probably perfectly all right, somewhere, and sooner or later Dot would hear from her.

Mendoza was delayed getting down to the legwork himself by a Fed who dropped in to discuss Kincaid and whether he could still be there, and he was still talking with a Fed, a nice fellow named Bright—which he was—at eleven-fifty when Jason Grace looked in.

"You busy, Lieutenant?"

"Killing time. Don't tell me, things to do. Come and meet—"

"Too busy to interview Samson?" asked Grace gently. "I've got him here."

"I haven't measured his shoes against the pretty casts," said Grace, "but I think he is. I really do think so. One Lee Beauchamp. Nice aristocratic name, isn't it? Which he isn't. I don't think it'll be much trouble to make him come apart. I just thought—"

"How the hell did you drop on him? You're sure? For God's sake—"

"I just sort of followed my nose," said Grace.

Chapter 8

THE FED said regretfully he'd better get back to work, and took himself off. Mendoza demanded chapter and verse from Grace.

"It was a fluke," said Grace. "Just luck. That name, Fred Holt—it's a common enough name, but I knew I'd seen it somewhere just recently, and it finally came to me—I'd seen it in the *Herald*. He got picked up for burglary. So I went down and asked Goldberg about it, and it turns out Holt is sitting down at the facility on Alameda because he couldn't make bail. So I went and saw him." He lit a cigarette. "I described Samson to him, far as we knew what he looked like, and what we've got on him, and asked him if he knew anybody like that. After all, if Samson knew him—it was a reasonable assumption."

"You're not telling me you've got a simple mind?" said Mendoza sarcastically.

Grace grinned. "Basically, simple as hell. I could see Holt was a nice enough fellow—"

"A burglar."

"Just part time. When his luck runs out at cards or the ivories. I told him about the murder and he was shocked," said Grace. "He says he doesn't hold with stuff like that, getting all violent and hurting folk. But he couldn't come up with any name—said he knows a lot of guys pretty big and who like to tie one on—until

I mentioned the rye. You know, the bottle of Old Overholt. Then he said right off, that'd be Lee Beauchamp, he always drank rye when he had the money for anything but *vino*. He told me where Beauchamp was living, with a couple of other men, an old shack the other side of the yards. So I went and took a look at him—when he came home—and I thought he looked interesting, so I fetched him in."

"Just like that," said Mendoza. He got up and went to the door.

"I fetched him," said Grace softly, *"in toto* as it were, to let you see the whole pretty picture at once."

Sitting on the straight chair there under Sergeant Lake's dubious eye was as unprepossessing a specimen of *homo sapiens* as Mendoza had ever beheld. Lee Beauchamp was probably under thirty, but he might have been any age by his gaunt appearance. He slouched there, a heady, heavy aroma rising from him composed of rye whiskey, long-unwashed humanity, long-unwashed clothes, and cheap wine. He was soaking wet and a little pond of rain had dribbled from him to the floor. "He'd been out walking around before I found him," said Grace apologetically. He was slightly drunk, no more, but long habitual drunkenness had left the blood-alcohol rate permanently affected, probably. He had on an ancient pair of brown wool pants too small for him, a dirty red shirt torn at the collar, no tie, an old tan garbadine raincoat which looked as if he'd plucked it out of a refuse can somewhere; and he sat with his long legs stretched out before him, so Mendoza had a good view of the clodhopper old shoes with the metal plate on the right heel, the much run-over left heel and the sizable hole in the right sole. There were many stains on the coat, but some down the front were rusty-brown.

"¡Qué mono!" said Mendoza.

"I thought you'd like him," said Grace. "I like him quite a lot."

Both Grace and Mendoza were somewhat fastidious individuals, addicted to the daily bath and the tidy grooming, but the incongruity raised no smile on Sergeant Lake's face. He rather liked Lee Beauchamp, too. It was always nice to get something cleared away.

"I thought—" said Grace, and Glasser came in. He was very wet and looked disgruntled.

"Not a smell of Kincaid anywhere I've asked. I think he's long gone—" He shed his coat, and looked again at Beauchamp hunched in the chair. "Oh-oh, what have we here?"

"You can help out on the questioning," said Mendoza.

"I don't know that we'll get much out of him," said Grace doubtfully. "He may not even remember much, you know. But we've got his shoes, and I'm taking bets those are bloodstains on his coat—"

They hauled Beauchamp up, into an interrogation room, and waste of time though it was they scrupulously told him about his rights and privileges and asked if he wanted a lawyer. Beauchamp blinked at them.

"Huh?"

So they started asking him about last Thursday night, and about Fred Holt. They got a response there.

"He owe me fi' dollahs, man. He do. Hidin' out on me, 'n' I need that money bad. You know wheah Fred is?"

"He's in jail, Lee. Were you looking for him on Thursday night?"

"Jail. Man, tha' so? He owe me fi' dollahs, he gotta pay. Welsh on *me,* he bettah try! I been lookin' for Freddy Holt—"

"Thursday night?" asked Grace. "You remember Thursday night, Lee?"

He blinked again. "I dunno. Whass today?"

"Sunday, Lee. All day. Were you out looking for Holt on Thursday night?"

He shook his head fuzzily. "I been lookin' for him.

Get my fi' dollahs. I need that money, he ain't got no right welsh on me. You lemme have a li'l drink, I maybe remember—"

It went on like that for quite a while. "I told you," said Grace. "What we get on him is going to be the nice laboratory evidence, all scientific. The shoes. The coat. It's on the cards he hasn't washed since and there may be some blood on his hands—under his nails."

Mendoza grimaced. "I wouldn't doubt." Beauchamp was getting restive by then, and alternatively demanding a drink or to be let go, and when they turned back they found he'd hauled a bottle out of his pocket and was taking a generous swallow. Grace took it away from him; it was a pint bottle of Old Overholt rye.

"Hey! You gimme that—" Beauchamp swayed to his feet, his eyes sparkling dangerously. He was well over six feet and despite his gauntness formidable. He took a swing at Grace, who dodged, and the three of them forced him back into his chair. "Whuh you guys think you doin', anyways? Wheah is this you brung me? You lemme go! Tell me Freddy in jail—I nevah see my fi' dollahs—I bettah go 'n'—"

"You're going nowhere, Lee," said Mendoza. They searched him then, and didn't find anything of interest—he had a dollar and a half on him and that was about all except the bottle—and then Grace took him down to the same jail where Holt was waiting trial, and booked him in as a material witness pending the warrant for homicide. He brought back Beauchamp's shoes and raincoat, having asked the jail doctor—who had wrinkled a fastidious nose at him—to glean some samplings of whatever was under Beauchamp's nails for the lab; and Mendoza turned over the shoes and the coat to the lab, asking priority on the examination.

"But it does look kind of open and shut," said Grace in satisfaction. "And what a hell of a stupid thing. Just blundering into a place like that, not even, likely, remembering much about it. Killing for nothing. Just the kind goes berserk with the liquor inside."

"Not the first time it's happened, Jase. And I tend to be one like that, too. Reason I don't drink much."

"I had heard. But then you're smarter than Lee Beauchamp, Lieutenant." Grace laughed. "Him hunting Fred Holt and his five bucks. Who knows where he got the idea Holt lived around there? And the Prothero house with all that cash and the diamonds—"

Glasser got out a cigarette thoughtfully. "Little windfall for the state, maybe. Nobody knew of any relations, both women sole alone. Why the hell were they hoarding it away, living down here, when they could—"

"That kind of thing," said Mendoza, "Can get to be a habit, Henry. Like the Old Overholt." He thought of his miserly grandfather, to whom he owed his affluence.

But it was nice—provisionally—to have one cleared up. The technical work would stretch out, it'd be some while before it came to trial, but at least, except for the remaining paper work on it, this one was out of their hair.

"Oh, yes," said David Daly rapidly, "oh, yes, that's him." He gulped and looked hastily away from the sheeted body lying on the morgue tray. "Mr. Trumbull." Hackett nodded at the morgue attendant and the tray was silently rolled back into the refrigerated case. "Couldn't mistake that big nose. But I can't understand how he came to get— A very nice quiet tenant. Not that I *knew* him at all, you understand. Not—not intimate, you know." He followed Hackett in undisguised relief out of the big cold room into the corridor outside, mopping his face.

"Well, what can you tell me about him, if anything?" asked Hackett. He had found Daly at home in the front ground-floor apartment at the address on Carondelet—Daly the manager there. Reluctantly Daly had agreed to view the body.

"Well, I didn't know much about him. We get a turnover in apartments these days, people coming and going." Daly mopped his face again. He was a little man, very hairy, with a small prissy-looking mouth and an unexpected bass voice. "Terrible to see anybody like that. Place like this. I can't understand how he came to have it happen to him. Killed like that. It must have been an accident. Though these juveniles running around, you don't know *what* they'll do. He wouldn't have had much money on him. He's been out of work for several months."

"He was a bookkeeper, wasn't he? How long had he lived in the apartment, Mr. Daly?"

"He did office work of any kind, I suppose. Oh, only since last May. The doctors said he had a little TB on one lung—he told me—and he come out to Arizona but he didn't like it and couldn't get any but part-time work so he come over here. And he had a job—that's when he moved in—but in August he took sick, some kind of stomach trouble I think it was, and he was in the General about three weeks. And he'd just got back on his feet, and he apologized to me, the rent behind some—I was sorry for him—he just paid up yesterday, I suppose out of his savings. He'd been looking for a job, he went to the state employment agency—"

Yes, they'd found the address on him, of course. "You saw him yesterday, then?" asked Hackett.

"I did, I said so, he paid me the back rent, and said he'd got a job. That's why I can't understand how the poor guy came to be—"

"Oh. What was the job, do you know?"

"I don't. He said something, but I don't rightly recall—All I know is, he paid up in full, ninety dollars it was counting what he owed for last month, and he left with his suitcase and that's the last I—"

"His suitcase? Was he going somewhere?"

"Yes, yes, didn't I say? I said he must've had some

good luck for a change, when he come to pay me, and he said yes, he'd got a good new job, he said—let me think now what he *did* say—yes, he said a different job than he'd ever had but it'd be more healthy for him, I don't know what he meant, but he'd have to be moving on account of the job, maybe it was out of town somewheres. And I saw he already had his suitcase packed. It's a furnished apartment, he'd just have his clothes. And he paid me and off he went."

"This was at what time?" asked Hackett.

"Oh, early. Fairly. About nine o'clock in the morning. I can't make out how he come to get killed such a terrible way. Was it a mugger, something like that?" Daly shook his head. "He was a quiet fellow. Not very talkative. Why, all I've told you about him, the little I know, I heard kind of piecemeal since he'd lived there. Just a little conversation when he paid the rent. I felt sorry for him."

"Did he ever mention any family?"

"No. That's another thing I can say—I do remember he said once, when he was sick that time—he called and asked me to call a doctor, he didn't know any doctors around here—he said there wouldn't be anybody to mourn him. I guess he was alone in the world, poor fellow. I mean, he didn't say it being sorry for himself, like that, but kind of cheerful really. The poor *guy,*" said Daly. "I don't think he was more than forty-five or so."

"He was found," said Hackett, "on the street outside a bar. Would you say—"

"A bar!" said Daly. "Oh, now, that certainly don't sound like Mr. Trumbull, Sergeant—"

"You identified the body."

"Yes, yes it's him," said Daly hastily, "know him anywhere, but what I mean is he didn't drink. Not unless he was what they call a secret drinker, but if so I'd have seen the bottles in the trash, wouldn't I, and I didn't, and anyway if he was like that he wouldn't be going in bars. He didn't, Sergeant. He was careful with his money, I know from things he said, he had to be, and he had this stomach trouble, he knew he shouldn't drink liquor. He said that to me once."

Well, thought Hackett, Mr. Garvin Trumbull looked like being a little mystery after all. It sounded a little funny.

"It must've been somebody knocked him down and killed him just for his money and maybe the suitcase," said Daly. "Terrible thing. He wouldn't have had much on him."

The suitcase. That was something new; no suitcase with the body. Hackett reflected that it was still the anonymous thing. And it could have been the casual on-the-make mugger, taking the chance that Trumbull had money on him, something of value in his suitcase.

Only, he thought, where had Trumbull been all day? Renting another apartment somewhere? Why? The new job. Why should a new job necessitate his moving?

And what had Trumbull—recently out of the General Hospital, an incipient tubercular with some vague stomach trouble—been doing out wandering around Grand Avenue late in the evening in a torrent of rain?

John Seeley had given Palliser a recent snapshot of his brother Jim, and Palliser was out wandering around, showing it to bartenders and regular patrons of the bars. About three o'clock, coming back to one of the bars on San Pedro nearest the alley where Seeley had been found, Palliser struck a little pay dirt. A little first, and then a lot. He'd had to come back because the bartender on duty at night didn't come on until three. The bartender was a weedy little man with cynical eyes; he'd been wiping glasses as a hard-faced blonde washed them, and he wiped his hands on a dirty towel, took the snapshot, studied it, and said, "Yeah, I seen that guy in here a few times. Here, Mabel, you look—you remember him?"

The blonde looked. "Yeah, he was here. Now and then. With another guy, I don't know any names."

"Not regulars we get in alla time, I don't think he lived around here. I couldn't tell you anything about him," said the bartender.

"Do you remember him picking up a girl while he was here?" asked Palliser.

The bartender's eyes hardened. "You insinuatin' we got set-ups operatin' out of here, cop? You callin' me a pimp? I don't hafta—"

"No, I just wondered if he ever picked up a girl in here, that's all. You know, the casual—"

"I don't let any dames on the make in here," said the bartender virtuously. "I see 'em, I chase 'em out. Don't I, Mabel?" The blonde nodded shortly. Sure, I bet, thought Palliser. I just bet. "No, I never seen that guy with a dame. In here."

"Do you know the man he was with? Or the men? Did you see him with more than one? You said—"

"I already told you, no. They was just customers. Off the street. I think they had highballs. Nothin' fancy anyways."

"Can you tell me the latest you saw this man in here? Thursday—Friday night?"

The bartender shook his head. "I don't know. I get the impression it was longer ago than that, maybe a week. That's all I could say."

"Well, thanks," said Palliser. He brought out the F.B.I. flyer on Kincaid. "Now I'd like to ask you—"

"Listen, cop, we're busy!" But he took the flyer. "Oh-oh. This a mean one, huh? Feds after him." He held it out, studying the picture. "I dunno."

But the blonde, looking over his shoulder, let out a loud gasp. "Jerry, baby, I seen *that* guy in here just last night! I did! I swear it was! He was only in here for maybe five minutes, it was on your break—he had a double Scotch and went right out, but it was this guy—"

Well, well, thought Palliser. She sounded positive and as Mendoza said, Julian John Kincaid was a distinctive-looking young man. . . . And so the odds were he was still around somewhere.

Only, where?

He went out to the street and walked up to where he'd left the Rambler parked a block away. Landers was just coming up. "Hi, how're you doing? I haven't had a smell. Nobody's seen him. Either one of them."

"Well, I have," said Palliser, and told him.

"Just fancy," said Landers. "One like that loose in our area. I tell you, John, I think the Lieutenant ought to hear about this right away."

"I'll find a phone and call in," said Palliser. They had dived into the car for protection; they were both soaking wet, and the rain was driving down as relentlessly as ever.

Carole lay bound and helpless and terrified on the bed in the room she'd had here before, and listened to the voices in the kitchen. She'd noticed that before—this big posh new apartment building, but it wasn't built solid, walls thin and all, you could hear people in the next room. She couldn't hear what they said when they were in the lounge, or anywhere else, but this rear bedroom was right next to the kitchen.

"Listen, you're the one to talk—all your fault in the first place, biffing her like that—for God's sake! It'd have been O.K., I could've—"

"But, Harry, when she just walked in, and he was *still* here, she could have seen—" Mrs. Newhouse sounded like crying.

"Well, she didn't! I could've thought up some tale to tell her, like you had a nosebleed or something—silly little fool'd believe anything—only you had to go and hit her, and *now* where are we? Try to tell her the plausible tale now! What the hell are we going to do with her? You trying to make me a mass murderer or something? If you hadn't—"

"I didn't mean any harm, Harry. I was only afraid—"

"What the *hell?* I had it all figured out. No sweat, I told you, just leave it to me. It was all *set.* And you had to—"

"I was only trying to help Harry!" She was crying now, open and noisy. "Oh, Harry, what are we going to do? You're sure—sure that nobody'll—"

"How will anybody know?" he asked roughly. "I *told* you. *That's* all right. But this damned girl—"

They'd been saying the same things over and over, when she could hear them, since—Carole's head ached terribly and it was an effort just to think. Remember. Back to yesterday, when she'd unlocked the door and come in and—*all that blood*—And Evelyn Newhouse, incredibly, had hit her over the head and knocked her out. She'd come to in here, all tied up with what she'd subsequently discovered were torn-up sheets or something, and gagged.

"I'll think of something if you just quit bugging me—you've done enough—"

"But, Harry—"

Oh, Mummy! thought Carole. *Home*—quiet Rowberrow village in green Somerset, the friendly country voices— Panicky, she struggled, then lay quiet. Why she'd ever come to this horrible country—

It had been a little funny—not funny-peculiar. When she thought. Mrs. Newhouse actually *apologetic.* "I didn't mean to hurt you, dear, but—" And they'd brought her dinner, one of those frozen TV dinners, and coffee, and untied her, and let her go to the bathroom to wash— But *he'd* been there, vigilant, with his cold light eyes on her all the while— "One peep out of you and you'll be hurt, sister!"

Carole believed him. One part of her despised herself for meekly eating the dinner and not even trying—

But the look in his eyes sent a cold shudder up her spine.

"But, Harry, they might find out—all the scientific things they've got nowadays—"

"Don't be a fool!" he said contemptuously. "Cops! Anybody knows how dumb they are—we can outsmart them any day! I told you not to fuss about that. It's finished. It's this damn girl—"

She'd never liked him. Mr. Newhouse's brother, they said, or half-brother or something, but it had felt wrong, him coming to see Mrs. Newhouse. She'd said to Dot—

They'd done something to Mr. Newhouse. Maybe even killed him. Yes, they must have killed him. *Murdered* him. That was why. . . . Carole had worked it out slowly, lying awake, miserable and terrified, last night. All that blood on the carpet in the lounge—a lovely silver-gray carpet it was, she'd always admired it—Mrs. Newhouse always telling about what a stick-in-the-mud he was, his piddling little job at the furniture store, and he wouldn't let her enjoy all the lovely money—talking about safe sound investments— And the other one, Harry, saying what a lot of fun they could have.

Perhaps they'd only just murdered him when she came in. Sudden weak tears welled in Carole's eyes. Nice, dull Mr. Newhouse, who had reminded her some of Daddy. His chess club and all.

But however could they get away with— There'd be his body, and—

American police, everybody *said* they were all crooked. And stupid. And he said, cops so dumb. Everybody knew. Carole didn't know. Maybe it was so.

"But, Harry, what can we *do?* It's not like *him*—people will miss her, and come asking, and that'll make them notice *us*—"

"Shut up," he said. "I'll think of—I could do the same as the other, maybe." He sounded suddenly thoughtful. "I mean, come spring, who'll know? . . . It'll be snowing heavy in the mountains, with this rain."

"What do you mean? I don't unders—"

"Or, hell, never mind. I've got to think about it. If you hadn't landed me with her—! The other was just perfect. Safe and easy. If you'd just—"

"I was only trying to help," she said humbly.

"Oh, for God's sake! Females! I want another drink."

They went out of the kitchen and Carole couldn't hear them any more. It wasn't any use to struggle; she was tied up *tight*.

And she was more frightened than she'd ever been in her life before, maybe more frightened than she'd ever be again her whole life— He was a gangster, maybe. They said in America—and she'd only been here six months, she didn't know much about—

But from somewhere, out of her panic and fear, came a calm logical voice saying to her, It's up to you. You've got to do *something*. You, yourself.

Logically, remotely, it said to her: people know you were here—Dot, Mrs. Spain's agency—but Mrs. Newhouse has only got to say you left. There's the motel room with all your things there, you paid for three nights, but they'll just think you went off somewhere, or—or were killed in an accident or something. Would they tell the police, investigate? But American police—

Nobody knows you're here.

Or about Harry. And whatever they've done to poor Mr. Newhouse.

It's up to you. Somehow you've got to get away.

Get to Dot—or the agency—or somebody, and tell. The police? Carole wasn't at all sure she would go to the police. American police. Everybody said—

The funny thing was, Mrs. Newhouse was—considerate. She came, with *him,* to let Carole into the bathroom, and—

They untied her then. For a few minutes. And to eat.

113

With *him* watching. But in the bathroom, only Mrs. Newhouse. Only he was right outside.

Could she—?

The cold little voice said, It's up to you. You'll have to *try*.

Sergeant Lake looked in the door of Mendoza's office. "Hit and run," he announced tersely. "Over on Broadway. A woman. Squad car just called in. A D.O.A."

"Oh, hell," said Mendoza and Palisser simultaneously.

Lake turned back to his desk as the phone shrilled again. "Homicide, L.A.P.D.," he said automatically.

"So Kincaid is still around," said Mendoza. "I'd better call the Feds."

"He's not just so bright," said Palisser. "But where he's holing up?"

"If we spread those flyers around, somebody's bound to turn him in sooner or later. He isn't leery of wandering around in the open, evidently."

"No. I suppose—"

"Lieutenant!" said Lake. "A new one. Squad car just called in. Male body in an alley off Wilshire. No I.D."

"*¡Porvida!*" said Mendoza. "They are keeping us busy. All right, Jimmy."

Chapter 9

MENDOZA GOT home at a quarter to seven on Sunday night, through the persistent drone of rain, to find Alison looking harried and harassed.

"I am about to go stark, raving mad," she announced. "Any minute. Those two monsters have been cooped up here for forty-eight hours and talk about excess energy—they're about to drive me out of my *mind*. Heavens, I wish Máiri was here! Dorothy's all right but not like Máiri." Distant screams confirmed her. "And the cats have been just as bad. El Señor is so mad because it's raining he's bitten everybody but the twins."

"I'll tell you one thing," said Mendoza. "I'm glad you insisted on a level lot." The headlines in all the evening editions told of houses slipping into canyons, canyon roads closed, and mudslides descending down hillsides.

"*Listen* to it . . . it's a night to stay in, all right. I hope to goodness it doesn't go on much longer. The twins—"

A night to stay home . . . Mendoza thought about his beat, sitting smoking and comfortable with Bast on his lap, after dinner. The twins seemed to be settled down at last. His beat down there, the derelicts like Beauchamp drifting around, some without a roof over their heads. . . . November wasn't usually quite so busy for Homicide, but in the big city, any month, you got the corpses.

He thought about the corpses, his finger idly marking a place in *The Collected Verse of Rudyard Kipling.* What they'd got or hadn't got on each, what more to do about them.

Shirley Corrigan . . . no roof over her head. Hadn't she? Funny. There hadn't been a key in her handbag. . . . Kincaid. Still loose and evidently still around Central's beat. And that was funny, too. He must know, however stupid he was, that there was a nation-wide hunt on for him. A little pattern showed there. Palliser had turned up that barmaid who'd seen him just last night; before they all went off duty and called it a day, Glasser and Landers had turned up a bartender and another barmaid who'd seen him in two other places. At night. After eight o'clock. San Pedro Street, Alameda, Los Angeles Street. Where was he holing up by day? Now the flyers were distributed, and the news passed around down there, it was to be hoped that somebody, seeing him again, would call in and tip them off while he was still there. Wherever.

May Gerner. That was something they hadn't got anywhere on. What with this and that, Hackett and Higgins, nominally working that one, had been intercepted from chasing down all the rapists out of Records. Jase's idea—well, he could check that out tomorrow.

What Art had turned up on this Trumbull, also a little funny. What had he been doing down on Grand Avenue at midnight, the respectable sickly bookkeeper with a new job? And where was his suitcase?

Seeley. And the damned B-girls. Should get the autopsy report on Seeley tomorrow. One of Hackett's pigeons had called in just before they all went home, and put the finger on two of the women. Probably. Annie Hammer and Lynne Shelley. There was a record on Hammer, none on Shelley. The pigeon had said, "They been rolling them guys—you know what I mean—and I don't hold with usin' dope like that—a plain drunk's one thing, but usin' the dope—I think there's more dames in on the deal but them two I know for sure."

Have a good hunt tomorrow for the women. *Dios,* this rain keeping all the petty little pros at home snug —along with the honest people—instead of drifting around their favorite haunts.

Have a look at Jim Seeley's friends, as named by his brother. Who had gone with Seeley slumming down there for the easy pickups? It hadn't, probably, been Seeley's idea: quiet young fellow off the farm.

That one. Still unidentified and possibly to remain so. Found in a covered doorway on an alley running off Wilshire, close in to Grand. A man about forty-five, banged on the head with the blunt instrument. Or something. He'd apparently lived for some time after-ward, because he'd bled some—from the nose, from the head wound. He'd been partly sheltered from the rain and that was visible. Labels all ripped out of his clothes, ordinary clothes anyway, false teeth, a very ordinary-looking man alive or dead. His prints weren't in their records, and had been forwarded to Washing-ton; but there were still a lot of people in the country who'd never been fingerprinted. . . .

This and that still to do on all of them. And the hit and run. Do what they could. . . . Shirley. No roof to her head. Oh, yes? . . .

"*Listen* to it," said Alison, buttoning the white nylon peignoir and reaching for her hairbrush. "I hope to goodness it lets up by morning. I'm meeting Angel for lunch."

"What? Where? You be careful driving—"

"I will be, I will be. Only over in Pasadena, at Robinson's. And thankful to get away from the mon-sters, if it *is* still raining."

Mendoza sat up in bed smoking, watching her brush

her long auburn hair. She had a birthday coming up. What should her get her?

Lee Beauchamp. Nice to have one cleared out of the way, at least. The stupid little violent people. Killing for nothing. They had, he thought suddenly, had a good many of that kind this week—the sordid, squalid, brutal and stupid things. . . .

"Something's funny?" said Alison.

"Not really, *cara*," The line from Kipling had slid quietly into his mind—

> Winnow him out 'twixt star and star, and sieve
> his proper worth:
> There's sore decline in Adam's line if this
> be spawn of earth.

Grace told his wife on Monday morning that it was just too much of a good thing—adding insult to injury. "Lucky if we don't all go down with 'flu at once, having to go around in all this rain." The rain had let up very slightly toward dawn, and then taken a new lease on life and was again drumming down steadily.

Virginia agreed that it was a nuisance and recommended a double dose of vitamin C. "Your father always says—"

"I sometimes think doctors try to create hypochondriacs," said Grace. "I'll be all right."

He called the office to say where he'd be, and spent a few minutes in the garage tightening the plastic top on the little Elva. At least today the city offices were all open. He drove down to the Department of Power and Light and inevitably got shuffled around, had to explain his request and show his credentials to a number of people. Bureaucracy was ever thus, he reminded himself. Finally, about nine o'clock, he got hold of somebody who seemed to be able to tell him what he wanted to know, a Mr. Trusdale who looked at large charts murmuring, "Pomeroy and Lord Street, corner of," and eventually said, "Yes, that would have been Tony Gilbert's crew. Working on the sewer line there. They're not there today—isn't this rain something, though?—the job's not finished, but naturally they're not there today."

"Where are they?" asked Grace. "Is the same crew together?"

"Should be, should be—except for any outside men. I'll just—" Ten minutes later he said, "Well, you could try the new bank going up on Wilshire—out near Beverly Drive. They might be there, one of the inside jobs, and Gilbert's supervising the water system there."

Grace drove, carefully in the heavy rain, out Wilshire to the new bank building. It loomed raw and half-finished; and there, of course, he had again to explain himself and show his badge here and there before he was finally brought face to face with Tony Gilbert, the foreman on the job.

"So what can I do for the fuzz?" asked Gilbert. "I got a brother on the Fresno force, always pleased to help out you guys. Like that bumper sticker says, hah, Support Your Local Police."

"Thanks very much," said Grace with a smile. "This job you were on last Thursday, downtown—corner of Pomeroy and Lord—there was a murder there that—"

"Oh, yeah," said Gilbert. "Cigarette? I heard about it next day. In fact, a detective asked me had I seen the lady that got killed. I hadn't. None of us knew anything about—we was busy on the job."

"Well, are all the men with you today who were on that job?" asked Grace.

Gilbert eyed him curiously. "Why? No, acourse not. A couple of the guys aren't needed on this job—the drillers and like that. No."

"Well." Grace debated. Lay his cards on the table? Gilbert seemed like a sensible, honest man. "Well, you can tell me this much, Mr. Gilbert. Just between you and me. Is one of the men in that crew—on Thursday,

I mean—a white man with a medium-sized or long moustache, and sideburns?"

Gilbert blew smoke. "Sam Keller," he said. "Now where the hell'd you get that? And what about it? Yeah, that's Sam. You got to kind of keep after him, he goofs off."

"Is that so?" said Grace softly. "How old a fellow is he?"

Gilbert shrugged. "Young fellow, twenty-five, twenty-six. Just a strong back is all. Unskilled."

"Was he working on that crew—on Thursday—up to the time you quit for the day?"

"Now *what* the hell," said Gilbert. "And how'd you know that? No, he wasn't. He said he wasn't feeling too good about noon, and he knocked off. Matter of fact I haven't laid eyes on him since, so maybe he really had the 'flu or something."

"Oh, really," said Grace. "Thanks so much."

"What you got in your—" But Grace, smiling gently to himself, had already turned away.

Grace thought this was a nice enough lead for the lieutenant to hear about; and it might also be an idea to have a look in Records. Just in case.

Hackett was being frustrated by bureaucrats too, at the State Employment Agency, but being an experienced and patient man he ploughed through all the red tape and at last found a Mr. Mullen who seemed to know what he was talking about.

"Trumbull, you said? Garvin? Yes. The files will— if you're sure he had been here—" Mullen bustled away leaving Hackett sitting on a too-small chair beside a very untidy desk, and came back ten minutes later with a manila folder in his hand. "Here we are," he said gaily. He was a very cheerful, round-faced little bureaucrat, with a large toothy smile. "It was Mr. Melvin had charge—ah, that is, interviewed Trumbull. Last—ah—Wednesday, yes. I'm sorry Mr. Melvin's not here, he's off today—picked up a touch of 'flu, all this nasty rain. But he probably couldn't tell you any more. It's all here in the forms."

"All I want to know," said Hackett, "is about the job you people found for Mr. Trumbull."

"Job?" said Mullen. "Job?"

"That's right. This is an employment agency—he came looking for a job."

"Why, yes. But we hadn't found one for him yet, Sergeant." Mullen looked surprised and a little offended. "In *that* length of time. It's very difficult at the best of times to find a permanent job for a man like this— I've just glanced over the forms, as I say it was Melvin who actually *saw* him—but you can see for yourself— a man of forty-six, in not too good health, an office worker, and his last full-time job a year back—oh, he seems to have had letters of recommendation, but that means very little. Few companies will take on a man that age. The insurance, you know."

"But he had got a job," said Hackett. "He told his landlord so. He—"

"He *had?*" said Mullen. "Well, I must say I am astounded. *Astounded.* And he certainly didn't get a job through *us.*"

"Well—" Hackett hesitated. "There isn't—you hadn't even suggested where he might try for a job? Where he might have been taken on?" But the job, whatever, had necessitated Trumbull moving. Any ordinary office job —unless, of course, it had been at the other end of the county, when logically he might have—

Slowly Mullen shook his head. "Indeed no. You can see for yourself, it's all here—Mr. Melvin was very thorough. His entire background—the jobs he'd held, everything. Mr. Melvin had advised him, I see, to apply to Welfare pending any *possible* employment."

"You're quite sure Melvin hadn't suggested any place—"

"No, no. It'd have been noted on his papers here. It

would be difficult to find any employment for a man like Trumbull, I must emphasize. No, you can see Mr. Melvin's data for yourself—"

Hackett did, to be thorough, and there was no mention of any possible job. Of course, Melvin might have said something casual which resulted—See Melvin for himself? There was another hiatus while Mullen bustled off, disapprovingly, to find Melvin's address for him.

"Thanks very much," said Hackett. "I suppose Trumbull could have gone to a private employment agency."

Mullen sniffed. "I suppose he *could* have."

Hackett sighed. That would be a long job, to cover them all. And Trumbull hadn't had a car, or money for transportation to the private agencies up in Hollywood, farther afield; but he could have written to them, of course. It posed some more tedious routine; but a lot of police work is tedious.

There was also the suitcase. For whatever reason, Trumbull had been hanging around Grand Avenue at that time of night—because it was after midnight when his body had been deposited there, or become a body, outside that bar, since neither the bartender nor the bar owner had noticed it on leaving after the bar had closed—had he had the suitcase with him? If he had— if it had been the casual mugging—the mugger had made off with it. But just to be thorough—because if Trumbull (and it all looked even funnier now) had had a reason to be waiting there, a date or something, he just might have stashed his suitcase somewhere first.

Hackett, braving the rain again, checked the Greyhound bus station and the Union Station, the two handiest places with public lockers. If Trumbull had stashed the suitcase, it would have been longer ago than twenty-four hours and these dime lockers were only good for that time; anything left longer would be picked up and held in the station master's office.

Hackett had got a description of the suitcase from Daly: an old brown leather suitcase, much scuffed, "the ordinary size," with double straps and faded gold initials on one side.

The station masters were cooperative. There was nothing, in the confiscated odds and ends from the lockers, that resembled Trumbull's suitcase. Nor was there among the checked luggage.

It was just enough of a little mystery to intrigue Hackett.

It was then getting on for eleven-thirty and raining as hard as ever. He was abstractly glad that when they were shopping for houses Angel had insisted on a level lot. The kind of soil Southern California consisted of, most of it could slide right out from under you if enough rain descended to turn it into sticky mud.

He found Higgins and Mendoza sitting around the office discussing the autopsy report on Jim Seeley, which had just been sent up. As expected, the overdose of chloral hydrate. "Those damn stupid women," said Higgins. "And that says there must be some bartender—"

"Not necessarily, George," said Mendoza. "Anybody wants anything under the counter, this city or any other, he can get it. What gets me, this is one very small-time operation. The kind of suckers these women are rolling. If the average one has ten bucks on him, it's a big haul."

"But they can take five or ten in an evening," pointed out Higgins.

"True. You look wet, Arturo. Is it still coming down as hard?"

"I think we ought to start maybe building an Ark," said Hackett.

"Don't let Piggott hear that. He'd take it seriously. Sodom and Gomorrah."

"And there are times I could agree with him. Luis,

there's something very funny about this Trumbull. His suitcase—and what the hell was he doing wandering around down there in the rain after midnight? It—"

"Maybe he wasn't," said Mendoza. "Nothing says— barring what Bainbridge has to tell us, we should get that report tomorrow—that he hadn't become a corpse somewhere else and just got left there later."

"Well, yes, but he doesn't seem to be connected to the Vice thing now. Banged on the head, and what we've got says he didn't drink or, presumably, chase after females. And where did he find his new job?" Hackett detailed his findings on that.

"That's queer, all right," said Higgins. "I suppose he could have met somebody, casually, you know, in a restaurant or somewhere, who offered him the job."

"He seems to have been a loner. What I'd like to know is, what was he *doing* down there?"

"Mmh, yes—a little mystery." Mendoza made a steeple of his hands. "We found Seeley's car," he added inconsequentially. "It was in the garage for a lube job and they were wondering why he hadn't picked it up. So he must have been with somebody who had a car. John got some names of his erstwhile pals from the brother, he's out looking at them. . . . And I would like very much to talk to some intimate girl friends of Shirley's. If any. Because—"

"Because why? We know that was Kincaid. At least—"

"A moral certainty, yes. But where is Kincaid? And she wasn't really so far down as that, you know," said Mendoza dreamily. "As far down as stashing the couple of changes of clothes in the twenty-four-hour lockers, and depending on the latest pick up to pay the three-dollar hotel bill for the roof over her head. She wasn't really—I don't think."

"The stupid damn females," said Higgins; and he said it with pity.

Hackett eyed Mendoza. "What you do think—wait a minute, I'll get there—"

Jason Grace came into the anteroom, shed his wet raincoat, hung it up and came on into the office. "Sitting around here while the underlings do all the work. Lieutenant—"

"I've been out," said Higgins defensively. "That stoolie tip on the females. But you can't expect to find that kind sitting around bars in the morning, I—"

"And God knows I've been out," said Hackett morosely.

"Well, so have I," said Grace, sitting down and lighting a cigarette. "And done us some good, I think. The little brainstorm—what Bobby said. There's a fellow who was on that crew working at Pomeroy and Lord on Thursday— one Sam Keller. He said he wasn't feeling so good, and took off at noon—foreman hasn't seen him since. Sam Keller, it seems, has got a longish moustache and sideburns. So I was sort of interested in him, and I came back to have a look in Records. And what you know, boys, Sam Keller is there. Assault, and—"

"I'll be *damned!*" said Higgins. "He's on the list we made up from Records, the known—"

"—Rape, and statutory rape back in 1960 when he was only nineteen. And so I figured, by all the rules and regulations, I'd like another officer with me when I went to look for him, and maybe question him."

"I will be damned," said Higgins. "So we'd have got to him eventually, the little brainstorm was just a short-cut—"

"How did we ever get anything done around here before you got transferred, Jase?" asked Mendoza.

"We'd have got there—routine," said Higgins. "But listen, you two with the crystal ball—"

"Let's have lunch first," said Mendoza. "Keller will keep. I hope." And Sergeant Lake looked in and said that pigeon of Hackett's was on the phone, wouldn't talk to anybody else. Hackett went out muttering.

He came back two minutes later to say resignedly that what the pigeon had to say was that Annie Hammer had just come into the Sweet and Low Bar and if they wanted her—

"Hell," said Higgins mildly.

"Remember your diet, Arturo," said Mendoza. "Do you no harm to skip lunch."

Hackett opened his mouth to utter a rude word and Higgins said, "Oh, come on. We can pick her up and then have lunch before we grill her."

"Listen," said Bill McCloy. "I'm a cautious man, Sergeant. I don't invite the trouble. I've got some sense."

"Yes?" said Palliser.

"I said to him—I said to Jim Seeley, you're seven kinds of a fool, I said. When he told me about him and Ray Webb going around down there. Now Ray's a nice enough guy, we all got to know each other in the union, see, lodge meetings and like that. I like Ray all right, but that kind of thing is just foolish. You get me," said McCloy earnestly.

"I get you," said Palliser. He had arrived at Bill McCloy via the sparse list of names Jim Seeley's brother had given him, names of acquaintances Jim had mentioned. McCloy was part owner of an electrical service shop on Western Avenue, where Palliser had just found him eating sandwiches from a paper bag in the rear of the shop.

"Sure. Even if I wasn't a married man, which I am. I *mean,* look, for God's sake, I said to Jim—this was two, three months back, he mentions it to me—I said, look, you find a nice girl and get married. Lotsa nice girls around. This Webb, it's his own business, I said, he likes to cat around, let him. His own funeral, I said. Jim didn't know his way around the big town yet. A

126

farm boy, see. And this Webb, he's kind of got the gift of gab and all, I s'pose Jim admired him like. And I don't s'pose, farm town he come from, was an easy dame in a hundred miles—"

"No bets," said Palliser. "You find them anywhere. Round heels aren't exclusively city, Mr. McCloy."

"Well, I *guess*," said McCloy, and laughed, and sobered. "It's Ray Webb's own business—though I'll also tell you, as I told Jim, nobody pours it down as heavy as Webb is gonna hold a good job long. I mean, you need a steady hand in this job, Sergeant. But it is the *hell* of a thing when such a guy can—you might say—be the death of a nice guy like Jim. Because you could say it was Webb's fault, Jim was down there. The hell of a thing. I told him—tried to. Jim, I mean. This isn't common sense, I said. What's he laying himself open for? The V.D. and all. You don't know, dames like that. But he was a farm boy—it was new to him."

"I see that," said Palliser. "So if he was with somebody—another man—it was most likely Webb?"

"I would guess. Devil's advocate," said McCloy surprisingly, seriously.

"Do you know where Webb works?"

"Olson's Electrical Service on Vermont. Down in Torrance. If he hasn't already got fired. I don't want you to think I got anything against him exactly," said McCloy. "You gotta be tolerant of people, Sergeant. It's his own business. But it's not his own business, he drags a nice guy like Jim into it. I told Jim, Webb's a damn fool and if he tags along with him, he's another. That's all."

"Well, thanks very much," said Palliser. He went out into the rain. He thought irrelevantly that in their search for a house they'd better insist on a level lot. All the headlines about the mudslides.

So, go and look up the devil's advocate Ray Webb. Who just might have been with Jim Seeley last Thursday night and might therefore be able to say which of the easy females had been picked up and might thereafter have added the inadvertent overdose of the Mickey Finn to Jim Seeley's drink. Jim Seeley the farm boy who hadn't listened to the common sense.

Raining again, and the twins were obstreperous, but Dot was firm with them. Mrs. Mendoza was going out —she looked ever so nice, thought Dot, a really smashing amber-colored tweed suit and a turban to match, a pity to cover up her red hair—and she said, whatever Dot wanted to do to keep the little monsters quiet, was all right. Even the TV, whatever was on. For once. This awful rain.

"They'll be all right, ma'am," said Dot.

Mrs. Mendoza smiled at her. "I suppose you're used to it for days on end, in England. But we're not."

"No, ma'am," said Dot. Funny ideas people had of England, she thought. Mrs. Mendoza had her own car—the police must pay awfully well here—a little foreign car, a Facel-Vega they called it—and after she'd backed out and left, Dot got the twins settled down over coloring books and went out to the hall and called Mrs. Spain's agency.

"—Miss Leslie hasn't called in? Are you sure? . . . May I speak to Mrs. Spain, please, tell her it's Miss Swanson. . . . She *hasn't?* But she's left her job. . . . Yes, I'm sure of that. At least I—"

Where could she have gone? She'd surely have called the agency at once when she left the job with Mrs. Newhouse. Row or no row. Or she'd have called Dot —Dot had given her this address and phone number.

Dot looked up the number and dialed the Newhouse apartment. After eleven rings she hung up, frustrated.

She felt suddenly, unaccountably and ridiculously frightened. Where was Carole?

Silly to be frightened. Carole had some sense. And some money, she'd said.

The twins were screaming at each other. "Now stop that, you two—give Terry the crayon, Johnny. Stop it now, I won't have it—"

Carole was all right. Somewhere. But, where?

Chapter 10

"Now, ANNIE," said Higgins, "we know you've been mixed up in this racket, you might as well be a good girl and come clean. Some of the suckers are going to identify you, you know."

Annie Hammer gazed up at him unblinking, but her mouth worked a little. She'd been down at the bottom for a while; her record of prostitution went back to 1950, and they knew she was only thirty-seven now but she looked fifty. Her hair was bleached to a light taffy color and her skin was raddled with careless use of too much makeup, and she was getting fat. She wouldn't be attracting the suckers much longer; she might be finding life hard, to go in for the Mickey Finns—by her record she'd never tried that before.

"I never done such a thing," she said automatically. "I never. I don't know anything about it."

"Oh, come on, Annie," said Hackett patiently. "We know better."

"I never—" She plucked at the sleeve of her cheap rayon dress. But her lips were less blue than when they'd brought her in, with only a thin gabardine coat over the dress.

"You can have it tough or you can have it easy, sister." Higgins loomed over her threateningly, his voice harsh. "Make up your mind. Just maybe your name'll go on the warrant for Homicide, too. Are you going to sing the pretty song, or would you like that?"

"*Homicide*—what the hell d'you mean? I never been mixed up in no murder—I don't know what you—"

"Well, the sucker did die, Annie," said Hackett gently. "Jim Seeley. Or did you know his name? Didn't you see it in the papers, Annie? And that turns it into homicide. Who got careless with the knockout drops, Annie?"

Her eyes rolled, showing white. "*Murder,* I never—" She sat as if stunned, breathing hard, looking straight ahead for a long moment. "I never see no papers. I been sick in bed since Saturday. I never— Somebody died. Of—of *that*? I didn't know a person could die—of *that*."

"Well, somebody did," said Higgins. "And not the first time. So, what do you know about it?"

"I don't—know any Jim Seeley." But her mouth worked and she said it dully.

"A big young fellow about thirty, sandy hair, navy suit. On Friday night. The Sweet and Low Bar maybe —maybe another one. I don't think he'd have gone for you, Annie," said Higgins, casually insulting. "The shape you're in. But you know the other females have been on this kick, and that's what we're after. We've got descriptions of some of them—I guess you're the one that was called an ash blonde."

"A young fellow?" she said abstractedly. "No, he wouldn't 've gone for me, would he?" She looked up at Higgins and incredibly the thin cheeks were blushing. "And he's dead. That's a terrible thing. Nor it wouldn't 've been Gloria neither. Not that Gloria's not still pretty sharp, but— Oh, that's a terrible thing. I never knew that stuff could *kill* anybody. Just like sleeping stuff, I thought." The two big men, close over her, were silent. She was going to talk. She was scared by the word *homicide*—but there was something else on her mind too.

"I'll tell you," she said. "I—I got to tell you, no matter what. I always thought it was a terrible thing for Gloria to do, but I never said nothing. Because I—I wasn't always like this. I started out pretty good—like lots of us did—" She was fumbling for words; it had been a long time since Annie had tried to express any philosophy. "You might not think so, but I graduated from high school. I had a job, pretty good job—I could've worked up. Some do. But I thought I was so smart—kids do—and like the fun was just everything, and eight-to-five for the birds. Kids. And there was Bill first and then I married that no-goodnik and after he got sent to Quentin I was sort of at loose ends and— You get pushed down by life," she said earnestly. "But I didn't *need* to. If I'd had any guts. I see it now, only it's too late. But it was my *own* doing—nobody forced me into it. And—and Gloria did. To her."

"Gloria did what, Annie?" asked Hackett. He exchanged a glance with Higgins over her bent head.

"I never said anything—it was just after I'd met Gloria, four years—five years back, I dunno, time gets away. But I thought it was just terrible to do. A kid ought to have *some* chance. So all right, Gloria's a set-up, on the street since she was sixteen, but she didn't need to go and bring the kid into it. Train her right up to it, like it's the only damn job a girl can *do*. And she's a pretty kid, she could've maybe gone places all legit, you know? It's been since she was fifteen—and all her life I guess seein' how Gloria is, and the johns brought home and all— you can't know she'd 'a' been any better, but she ought to 've had the *chance*."

"Annie—"

"And you said—a young fellow. He wouldn't have gone for Gloria. It could've been Lynne Shelley, but I think likely it must've been the kid. A *terrible* thing. But I better tell you—because—she's only about nineteen now, and maybe if she gets caught up to and maybe does some thinking—" Annie looked at them in

132

sudden horror. "She wouldn't get the *gas chamber*, would she?"

Hackett shook his head. "Involuntary manslaughter, probably a five-to-fifteen."

"Oh. Well, anyways, I got to tell you. I see that. Because we never meant nobody to get killed. I never knew that stuff—"

"Some names, Annie," said Higgins.

She nodded. "Lynne Shelley. She lives over that bar, like I do. A room upstairs. She—"

"There's a man in it, we know that too. Who?"

"C-Carlos Feliz. He owns that bar on—"

"Uh-huh," said Higgins. "Who's Gloria? and the kid?"

"Gloria Hamilton," she said dully, and then sat up straighter and her tone was suddenly vindictive. "She calls herself that but her real name's Mary Jane Blackwell. Her own *daughter* she brings into it—as if it was the only damn life a girl'd want to—And Sue's the prettiest kid, she could've gone places and made it straight. I don't know, she never saw no other kind of life, but if Gloria hadn't—I thought it was terrible."

"You know where they live, Annie?"

"They've got a place together—an apartment on Diamond Street. It must've been the kid. Did that. With the stuff. Feliz got it for us, I don't know where. He always said, just a teaspoonful. But the kid—"

"All right, Annie, thanks very much." Hackett put his notebook away.

"You're goin' to book me in, I guess." She looked very tired, sitting there in her cheap clothes, clutching a big green plastic handbag. "I never done any time at all, you know? It was always fines, and probation. Are you going to put homicide? I never knew—"

Hackett shrugged. "Technically, it's assault with intent to rob," he told her. "We'll forget about the accomplice-before. You might get a one-to-three, or a three-to-five."

"I'll be forty-two," she said. "Too old anyways." She got up draggingly. "Well, I guess it can't be helped, huh? I guess you could say it's my own fault. For bein' a plain damn fool. But life pushes you down."

As they took her out of the interrogation room, they met Mendoza and Grace shepherding a man down the corridor. The man was young, and he had a thick black moustache and hairy black sideburns. Grace was looking pleased, and Mendoza gave Hackett a rather wolfish grin as they passed each other.

Carole Leslie was still having moments of despising herself for being a coward, but mostly she was just scared silly. She sat bolt upright in the front seat of the car, between the man and Mrs. Newhouse, and looked at the road ahead, and the places they were passing.

He had stayed at the apartment all the time, and they'd gone on arguing, sometimes where she could hear them. She knew now, from some of their talk, that they had killed Mr. Newhouse. *Murdered* him. The man said something about a perfect murder, and she'd gone and ruined everything. Mrs. Newhouse cried and kept saying she'd only meant to help, and Harry snarled at her.

Then, sometime yesterday, they were in the kitchen again and she could hear, he'd seemed to give in—as if he'd been arguing with himself really—and what he said had set Carole shaking so the bed nearly shook with her. All right, he said, she'd just have to go, let the devil take the hindmost, God knew it wasn't any of his doing but there she was, going to foul the whole thing up, she'd just have to *go*.

"But, Harry—people'll miss her, people knew she was here—"

"It's a mess," he said. "One sweet mess. It won't be nice and neat like the other one, but it can't be helped. But we've got to find out things first."

When they came in, Carole was terrified he was go-

134

ing to *do it* right then, but he only stood over her and untied the gag over her mouth. Her tongue had swollen and she swallowed painfully, looking up at him.

"You just answer me nice and quiet," he said. He had his hand ready to clap over her mouth. "And answer me *straight,* see?" Carole nodded once. "OK."

"Oh, Harry, you won't hurt her? I don't like—"

"Be quiet. Now look, kid. When you left here Friday afternoon where'd you go?"

"A—a motel," quivered Carole.

"Which one?"

For a moment she couldn't remember. "Come *on,* which one?" he rasped. The name came into her mind thankfully.

"The—Sunset Palms. On Sunset B—"

"How long did you pay for?"

"Th-three nights."

"All *right,*" he said. "That's good. Up to tonight. That's just fine. Did you talk to anybody—any of your pals—on the phone, or—? Tell anybody about Evelyn firing you?"

Carole shook her head, and he frowned. "That's bad," he said. "I'd like it a lot better if you had. If somebody knew you'd left here and weren't coming back. So all right, you'll just write a little note to one of your girl friends and date it Friday and when people come to look there it'll be to tell them we never saw you since."

"I—I—"

"You'll write it," he said. "By God you'll write it. Where's the motel key?" He hunted through her bag and found it. "Now I'm going to untie you, and you'll write that note."

"I won't," said Carole faintly. "You can't make me—"

"Look, kid," he said hardly, "you're going to get it anyway. Do you want it easy or tough? I can use the

135

matches—I can maybe break your arm. I can do a lot of things. You'll write—"

She looked up at him, terrified, and all she understood clearly was the threat of torture. She didn't recognize his own deadly fear, the desperation of the man who sees himself trapped, an essentially weak man of limited imagination who, turning like the cornered rat, saw only one way out and went for it blind, though in reality it led deeper into the trap.

They stood over her, and he dictated what she was to write, and Carole wrote it with a shaking hand. He looked in the little address book in her bag, and picked out Dot's name at random, but the address was wrong now, Dot had left that place. She didn't know where Dot was now. Oh, Dot, she thought. *Oh, Mummy.* She hoped perhaps the old address on the envelope would tell somebody, sometime, that it was all false and she hadn't meant to—

She wrote obediently that the Newhouses were giving up the apartment and going to travel, so they had given her a little present for such short notice and she'd left. And then something funny, which he dictated to her slowly. "I am going to give myself a vacation and go to a winter resort somewhere. Will contact you later."

Fuzzily Carole realized, with a little surge of hope, that Dot—if she ever saw it—would know that was all wrong. She'd have said "holiday" and she wouldn't have used "contact" like that. But before Dot or anybody saw it, he'd have murdered her too and it'd be too late.

"Do you want me to go get her clothes, Harry?"

"Why the hell am I sending you down there? And *don't* let anybody see you. You'll go tonight, late. Clear everything out, and mail this thing at the nearest mail box, see? She's not connected to you any more then. She left here Friday, she stayed at the motel, and now she's gone off to the mountains."

"Why'd you put that, Harry? What are you—"

"Never mind. I'll tell you later. One thing at a time."

They'd tied her up again, and gone off. And now it was another day, and they were taking her away somewhere to murder her.

She ought to have *tried*. She ought to try now. If she was going to get murdered anyway, she ought to try to do something so that somebody would know it was Harry who had murdered her. But she couldn't think of anything to do. Her brain felt numb.

He'd thought of everything, he was being careful. They'd given her a cup of coffee, but no breakfast. She didn't feel hungry, only empty. All her things were there; Mrs. Newhouse had brought them from the motel last night. He looked at them, and made her put on her heavy wool slacks and a thick sweater, with her car coat over it, and a scarf tied round her head. "It's got to look natural," he kept saying, "in case—"

"Harry, what are we going to do? I don't—"

"You just do as you're told, damn it!"

And when they went out, he was careful, too. It was still raining hard; he made Mrs. Newhouse go and look to see if anyone was around, and took Carole down the back stairs of the apartment building, holding her tight by the arm with his other hand cupped over her face. Even then she didn't try to scream. She felt like a robot. *Scream,* the voice in her mind told her, try to get away from him just long enough to scream—there were people in the apartments all around—but somehow, too soon, they were there at the car, its engine running, and he thrust her into the middle of the front seat and crowded in himself too close to her and slammed the door.

"You drive, Evelyn. Till we're out of town. I want to keep a close eye on her."

"W-where, Harry?"

He told her. The names meant nothing to Carole. She'd only been here six months. While she was with the Millers, they'd gone down to the sea once, a place called Balboa where they had a cabin. She knew a little section of Hollywood fairly well, and Randy Bearley had taken her around in his car but she hadn't paid any attention to directions. She had a very vague notion of the geography of Southern California.

They drove and drove. The rain was just a thin drizzle, but enough to slow down Mrs. Newhouse's driving. They drove through Hollywood, and once farther on Carole saw a sign that said *Glendale,* and there was more town, and then they were on a wide street—she saw the name once when they were stopped at a traffic light, Foothill Boulevard. There wasn't much traffic. Then a main road with businesses, restaurants and a few shops—and just awhile ago they had turned and were on a wide curving road that climbed. It was suddenly much colder, and there was no traffic at all. Only themselves in the one car.

"Everybody came down last night," he said as if to himself. "Sure. Weekends, it'd be jumping. I should've thought of that, I had a job of it on Saturday. But now —just perfect. For us."

"Harry, I'm not used to mountain roads—"

"Just a little further, honey, I'll take over. We're O.K. now. We won't be meeting anybody."

It was very cold in the car; the rain had stopped. The empty road climbed and climbed, and on one side the mountain rose steeply up and on the other, where they rounded curves, there were dizzying panoramas of steep slopes falling away, and a thick stand of great trees everywhere—pine trees and others she didn't know. Were they going to throw her off a cliff? Carole shuddered and couldn't stop. She hadn't gone to church much but incoherently she tried to pray. *Please don't let—*

"Stop here," he said suddenly. "I've got to put on the chains. There's a ranger station just ahead where they'd stop us if—" He got out and opened the boot, and here was swearing and fumbling for what seemed a long while. The car lurched now and then as he worked. When he got back in, he was sweating and his hands were dirty. He slid under the wheel and made Mrs. Newhouse go round and sit on the outside so Carole was squeezed between them. "And you hang onto her, for God's sake, while we get past the damn rangers—I can't take it too fast, and—"

But he did take it fast, she thought; she hadn't a chance to try. They came round a curve and there was a sign, All Cars Going Beyond This Point Must Be Equipped With Chains, and there was a kind of portable kiosk and two men in uniform standing beside it, and before Carole could open her mouth they were past, Harry waving an affable arm out the window at them.

"Harry, I don't like it. I know you said—but—how did we ever get into all—"

"You know who got us into it!" He was breathing roughly. "Just be quiet and keep an eye on her."

The road climbed, and now there was snow. What looked like deep snow, everywhere—mantling the trees and the mountainside going up and down, and still they climbed, and still Carole sat as if she was already dead, numb and hopeless. No good to scream—no good to try anything now, here. A few flakes of snow were falling, and he turned on the windshield wipers, muttering, peering ahead.

"I don't want Big Rock Creek—that's where—"

"Harry—"

"Shut up!" And what seemed a long time later, he said in satisfaction, "Big Pines Road. That'll do." The car turned, slithered sickeningly for a moment, and righted itself. And then a little farther on it stopped. "All right," he said, "get her out."

"What? What are you—"

He came round to the right side of the car, opened the door and Mrs. Newhouse got out, obediently. He reached in and pulled Carole across the seat and out. There was a fairly deep drift of snow at the roadside; stiff, she floundered and fell in it. He dragged her up. It was bitingly cold, the air fresh and icy.

"It's *cold*," said Mrs. Newhouse.

"So get back in the car," he said. "Cold, yeah. That's the whole idea. You wait for me, and if anybody comes along, God forbid, one of these snoopy rangers, you're just sitting here admiring the lovely winter wonderland, be as silly as you like and God knows you can be!" He held Carole tightly by one arm. Suddenly she saw that he had a big wrench in his other hand. He must have brought it into the car with him when he put on the chains—he was going to—

"Harry, what—" She was a silly, silly woman, thought Carole. A bleating sheep of a woman.

"Up here, nobody'll find her till spring," he said. "I hope. I'll be back in five minutes." He turned and shoved Carole ahead of him, off the road, under the big trees. She stumbled in the snow and he held her upright roughly, forcing her ahead. Here the ground was level, and there wasn't as much snow under the trees but it was thick enough—halfway up her legs. She floundered blindly, propelled by his hand. It was so *still*. They might have been on the moon. She found that for the first time in two hours she was making a sound—a little breathless moan, "Please, please, please," over and over.

"I'm *sorry*," he said desperately. "But I've got to— you would come walking into it, damn little—" They were out of sight of the road now, under the close-growing great towering trees. He let go of her arm, and his other arm raised, and she saw the silver glint of the wrench in the thin icy sunlight. She opened her mouth to scream at last, and then in the last moment the naked instinct of self-preservation claimed her and she dodged, whirled, and ran.

Tried to run. Impeded by the clinging snow, she fled

lind, sobbing. She heard him swearing, coming after
er. But she was much lighter weight, and made better
rogress. She ran into a tree, branches scraping her
ace, pulling the scarf loose round her head; she got
round it, and thought he was farther behind—

"Hell, hell, hell," he was saying, and she fell into a
reat drift of snow, and clambered out of it, panting,
o something like solid ground, and was under even
aller trees where the snow lay much thinner and she
ould really *run*—

She couldn't hear him now, but her heart was pound-
ig and her breath came in gasps. She mustn't stop—
e'd catch up—

She blundered on, out of the trees, the mountain slop-
ig steeply down under her feet now, the snow deep
gain, and there was a little stand of young trees ahead;
he came round it and ran straight against a thing that
oved, and snorted, and puffed a great warm breath
gainst her.

She screamed, shrill and loud, and collapsed into the
now.

The great buck deer, startled, snorted again and
tepped back. But his harem was all about him, and
moment later he lowered his antlers and sniffed curi-
usly at the heap in the snow. It was starting to snow
gain, and the new flakes were rapidly descending on
he little inert form.

The buck and all his harem had lived their safe
leasant lives in this great forest sanctuary where the
uman animals, well-known, meant only tidbits of
ood. He sniffed at this human animal, but it did not
et up or offer him anything to eat.

The buck pawed the snow around it, and presently
ed his little band down toward the nearest ranger sta-
ion, where the generous handouts would be waiting.

"I wonder if we'll ever find out who he was," said
Piggott sadly.

"Sometimes we don't," said Glasser.

"Of course Washington might have his prints."

"That's right," said Glasser.

"I wonder," said Piggott, "whether they're getting anything on those B-girls."

"Hackett seemed to think they would."

"That's a wicked bunch," said Piggott.

Glasser agreed, aware that Piggott meant the word in its literal sense. They were down here nosing around on that new body, as yet unidentified. They hadn't got much.

The doorway where the body had been found was the back entrance to a men's clothing store. They had asked the store owner and his two employees to look at the body, but none of them had recognized it—or said so, anyway, and they seemed honest enough.

"Not that I can say positively he wasn't one of our customers," said Mr. Abraham Wolf. They had showed him the clothes, and he felt the collar of the jacket. "Cheap stuff. A crying shame it is, the stuff I got to sell—I did my apprenticeship to Kleinert in New York. Kleinert. The finest there was. In gents' tailoring. He had clients—well, gentlemen, high society is no word. Titled gents yet. From abroad. And I come down to this ready-made stuff, it's a crime, the prices we got to ask. I tell you. This, it's not worth more than fifteen bucks and I'm betting you he paid fifty. A crime."

"Was he one of your customers?" asked Glasser.

Wolf peered stolidly at the corpse in the morgue tray. "I couldn't say, gentlemen. They come in off the street. Down here, how often does a man buy a new suit? The clientele isn't the same—no regulars, like a regular tailor has. How can I say? I could have sold him a suit. I might not have."

"Well, is this suit one of yours?"

Wolf shrugged. "The ready-made stuff, who's to tell? It's all alike. This could be some of my merchandise or not. Cheap line a lot of stores handle—me included."

It was very inconclusive. Of course, as Piggott said, his prints might be known in Washington. And Wilshire Boulevard might sound exclusive, an unlikely place for a nondescript corpse to be found, but down here where it ended (or began) at Grand Avenue, it wasn't exactly exclusive. Just downtown L.A.

Wolf had left by the back door the night before the body was found, and it hadn't been there then. So it had been deposited after ten o'clock that night.

Unidentified bodies were always depressing.

"Satan going up and down to find who he can convert," said Piggott. "And these days, Henry, he's getting a lot of converts."

"I would say you're right," said Glasser. They had knocked off temporarily to have a belated lunch, and were sitting in a drugstore on Flower Street. It was raining harder than ever, and there were few people in the place.

"Spiritual wickedness in high places," said Piggott.

"You can say that again," said Glasser.

A slatternly waitress put their sandwiches in front of them, and Glasser took a bite of cheese on rye reflectively. "You think Sergeant Higgins will ever make it with Dwyer's widow? I was having a word with Lake yesterday—"

"Well, I'll wish him luck," said Piggott. "The sergeant is a good man."

"Yeah. But when she's had one husband shot—"

"I understand there are a couple of kids. Kids need a father."

"Yeah. You wouldn't think it to look at the sergeant, quite a guy, but I guess he's kind of shy about asking her. Well, in a way you can see—he's a bachelor but I guess not what they call an ascetic," said Glasser, "and maybe she's the only nice woman he's—"

"I wouldn't like to think that of Sergeant Higgins," said Piggott. "But Mrs. Dwyer could certainly do worse. What with the kids, and he makes good money."

"Oh, sure," said Glasser. "But you can see why he'd be kind of shy of trying. Seeing as she's had one cop husband shot, she might not like to risk another cop at all."

"I suppose," said Piggott, finishing his ham on rye. "But we have to go on trying, Henry. The good guys against the bad guys. Those B-girls. The Lieutenant said— *And* that rapist." Piggott shook his head. "Satan pretty active these days, Henry. Going up and down the world."

"I wouldn't say you're wrong, Matt." said Glasser. "Another cup of coffee please, miss."

Chapter 11

MENDOZA AND Grace had located Sam Keller without much difficulty, at his home address. His mother was more alarmed than he was. "What's he done now? He in trouble again? My dear Lord, I knew he'd done something when he come home early that day and hasn't been to work since! Oh, my Lord—"

Keller maintained a sullen silence. He went on maintaining it at headquarters for quite a while—they got indifferent denials, and Mendoza got tired of him. They'd told him all about his right to silence, and he was taking advantage of it, if not asking for a lawyer.

Finally it was the little nudge from Grace that did the trick; sometimes the little things did it, with the chancy ones like Keller. "Come on, Sam," said Grace, "you might as well tell us—it was either you or your twin brother raped May Gerner. There was a witness."

Keller looked up under his heavy brows. "Witness? I don't—"

"Bobby was there. He saw you. The little boy. He told us what you look like."

After a moment Keller said, "Oh. Yeah. I'd forgot that. I'd forgot the kid. I guess that was my mistake. But a kid—I never thought."

Just like that. "How'd it happen, Sam? Did you see her walking past and get a sudden yen?"

"Why should I tell you? Nah, it wasn't. All right,

you don't know everything, hah? No, I'd seen her before. Up that block. We'd been workin' there a couple days. She—I dunno, there was just something about her—" he stopped, and then went on. "I just—I just wanted her, 's all. Something—I wasn't going to *hurt* her, understand. For all I—all I knew, she'd be willin'. Well, she wasn't. That's how it goes."

Mendoza exchanged a glance with Grace, who shrugged. "You quit work at noon—did you have Mrs. Gerner in mind then?"

"Well, yeah. I suppose. I didn't go home, I went to a drugstore up on Marengo and had a malted, and then I just hung around. I didn't have no plan. I just thought maybe I'd go down there. Where she lived. Only pretty soon I saw her goin' into the market. So I just followed her. That's all. You know it from there, I guess." Suddenly he raised his head entirely and stared at Mendoza. "The kid?" he said. "The kid told you? What about her? The way she fought I'd sure think she'd tell you quick enough—I kind of been expecting—"

"Don't you read the papers, Sam?" asked Grace gently. "She's dead—that's why she didn't tell us. You killed her, Sam."

Keller moistened his lips. "Dead?" he said dully. "Dead? She's—is that level?"

"You like to see the autopsy report? She's dead and buried."

"Oh," said Keller. "Oh. Well, that's—I didn't know. I didn't mean to do that. Just—I don't see how I *did* that, I didn't think—" And he sighed. "I guess that means I'm in bad trouble, don't it?"

"I guess it does, Sam," said Grace. "Come on."

And Keller stood up slowly. "What'd you say her name was?"

"May Gerner."

"Oh. That's a nice name, isn't it? I'd never heard what her name was."

And Mendoza and Grace exchanged another eloquent look.

Grace took Keller down to the facility on Alameda to book him in temporarily, and Mendoza started the machinery going for the warrant. He had just finished a long phone conversation with a judge over in the Hall of Justice when the office door opened and Hackett's broad top half was thrust in.

"You like to take a look at a pretty pair of females? Pretty meant all sarcastic, not that one of them isn't?"

"Need you ask? I used to be quite a ladies' man."

"Come, birdie, come," said Hackett. "This is quite a pair. And the hell of it is—"

Quite a pair indeed, Mendoza agreed, surveying them. Gloria Hamilton, alias Mary Jane Blackwell, was a raddled big woman, probably around Annie Hammer's age and like her looking older; the broken red veins showing in cheeks and nose told part of her story. She was defiantly hennaed and incongruously clad in a red silk sheath under a swashbuckling black trench coat, with a big transparent plastic bonnet tied over her head. She was also wearing deep purple lipstick and false eyelashes. But she wasn't getting the attention the other one was.

The kid, Sue, whom Annie Hammer had mentioned. Here was the bashful young sailor's real nice girl, the pocket Venus with the big brown eyes and short black hair, with a feathering of bangs. A looker, all right. She had beautiful creamy skin, a delicately cut mouth, an aristocratic look somehow, and they were all wondering what unlikely genes in Mary Jane and some unknown male had combined to produce her. She was dressed quietly in a black wool suit, with a lot of jangling bangle bracelets on one arm, and discreetly made up; and she was eyeing them back in open contempt.

"You've got a nerve, bringing us down here. You haven't got a thing on us and you know it."

147

"Just a few questions, Miss Blackwell."

"Hamilton!"

"It says Blackwell on your mother's pedigree."

She answered that with one spat-out obscenity, and even Higgins looked startled. "You can ask questions right here, cop, and starve to death waiting for an answer!"

The other woman smirked. "That's the way to talk up to 'em, honey. We don't know nothin' about nothin'."

They asked the questions, of course. Did they know Annie Hammer? Never heard of her, or Carlos Feliz. It was two other girls. Knockout drops? What were those? And so on.

Halfway through the session Palliser came in and beckoned Mendoza out. "I think Feliz has run. Or gone to ground somewhere. Maybe somebody tipped him off."

"Hell," said Mendoza. "If we could get him to talk—"

"Yeah. And that Lynne Shelley—not a smell. If we could get a warrant for her room, see if she has taken off—. And damn it," said Palliser, "I can't find Ray Webb anywhere. That pal of Seeley's. He hasn't been to work, I can't raise him at his apartment, and nobody's seen him for a couple of days."

"Dios me libre," said Mendoza, "let's hope he didn't get an overdose too and we just haven't found him yet. Yes, he'd be a little help, wouldn't he? He could probably say right away whether Sue was with Seeley on Friday night. Barring him, we'll have to get that sailor back to identify her. And it'd be just our luck to find he's already shipped out somewhere. I think just to be thorough—" He went down to Lake's desk and told him to call the naval base at San Francisco, get hold of somebody in authority and request politely that the sailor be given leave to come down and help the L.A.P.D.

In the end, of course, they had to let the pretty pair go. Mother and daughter; and what a pair. They hadn't any evidence that the Blackwells had been involved in Seeley's death; only Annie Hammer's word that they were in the racket, and by all implications, Sue one of those to go after the young suckers, with Lynne Shelley. Which was understandable.

They watched the pair swagger out, very pleased with themselves, and Higgins said, "Goddamn. It's aggravating. They're guilty as hell. Matt would say, servants of Satan. When you think of the harm they're doing—"

"Have faith in the U.S. Navy, George," said Mendoza. "Let's hope we can nail Sue at least."

The rain had thinned out to a fine drizzle, but was still coming down. Mendoza got home at six-thirty, locked the garage door on the Ferrari and Alison's Facel-Vega—which showed signs of having been out today—and opened the back door to the service porch.

"*¡Cuidado!* Oh, damn," said Alison. El Señor had streaked between Mendoza's legs and was out.

"*Non importa,*" said Mendoza, and held the door open. El Señor, frustratedly imprisoned within for three days, discovered two seconds later that it was still raining, and retreated back inside, where he spat loudly to indicate his opinion of matters in general and stalked sullenly into the kitchen.

"They hate being cooped up, and I don't blame them," said Alison. The kitchen looked peaceful, with a casserole visible in the lighted oven, assorted pots on the stove, and the coffeemaker purring to itself. The house wore a deathlike stillness.

Mendoza kissed her and cocked his head. "Have you murdered the offspring?"

"I had a brainstorm," said Alison. "I really did. They were driving Dorothy and me mad. I tell you. All that confined energy. So I packed them in the car and took them out to the County Museum. Of course on a day like this there wasn't another soul there—well, hardly anybody—and I don't know if any of the intellectual exhibits made any impression—though Terry was fascinated by all the stuffed North American Mammals, and called the mountain lion Nice Kitty—but they wore themselves out chasing up and down all the nice slippery halls. They were so tired they ate their suppers without a murmur and went to bed like lambs."

Mendoza laughed. "Well, that's one use for a County Museum."

"You can go and sit down, everything's ready. You might take the coffee in. Oh, and Luis, I'd never heard a dozen consecutive words from our Dorothy before— a nice girl, but not talkative—until I came in. Very apologetic, would it be all right for this former employer just to stop by this evening? Something about a letter, I didn't get the details—it seems a letter was sent to her at the former employers', and they called the agency to find out where she was. Of course I said—"

"Mmh." Mendoza was uninterested.

"I know we're noted for unusual weather, but I have really had enough of this. . . . And how are all the corpses? I didn't see any headlines about Kincaid the mass murderer."

"But you just might," said Mendoza, taking up his fork and looking at it intently. "About Kincaid I have a small idea. A very small idea. . . . We'll just see."

"A hunch," said Alison.

"I wouldn't go so far as to call it that. *Sí será cierto.*"

As he held out his cup for more coffee, the front doorbell rang, and Dorothy's light steps could be heard hurrying down the hall. "Probably the former employer," said Alison. Presently Dorothy came back down the hall, to her own room next to the twins', and they heard the door close.

"Did I have a nice day?" repeated Angel. Her face was flushed with the steam from the oven and her hazel eyes sparked dangerously at Hackett. "When you say that, smile! These offspring of ours are driving me *crazy*, cooped up here! Will it *ever* stop raining? I never remember such a siege—"

"It's bound to eventually," said Hackett. "Be a philosopher, woman. Just think, two months ago you were creating all hell about getting the place air-conditioned."

"What's that got to do with it?" asked Angel crossly.

Hackett laughed and went to find the offspring.

Dot read and reread the puzzling little note from Carole. . . . Awfully kind of the Fosters to fetch it to her, thinking it might be important. And maybe it was, at that. But what on earth did it mean?

She was leaving the Newhouses. Well, Dot knew that. No mention of a row, but an "extra present." Money? As Carole had foreseen, Dot boggled over the vacation" and "contact," but the mention of a winter resort wrinkled her brow further.

It just didn't sound like Carole. But it looked like her writing, if hurried and crooked. Dot couldn't imagine what it might mean.

The first instant notion that came into her mind— Carole an impulsive little idiot some ways—was that Carole was eloping with the Bearley type. And putting Dot off with this queer concoction until it was too late for anyone to interfere.

Well, if she was, Dot washed her hands of her. Carole was no responsibility of hers, after all, but on the other hand she was only nineteen and not very experienced; but if she was such a fool as to—

She decided after rereading the peculiar note for the tenth time that she'd call Mrs. Spain and tell her all about it tomorrow. Mrs. Spain was very careful of the reputation of her English girls, and considered herself a sort of guardian while they were here. She'd cer-

tainly be concerned about Carole, and perhaps she'd
have some idea just what to do about it.

Dot hoped so, because she hadn't.

On Tuesday morning all the headlines were about
the weather. RECORD STORM DUMPS SIXTEEN
INCHES ON SOUTHLAND. END NOT IN SIGHT.
BLIZZARD IN MOUNTAINS—ALL POWER LINES
OUT. WINDS AT GALE FORCE IN ANGELES
FOREST. RANGERS REPORT BLACKOUT OF
WINTER RESORTS. GALE WARNINGS OUT
FROM SAN DIEGO TO 'FRISCO.

It was unusual, but it wasn't unprecedented. Occasionally God, or whoever arranged the weather for
Southern California, got absentminded and left the
faucet running up there.

Palliser was not much of a philosopher. Raining
again, he thought as he jockeyed the Rambler into the
parking lot. He'd spent a good deal of yesterday chasing that Ray Webb, and he supposed he'd be doing the
same today. In the damn rain.

Hackett and Higgins, those good wheel-horse sergeants, accepted the weather good-humoredly. Unen-
viably, they were going to try to trace down some of
the regular patrons of the several bars where Jim Seeley
just might have been on Friday night, hoping for some
concrete evidence on Sue Blackwell.

"And, Arturo," Mendoza said, "I am burning with
a secret desire to have a heart to heart talk with some
pal of Shirley Corrigan's. Male or female. On your—
mmh—wanderings, just ask around and keep an eye
out, will you?"

"Why?" asked Hackett.

"Just my 'satiable curiosity,'" said Mendoza, who
had only recently reached *The Jungle Book* in his perusal of Kipling.

Hackett shrugged. "Will do."

Piggott, looking resigned, and Glasser, looking

ournful, went on trying to find some lead on the un-
lentified corpse. Washington hadn't answered yet.

At least there was nothing new in.

Landers teamed up with Palliser to look for Webb.
ut he didn't show up at his job, and just where were
ley going to look? Find some other pals of his and
sk about favorite haunts? Sometimes you were re-
uced to going through the motions.

"And this damn rain—" said Landers.

The business area has mail delivered early. At about
ne same time the men in Homicide were setting off on
heir daily round, Mr. Felix Hill was saying to his
rusted employee Jacob Artz, "It's funny. It's not like
ames at all. Is it, Jake? After the way he talked—
vell, read it for yourself."

Artz read the letter and said, "It's funny all right,
ʾelix. It doesn't sound like James worth a damn."

"That's what I thought. Going around the world—
Tosh!" Hill took off his glasses and polished them
vigorously on his handkerchief. "That fool wife of his
:oming into all that money and just dying to throw it
away. She'd never have persuaded him in a thousand
years, Jake. I know James. Stubborn as hell, and *in*
his case, more power to him, I say."

"So did I," said Artz. "He told me about it, too.
We both belong to this chess club, you know."

"Yes, yes," said Hill. "There's something very funny
about this, Jake. Twenty years he works here, all one
big happy family together—well, you been here eighteen—and we know him. Maybe even better than his
wife we both know him, would you say, Jake? And all
of a sudden, no notice, this. 'Dear Mr. Hill.' I ask you.
That's not James. And I don't like it."

"Neither do I, Felix. What can we do about it?"

"What can we do? Listen, Jake James is a friend of
mine. I'm going to find *out* about it. Going around the
world, you don't decide to go Saturday and leave Mon-

day, for God's sake. I'm going up there—to the damn fool expensive apartment she made him move into, waste of good money, and I'm going to find *out* what gives. What's got into him."

"That's a good idea," said Artz.

"Because this just doesn't sound like James, Jake."

"No, it sure doesn't."

"And so I would like to know," said Hill, "just what the hell is going on."

"And I would like to know," said Mendoza, "what has happened to that Ray Webb. By what John got, he could probably tell us about whatever female was with Seeley that night—even identify her. *Dios,* that Sue. It sometimes makes you wonder, Jimmy—that human nature can be so very damn human."

"It does," said Lake inattentively. He was doing sums on the back of an envelope, and wondering how the hell they were going to manage to pay for the teeth-straightening job the youngest Lake offspring needed. Caroline said it was necessary and come hell or high water, if she had to go back to work herself—Well, he wasn't having that, but—

"Trumbull," said Mendoza. "Something very odd about Mr. Garvin Trumbull and his new job. *De veras.* And then there was Shirley—mmh, yes—she really wasn't as far down as all that. And Kincaid—Kincaid's a very stupid fellow, Jimmy. Dangerous, but stupid. Like so many of them."

"I've no doubt," said Lake. The Lieutenant got like this sometimes, nervous as a cat, fidgeting around, pacing up and down: maybe when he'd had a hunch and was waiting for it to break.

"At least there's the U.S. Navy."

"Yeah," said Lake. He had made contact with the U.S. Navy, and the young sailor was probably en route now to identify Sue for them. They could hope.

The door opened and a man in uniform laid a

manila envelope on Lake's desk. Lake glanced at it: something to occupy the Lieutenant a while, anyway. "Autopsy report on Trumbull."

"Ah." Mendoza seized it and went into his office. Five minutes later Lake heard him talking to himself.

"*¿Qué es esto? ¿Qué se yo?* Just what in hell's name—"

"You want anything, Lieutenant?" asked Lake patiently.

"No. I'm thinking," said Mendoza.

He was. Hard. He'd known how Garvin Trumbull had died: a bang on the head. The rest of the autopsy report was a surprise. Quite a surprise.

Dr. Bainbridge was a precise man. . . . "—the body of a well-nourished male, Caucasian, between forty and fifty years of age . . . appendectomy scar. . . . Has all natural teeth with exception of last three molars lower right side, an artificial bridge being present in mouth to replace. . . . Organs sound, normal. No present or past evidence TB, V.D., any organic injury or disease. . . . Death did not occur at once after injury; possibly four hours to six hours later. Hemorrhage from nose and mouth assumed by area and nature of blow to head."

And, even more astonishing, in a subtle sort of way, reflected Mendoza, was the notation: "Stomach contents: at time of death subject had within approximately three hours consumed a probable full meal consisting of Mexican food: green pepper *burritos, tacos, tamales* with spiced tomato sauce, refried beans with cheddar cheese, and Spanish rice."

"*¡Qué hermano!*" murmured Mendoza. Oh, yes? Oh, really?

Mr. Garvin Trumbull—

There was something very funny indeed about Mr. Garvin Trumbull.

He swiveled around in his desk chair and stared out the window. Rain. The line of the Hollywood foothills was obscured by gray overcast and rain. He wondered about Mr. Trumbull. He wondered what the boys were getting, out hunting.

It was a quarter to twelve.

Mendoza got up and went out to the anteroom. "You know, Jimmy, there is something very funny about this Trumbull. I can't—"

"Yes?" said Lake, and the phone shrilled on his desk and he picked it up. The door opened and Hackett and Higgins came in with a woman between them.

"—Homicide, L.A.P.D.," said Lake. "Yes?"

Hackett and Higgins and the woman were all very wet. The men's hats were dark and limp with rain; the woman began to divest herself of a navy-blue gabardine raincoat, untied the neat navy-blue pillbox bonnet covering her head. Her dark eyes were curious on the office, on Mendoza.

"Oh, my God!" said Sergeant Lake. "Oh, no— Who is this? All right. All right, I'll see that—" They all turned to stare at him; his tone had held naked shock. "Yes, I'll—Thank you." He put down the phone. He got up and turned to Higgins. "George— damn lucky you just came in—I'm sorry. That was a nurse—up in Wilcox Receiving Hospital—Mrs. Dwyer asked her to call and—"

"Mary," said Higgins.

"No, it's the kid, George. Stevie Dwyer. He got hit —a hit-and-run—on his way home from school to lunch. They don't know—I guess it's bad—"

"Oh, my God," said Hackett. Higgins didn't say anything. He just turned white, snatched up his hat and was out like a shot. The door slammed shut behind him.

Mendoza said, "As if it wasn't enough, losing Bert. Do we say Fate, Arturo?"

"I don't know. What a *hell* of a break. That poor woman. . . . I'll ask Angel to—"

"Well, what can we do? There it is. Jimmy, you

might use the almighty power of police authority and try to get to the doctor. Find out how bad it is."

"I will," said Lake, shaken. He felt, suddenly, immensely thankful that all he had to worry about was the dentist's bill. They were all safe and sound, Caroline and the three hostages to fortune. That poor woman Mary Dwyer. The good cop Bert Dwyer shot by the bank robber last year, his name on the Roll of Honor downstairs. And now maybe losing her boy, too. George Higgins thought a lot of Bert's kids, Lake knew.

The hell of a thing. These Goddamned hit-and-run drivers. Maniacs. Drunk, or fools, or junkies. Whatever. And not that Mary Dwyer or Higgins would be thinking of that aspect right now, when it was a hit-and-run and the Hollywood boys couldn't find him, no insurance money to pay all the medical bills.

Sergeant Lake said aloud, "Goddamn the bastard." He hoped very hard that Stevie Dwyer would be all right.

And of course the job had to go on. To be done. They were both thinking about Mary Dwyer and Stevie, but it was the middle of a work day and they were still the good guys trying to catch the bad guys.

After a few minutes' talk in Mendoza's office, Hackett brought the woman in and introduced her. He and Higgins hadn't dropped on any of the regular customers maybe to back up Annie Hammer, but they had found, inadvertently, Miss Jean Loftus. Who had known Shirley Corrigan.

Jean Loftus wasn't a play-for-pay girl, just a casual all-for-fun girl. She hadn't gone so far down as Shirley —yet. She hadn't any pedigree and she didn't dislike cops: she had a job as a waitress. She'd known Shirley Corrigan, but she probably hadn't realized just how far down Shirley was. She was the kind of girl who knew, casually, a lot of different people, good and bad, and didn't draw lines or delve very deep into them.

And Mendoza said to Hackett abstractedly, "It figures." He'd summed up Jean Loftus with a look. "Shirley was still putting up an appearance of sorts. I said so. Q.E.D."

"How much?" said Hackett.

"Never mind. Now, Miss Loftus——"

They listened to her. Thinking with another part of their minds about Mary Dwyer and Stevie, eleven years old.

"I couldn't believe it, Shirley *murdered*—see, I been over in Palm Springs with my boy-friend Eddy, a little vacation over the weekend, and I didn't see any papers till we got back last night. Gee, I just couldn't believe it! And the things the paper kind of hinted— I always thought Shirley was OK, she *seemed*—well, I mean, ordinary. . . . Why, gee, I saw her just last Wednesday night, she was right on top of the world, having a ball, she'd got a new fellow she really went for, an easy spender and handsome too, she said. She was waiting for him then—it was in the same bar where Eddy works, the Deuces Wild over on Broadway. . . . What d'you *mean?* I don't—Well, of *course* she had a place to live! Who doesn't? I don't get— Well, of *course* I know—I was a friend of hers, I knew her a couple of years. She lives—lived, my God, Shirley *murdered*—she lived on Stanford Avenue, she had what they call a bachelor apartment, I been there to parties sometimes——"

And Mendoza said tautly, "OK, that's all we want —the address. Thanks very much, Miss Loftus."

And when Hackett came back from shepherding her out, arranging for a squad car to take her back to work, incredibly Mendoza had his jacket off and was buckling on the shoulder holster, the gun he never would carry.

"What the *hell?*" said Hackett. And suddenly dawn

broke and he clapped a hand to his forehead. "My God, you think——"

Mendoza gave him a mirthless smile. "We don't know," he said, "whether Kincaid has got in a home supply and is maybe under the influence. Which seems to predispose him to homicide."

"You want me to call the Feds to go along?"

"They're busy fellows. Let's—I hope—bring him in all by ourselves and hand him over as a surprise."

Chapter 12

BELATEDLY, as Mendoza locked the Ferrari and they started back up Stanford Avenue hunched against the rain, Hackett remembered the massacres in Arkansas and Iowa and thought they weren't just so smart. He said so.

"But think what nervous Nellies we'd look if we showed up with a posse of Feds and he'd never been within a mile of the place," said Mendoza.

Shirley's room was on the upper floor, presumably, of a dingy two-storeyed building that stretched for half a block of small store fronts. The girl Jean Loftus had told them the number on the door: fourteen. They found the street entrance to the upper storey round the corner on Ninth and Mendoza said, "You go round and reconnoiter for a back entrance."

Hackett hunched his shoulders deeper against the steady rain. "We're going to look like damn fools if he isn't here, Luis."

"Wish ourselves Good Hunting. We may as well go by the rules."

"Oh, all right." Hackett plodded on around the building and came back five minutes later to report that there was no other entrance.

"*Bueno*. The Fire Department would not approve," said Mendoza. "Come on."

"How do we play it?"

" 'What is the Law of the Jungle? Strike first and then give tongue.' There's a lot of common sense in Kipling," said Mendoza, and opened the street door and went in. There was a narrow square landing from which stairs rose: old and creaky stairs. At the top, there was a long dark hallway, uncarpeted, with doors either side, and no light showing at all. Hackett tiptoed to the nearest door and had to use his lighter to read the number: two. He tiptoed on and found three.

"Diogenes with his lantern," breathed Mendoza behind him, "or, if at first you don't succeed."

"You will try to be funny at *such* moments." They went on as quietly as possible, Hackett giving up the lighter in favor of less noisy matches, and came to a cross-hall with a skylight above. They tried left first and found eight, nine and ten. They turned right and found twelve, thirteen, and down at the end where a tall window gave on a rusty fire escape—"Ah, a sop to the Fire Department after all," said Mendoza—fourteen.

Hackett put his eye to the crack in the door; there was no light inside. He eyed the door. A very flimsy-looking door; he could probably shoulder it in. He shrugged a question at Mendoza.

Mendoza took out his Police Positive; Hackett emulated him. Very gently Mendoza laid a hand on the knob of the door. It turned quietly in his grasp, and he eased it open and looked in, gun held at the ready. Hackett looked over his shoulder.

It was a large square room, with another door open on a bathroom in one corner. Gray light came from a large window where torn nylon curtains kept out no light. There was a studio couch tucked in one corner, a rickety table with a miscellany of litter on it, dirty dishes, cups, a half-full bottle of Scotch. There was a dressing table with a litter of cosmetic bottles and jars, a couple of bright-colored scatter rugs, and a cheap fiberwood wardrobe opposite the studio couch.

On the couch, peacefully asleep and snoring slightly, was Julian John Kincaid.

Mendoza tiptoed over, Hackett behind him, and regarded the man off the Ten Most Wanted list. He looked young and completely harmless, defenselessly asleep.

"Isn't he pretty?" said Mendoza under his breath.

Hackett thought Kincaid would look prettier in cuffs. He shouldered Mendoza aside, bent and shook Kincaid roughly by one shoulder.

Kincaid's eyes opened and focused hazily on Hackett. He sat up, bracing himself on one elbow. "Hullo," he said. "Who're you?"

Hackett told him. He kept his gun on Kincaid, vigilant. "Get up. Move! All right, now get dressed—we're taking you in now."

Kincaid looked bewildered and aggrieved. "Hey, now. Hey. You got me all shook—I just woke up—I ain't rightly taking you in, mister. You the law? You want me for somethin'?"

"You know damn well what the law wants you for, Kincaid."

He gave them a rueful disarming smile. He was a handsome young man, built like Tarzan, standing there in just his shorts and socks. "Man, I guess I do," he said. "I did for Shirley, too, didn't I? I kind of figured when she didn't show up—this is her place, you know. I musta took her key. I kind of remember that, all hazy. We was in a bar someplace, some night, and I was real hot for her—too far come back here—I think we was in a hotel, someplace. Last I saw her, and I kind of figured afterward maybe I done something to her." He shook his blond handsome head, a child confessing he'd been naughty.

"Get dressed."

"Don't be rushin' me. Did I? Do that? I'm really sorry." He picked up his shirt from the end of the couch. "I tell you how it is, it's the fire-water. The stuff. I didn't ought to use it. Some reason, it sends me off—I get enough—doin' these things. I can't figure why. Don't to other guys. It's a shame—a real shame." He started to climb into his pants.

"Then why do you go and get tanked up?" asked Hackett irritably. He felt as if he'd come out armed for tiger and found a bleating little lamb; it was confusing.

"Man, you asked a question," said Kincaid, shaking his head dolefully. "You sure did." He stepped into his shoes and looked sadly at his captors. "Only I don't know no answer."

"I don't know about you, but I feel kind of like a damn fool anyway," said Hackett.

"We'll keep it to ourselves, Arturo," said Mendoza, and put the Police Positive back into the top drawer. They had dropped Kincaid off at the jail on Alameda. "Jimmy, get me the Feds."

He spoke to Bright, who was very excited and congratulatory, not to say adulating, and Bright probably never knew Mendoza was being sarcastic when he said, "Anything to oblige. The L.A.P.D. aims to give superior service. You can go and pick him up any time—he's all yours. . . . Jimmy, get me Wilcox Street."

There he got a Sergeant Barth who, put abreast of the facts, was sympathetic. "My God, I didn't know that, Lieutenant—widow of one of your boys, hah? We'll do all we can on it, but I'm bound to tell you I think it's dead. Just nothing to get. It happened at the corner of Berkeley and Silverwood Terrace—the kid was riding home on his bike from the elementary school on Waterloo Avenue. This rain—probably a pure accident and the driver panicked. There wasn't a single witness—the woman who called in heard the brakes, and then a car gunned off, and looked out and saw the boy in the street. . . . Yes, I checked back with the hospital just now. He's got a skull-fracture, one leg badly broken—compound break."

"*Dios*. As if she hadn't had enough trouble."

"Well, the way the ball bounces." Barth sounded tired. "If he ever comes to he might give us something on the car. The hell of it is, the damn rain, even if any evidence was on the car, it'd have been washed off within a block, barring any dents from the bike, which is a total loss. I've got experts looking at it, but it'll probably be n.g. And—"

"Well, I know you'll try."

"We will. We've been kind of busy, and now, my God, it looks as if we might have a mysterious homicide on our hands. Funniest damned thing I ever ran across. The indignant citizen—he owns a furniture store over on Vermont— and the manageress of an apartment up on Sunset Plaza, agitating at us to come look at an empty apartment. What do you know, there's blood on the floor—manageress wailing they've cut her nice wall-to-wall carpet, but the blood had soaked through. Only we can't figure out who killed who, if anybody *was*. It's all very funny."

"It sounds funny. Well, you'll let us know if you come up with anything on the driver."

"Sure thing. I wouldn't hope for it. I don't suppose Mrs. Dwyer is so well fixed. We might take up a little collection," said Barth.

"If you'd like. We probably will, too. Thanks very much."

They went out to Federico's for a belated lunch, and were pounced on by Piggott, Glasser, Palliser, and Landers who on reporting in had heard about the accident and wanted details. They kicked that around over lunch, Grace appearing halfway through; but there was only so much to say about it. They talked about Kincaid.

Piggott said there was just nowhere else to go on the

nameless corpse, and Palliser said he thought Ray Webb had vanished from the face of the earth.

But there was still part of a working day left, and they had to go through the motions.

Mendoza took Hackett, Palliser, and Grace back to the office with him, sat down at his desk leisurely, lit a cigarette, and handed over the autopsy report on Garvin Trumbull. "We have here," he said, "something very, very peculiar. Just read that and tell me what it is."

Hackett held the stapled sheets and the other two leaned on either side. They read at about the same rate. Mendoza considered these his top men, and was gratified at the muttered comments.

When they looked up simultaneously from the last sheet, he said, "Any bright ideas?"

"About," said Grace, "Mr. Garvin Trumbull who came out west because he had a little touch of TB, and had recently been in the General with some stomach trouble?"

"Por fin ha dada tu en el claro. Very funny."

"I haven't got chronic stomach trouble," said Palliser, "but Mexican stuff usually does give me a little indigestion."

"But he's been identified as Trumbull," objected Hackett. "If the corpse isn't Trumbull, who the hell is it? And where is Trumbull? Trumbull's a real person —all that identification—"

"One man identified him," said Mendoza. "I think now we ask some other people who knew Trumbull to have a look."

"Who is Trumbull, what is he?" murmured Grace. "I'll go along there—the corpse has no signs of TB, of chronic stomach trouble, and nobody who was liable to indigestion is going to go inviting disaster with a meal like that. But I will also say—"

"But he had all Trumbull's ID," said Palliser.

"Exactly," said Mendoza.

"Oh. I see," said Palliser. "Yes. But look, according to the ID Trumbull *is* a real person. The birth certificate. The driver's license was eight years old. And—"

"I will point out," said Grace, "that there must be some superficial resemblance between Trumbull and the corpse, or nobody would have identified the corpse as Trumbull, even mistakenly."

"Yes. But I did just wonder," said Mendoza dreamily, "whether Mr. Trumbull—the quiet, untalkative Mr. Trumbull—had possibly been on the lookout for somebody who looked a little like him."

"You just like them complicated." Hackett was glancing back through Bainbridge's report. "This is a funny one, all right. But who the hell is Trumbull?"

"I will likewise point out," said Grace, "that he had evidently been known as Trumbull for a good long time, by the ID—all his life by the birth certificate."

"You can get phony birth certificates—" Palliser's voice died away. He rubbed his chin. "It's very damned peculiar. I'll grant you, by what Trumbull *said* about himself that corpse is all wrong. But how do we know Trumbull was telling the truth about his reason for being here and—"

"We can check with the General." Mendoza looked into the anteroom and asked Lake to do that.

"But why should he have lied? If he was running from something—a bank robbery back east or a nagging wife or even a murder—would he use his own name?" asked Hackett. "We haven't had anything at all about him, or a likely description of anybody wanted for anything."

"So we haven't. But I think we now ask Chicago about him, and also send the corpse's prints to Washington, just to be thorough. If Chicago knows anything to the detriment of Mr. Trumbull—"

"Yes, I see that," said Hackett. "What a hell of a funny thing. Do we suppose Trumbull killed him? Whoever he is?"

"One thing, he wasn't a bum," said Palliser. "Well-nourished and his hands had been taken care of, and he was clean. But he must be somebody Trumbull was sure wouldn't be missed, which is funny in itself."

"Yes. It's a little tangle," said Mendoza, "and I think the first thing to do is try to establish definitely that—"

Lake looked in. "I got an efficient office help for once. She found the record right off. A Garvin Trumbull was in from August nineteenth to September fourteenth. For observation and medical treatment—they decided not to operate. He had a bleeding ulcer and chronic colitis. They've got X-rays on file."

"So," said Mendoza. "That's definite. Bainbridge wouldn't have missed that. The corpse is not Trumbull, and the first thing we do is establish that legally. Art, you go and round up some people who knew him. He'd lived in that apartment for six months—and try whoever employed him, if Daly knows who it was. Also there was that clerk at the state employment agency who saw him most recently, if he didn't know him well. No harm to run the corpse's prints through our records—"

"Just to be thorough," said Grace.

"*Pues sí.* And also query Phoenix—he had a post-card on him from there." Mendoza glanced at his watch. "Get busy on it. I'm going to chase up to the hospital." They didn't need to ask which one.

"No," said Bruce Cassidy definitely. "That's not Trumbull." He peered carefully at the body in the morgue tray.

"You're positive?" said Hackett. He had found Cassidy through Daly, the manager of the apartment where Trumbull had lived.

"Oh, yes," said Cassidy. "Certainly. I employed him, didn't I? Trumbull, that is. But what on earth was this poor fellow doing with Trumbull's identification? Of course, I can see that at a first glance someone who didn't know him very well might have said this was Trumbull."

"Is that so?"

"Trumbull," said Cassidy, "has got the same kind of nose. A big high-beaked nose. Very distinctive. But I've never laid eyes on this man before in my life."

"I see," said Hackett. "Well. If you'll come out to the corridor, sir—" He nodded at the morgue attendant. "Now, we'd appreciate anything you can tell us about Mr. Trumbull."

"About Trumbull? But that's not Trumbull." Cassidy was bewildered.

Hackett was feeling a little bewildered himself. But he pressed on with the questions. Cassidy owned a small blueprinting and lithography firm out on Western Avenue, and he had, up to August, employed Garvin Trumbull to come in three times a week and keep up his books. He had employed him since last May. He must have had some conversation with the man.

But he wasn't a great deal of help. "He never talked much about himself," said Cassidy. He had heard this and that, at different times, from Trumbull, as some casual talk brought up personal facts. Trumbull had never been married. He'd lived in Chicago until last year, come west because of incipient TB. He hadn't any relatives—"that he knew of, he said." He'd been turned down by the Army for physical reasons. He used to bowl some, but had given it up of late years. He didn't like the movies but when he could afford it he enjoyed a good stage play. He had complained because you couldn't get vests with suits any more. He always dressed quietly. . . .

Obviously it had never crossed Cassidy's mind that Trumbull was not the genuine article, the quiet unobtrusive fellow he seemed to be. Or had really been? Or was?

Grace and Palliser had been at the apartment asking

around; but they didn't turn up anything at all useful. It was the kind of apartment house where working people lived who were mostly away all day and hardly knew the other tenants by sight. They turned up one old man, a pensioner, who had talked with Trumbull. "He useta go down to the drugstore on the corner for his dinner, like I do. The food's not bad, and it's cheap. I'm not much of a hand to cook for myself, and he wasn't either. We ran into each other sometimes, and walked back together. He was a nice feller—quite the gentleman. Office man. You coulda knocked me down with a feather, I heard he got mugged like that. But these here jubilant delinquents like they say—"

Grace, duly appreciative of the jubilant delinquents, said only, "It just occurs to me that a man running from something might act just that way, you know—drawing no attention to himself, quiet, untalkative. Take some piddling little job, an obscure apartment, all anonymous, down here."

"But using his own name?"

Grace didn't say anything for a minute. They were sitting in Palliser's car with the rain drumming steadily on the roof; Grace's not unhandsome regular profile was immobile as he stared out at the rain. Then he said, "The name could be legit—likewise the birth certificate and driver's license. Most of the pros—*and* the amateurs, Sergeant—are very damn stupid, but once in a while you get a halfway smart one. The name could be legit. But what tells us it was the one he's been using recently, back east? He could have said he came from Chi. Maybe he did, originally. But he could have come, a little bit more recent, from Philly or Florida or Manhattan, maybe with a suitcase full of bank loot or leaving a couple of corpses behind him. And maybe he was smart enough to realize that sooner or later the boys in blue back in Philly or Florida or Manhattan were going to link up the legit name Trumbull—who he really is—with the name of Lucius J.

Guggenheim or John Smith or whatever he'd been calling himself. So he went to ground, and kept an eye out for some fellow with no near relations to miss him, who could be mistaken at the casual glance for the real Trumbull. You notice he seemed to take care not to get too intimate with anybody—nobody knew him really well. So when the flyers get circulated, Have You Seen This Man, we efficient peace officers wire smartly back, Yes, we have, he's dead and buried. So the hunt is shut down. And all the while the real Trumbull is relaxing down in Argentina or somewhere."

"You've got an imagination, Jase," said Palliser.

"I've never denied it. Can you deny that it could be?"

"I can't. It could indeed be. And if we never get the corpse identified—"

"There's some dental work, by the autopsy. That might help."

"Oh, yes? If it was done around here. It might have been done," said Palliser, "in Philly, or Florida, or Manhattan."

"Policeman's lot," said Grace placidly. "I do wonder how the little Dwyer boy is doing."

They were all wondering about that.

Mendoza went home feeling depressed at the memory of a white-faced Mary Dwyer sitting dumbly on the waiting-room couch, with an equally miserable Higgins in the chair nearby surrounded with overflowing ash trays. The doctors weren't saying for certain yet. . . . Somnolent and abstracted over *The Jungle Book,* with Alison writing letters at the desk across the room, he only grunted absently when the girl Dorothy came and said apologetically, "The telephone was for me, sir, I hope you don't mind—"

"And of course I was concerned—it seemed so peculiar," said Mrs. Spain on the phone. "I went right up to Mrs. Newhouse's apartment, when I could get away—it was about three-thirty—and, Dot, the *police* were there! Two men in uniform, and a young man in plain clothes, and another man, and the apartment manageress. I couldn't make it out—they wouldn't tell me a thing! The manageress kept talking about some carpeting, and the detective said something about blood on the floor. I told him—the detective—about Carole, and he took my name and address, but—what *do* you suppose it can all mean?"

"Oh, dear," said Dot inadequately. "Oh, Mrs. Spain, I *am* so worried about Carole! We've got to find out where she is—"

"I've been trying to get the detective on the phone. His name was Barth, I remember *that*. To impress on him how important— But Mrs. Newhouse seemed to be such a nice woman—what *do* you suppose has happened?"

About two o'clock on Wednesday morning, quite suddenly it stopped raining. After the long and relentless sound of the rain falling, the sudden stillness was uncanny. And, as per the general rules of Southern California weather, the rest of the night it turned steadily colder.

The rain had been snow and ice above fifteen hundred feet, and when the rain stopped below the air chilled by the ice and snow descended, until the temperature dropped below freezing in the coastal valleys. When L.A. County woke up on Wednesday morning, it was to a typical day after a hard rain, a beautiful day of golden sunlight, slow-dripping trees, intense blue sky without any cloud, and a temperature of thirty-eight degrees mean, with an icy cold wind bringing more than a hint of the deep snows above on the towering Sierra Madres.

Normally it wasn't often that residents of L.A. caught a glimpse of the back mountains—the great range lying beyond the Hollywood foothills and the hills enclosing Pasadena and environs. Today, in the sparkling clear air, where tall buildings didn't intervene, they stood tall on the horizon with Old Baldy hoary-crowned above them all. There would be a total influx of the winter-sports fans on the coming weekend, to the mountains.

Mendoza, never operating on all cylinders the first thing in the morning, winced at the twins' loud outcries of joy at the sunshine. The cats paraded excitedly before the back door and Alison let them out. "Yes, you can go, too, just wait till I get your coats—"

"¡Brillo del sol!" chanted Johnny, jumping up and down.

"Nice an' sunny!" corroborated Terry.

"Thank heaven!" said Alison, and came back and sat down and sipped coffee.

Within ten minutes the cats were clawing impatiently at the door. Too cold to be out, announced Bast. Nearly froze to death out there, complained Sheba and Nefertite, making determinedly for the nearest floor furnace register. Icicles on my whiskers, charged El Señor loudly, galloping in after his mother and sisters.

Five minutes later the twins were back.

"¡Frio!" said Johnny crossly. *"¡Frio tambien!"*

"Too cold," translated Terry solemnly.

"Honestly!" said Alison. "You can't win!"

When Mendoza got to the office, this and that had come in for his perusal. He read reports from Hackett and Palliser. Washington had no record of the prints of the nameless corpse found at the back entrance to Wolf's shop. Chicago's records had yielded no mention of Garvin Trumbull under that name. The prints L.A.P.D. had forwarded would be checked, and a report sent later.

The sailor, Scott Robinson, had called in: he was

again at the Grant Hotel, available to identify his real nice girl. So first of all Mendoza sent Hackett out to find her and bring her in.

Next order of business—he called the hospital and got the usual "doing as well as can be expected." At least Stevie Dwyer was still alive.

He called Grace and Palliser in to talk about Garvin Trumbull. The peculiar case of. They kicked it around and decided they were doing about all they could do for the time being.

Patrolmen Barrett and Gomez were peacefully on tour along Spring Street down toward Maple, about ten o'clock, when Barrett said, "Hey, what was that?"

Gomez trod on the brake. "Shots. Where—"

They looked, and in the beautiful bright sunlight, ahead of them down the block on the right side of the street, they saw a woman come running like a deer out of a doorway. She fled down the sidewalk, dodging among the relatively few pedestrians along there of a morning, and after her there came running a man waving what looked like a gun. The woman screamed once, short and shrill, as she ran.

"For God's sake," said Barrett. "What the hell—" But he reacted automatically, as a good cop should. He was out of the patrol car instantly. Gomez nosing it into the curb and reaching for the mike.

"Car 3-0-4. We have a 415, heavy, repeat a 415 heavy, on Spring near Maple, pursuing female along street—"

Barrett ran, dodging the people. The man ahead of him fired more shots. Barrett shouted, and suddenly the man stopped and just stood, by the curb. Barrett came up and laid hold of him, not tenderly.

"Just what the hell you think you're doing, mister?"

"I got her," said the man. "I got her. The little bitch. She killed my pal."

Gomez was there by then. The woman was lying

still, half on the sidewalk, half in the gutter, with the inevitable crowd collecting. Barrett slapped the cuffs on the man and took the gun away from him, while Gomez went to look.

The woman wasn't more than a girl, a very pretty girl, a small girl—black hair and a nice figure, and she died while Gomez looked at her, her blood pumping out in the gutter from the bullet holes. She looked up at him and uttered one faint word, a gutter obscenity, and died.

Shaken a little, he went back to the car to call in. Barrett had the man in the car. The man was weeping bitterly. "It was my fault—all my fault—killed him they did, the bitches, the dirty bitches—a good guy, Jimmy was—"

"Hey—hey, you cops!" An excited man thrust his head into the car. "It was my place it started—you better come up there—he started shooting, my God, and there's a dame lying dead on the floor right in my door—my God—"

Another car arrived then, so Barrett and Gomez went back to the doorway the girl had run from. It was a bar and grill, and there was another woman on the floor there, shot dead.

The new arrivals were frisking the man, and turned up his ID. He was one Ray Webb. He was still weeping.

"I guess we better call Homicide," said Barrett.

Chapter 13

"WELL, we seem to be making a little progress," said Mendoza, looking into the sergeants' office and finding only Landers there. "Squad car just called in. Ray Webb has just shot two women over on Spring. One of them was Sue Blackwell—the other one seems to be Lynne Shelley. The squad car men are fetching Webb in."

"Well, do tell," said Landers. "John'll be pleased—he was thinking Webb had been kidnaped by Martians or something."

When Barrett and Gomez brought Webb in ten minutes later, he was quieted down and subdued; he just looked unhappy, standing there with the cuffs on his wrists. He was also unshaven and dirty; he looked as if he had been sleeping in his clothes.

"Would you like to tell us something about this, Mr. Webb?" asked Mendoza. "You can sit down here. Now—" But to the necessary recitation of his rights and privileges, he only shook his head.

"Maybe I'll see about a lawyer later. It don't matter—you know what I did, and I'd do it again. Little bitches. And I got to feeling—all my fault. All my fault. Me taking Jim down there, pick up the easy girls!" He looked desperate. "I tell you how it was, I don't remember the last part o' Friday night atall—we was together, I forget which place too, but the girls I remember all right. I sure do! That Sue and the one called herself Lynne something. She was with me and the Sue girl was sweet as honey all over Jim. And next thing I know, I'm coming to in a dirty alley with a head like to split and my two weeks' pay gone. Goddamn, I get my strength and get back to where I parked the car, damn if there isn't a parkin' ticket under the wipers. Insult to injury. But when I seen the papers next day—Jim—Jim *dead* down there, and how you all think it was the knockout drops, like I guess they slipped me, too—my God, I never had *that* happen to me before—"

"You're lucky, Mr. Webb."

"I suppose. I didn't feel so damn lucky. But Jim— and I'm the one took him down there—all my fault! Up to then I'd been thinkin'—well, I dunno, but I figured he'd got home some way himself. Listen, I thought a hell of a lot of Jim. And I seen what a plain damn fool I'd been—Bill McCloy, he'd said somethin' to me, and Jim, too, but like a fool I—anyways, I was so mad at those two little bitches, by God, I said to myself, I'm goin' to get those two— Don't I know the damn judges? Call it manslaughter or somethin' and they get off with three years or— It was plain *murder*. Not to mention they mighta killed me too." He glared at the two men listening to him, defying them to deny it.

"Where'd you get the gun, Mr. Webb?"

"I *had* the damn gun. Never used it, just got it to have one. And God knows I'm no shot, but I got a lot of ammo and I figured to myself, when I find 'em, when I find those bitches, I'm gonna keep shovin' bullets in fast as I can until I kill them both dead— Dead as Jim.

"I been down here lookin' for 'em ever since. All the bars. The likely places. I never did lay eyes on 'em till this mornin', I'm a little bit out of their territory I was thinkin', up on Spring, but I wanted a decent breakfast. The crummy joints down on Main—when I see 'em, by God, together too, just goin' in that place. Time I got there, have a good look to be sure, by damn they're sittin' there in a booth drinkin' coffee and laughin' and talkin'—so damn pleased with themselves, thievin' little bitches—and killin' Jim—and I just up and started shootin'. And I'd do it again." He looked at them defiantly. "And don't let anybody tell you I didn't know what I was doin', neither! I knew exactly what I was doin', and good riddance to 'em—dirty little bitches—"

There was a good deal more, but that was the gist of it.

They booked him in, and while it was an academic point now they sent a car for the young sailor and took him down to the morgue to see if he would identify Sue. He took a look, turned a little pale, and said "Oh, yes, that's her. She *seemed*—"

In the corridor outside they met a screaming tirade from a hysterical Mary Jane Blackwell, who had just shouldered aside the protesting attendant and walked in—"To see my little girl, what you bastards done to my little girl? Joe come an' say she's *shot*—killed—my baby! All you bastards—murderin' my own sweet baby, own flesh 'n' blood—" She sobbed and hiccuped, obviously still in the throes of a king-sized hangover, and Mendoza looked her over coldly. "All you men bastards—"

"You're the one who murdered Sue, Mary Jane," said Mendoza gently; but she probably didn't hear him.

"Awful shame, all this," ventured the sailor as they went out, leaving the morgue attendant to cope with Mary Jane.

"Depressing," agreed Mendoza. "Crime is always depressing, because it's so very damned stupid."

Hackett was having a very unproductive morning back-tracking Garvin Trumbull. Mr. Trumbull had either been deliberately lying low or he was just naturally an unobtrusive man. He was vaguely remembered at a laundromat in the vicinity of the apartment; the waitress at the corner drugstore remembered him as "a nice man," who was polite and never made suggestive remarks, but that was all she knew about him. A couple of clerks in the drugstore also vaguely placed him as the fellow who bought this brand of shaving cream and that kind of candy bar, and that was all. One thing, the distinctive big-beaked nose seemed to have stuck in everybody's mind. The man at the newsstand on that corner remembered him, but had never exchanged more than a word with him.

At least it had stopped raining.

Hackett went back to the state employment agency and saw Mullen. "The fellow who actually saw Trumbull when he came in—I'd like to talk to him. Is he—"

"Oh, dear, that's a pity," said Mullen. "Mr. Melvin's still off. This flu—so much of it around, and it seems to hang on."

"Oh," said Hackett. "Well, if you could give me his telephone number—" Melvin had seen the man most recently, and in the course of a personal interview something might have been mentioned. Mullen was obliging.

He found the nearest public phone and tried the number. No answer after seven rings. Well, well, thought Hackett, Mr. Melvin is playing hookey maybe? And if he had sick leave accumulated, why shouldn't he? Come to think, that must be a dull job. Sometimes, on a particularly dull job like this, Hackett wished he could play hookey, too.

Palliser and Grace, on the other hand, were having a little luck. Both of them had the same combination of imagination tempered with caution, and when Palliser had said an hour ago, "Look, Jase, he was only working part time—not at all lately—and whether it was an act or not, do you suppose he'd have sat around in some park, the way a lot of people with time on their hands do?"—both of them had approached the idea with caution.

"So what's there for us if he did?"

"There are regulars in the parks—sit around, get talking. Sure, a lot of them old people, pensioners, and he wasn't a senior citizen as they say. But he might have struck up an acquaintance here and there, and if—"

"Longish way to go from that apartment to any park," said Grace.

"Well, didn't somebody—I seem to remember—say he liked to walk? And so he didn't have much money, he could get to Echo Park for a dime on the bus. And MacArthur—"

"I'll go along enough to say let's have a look. Just," said Grace, "to be thorough. And I'll cast a vote for Echo Park even though it's farther away than MacArthur."

"Why?"

"More to attract the bench-sitter. The lake—swans—and the boats," said Grace. "And a hamburger stand, where he could get milk."

"Milk?"

"The ulcer, the ulcer," said Grace, whose father was an M.D.

"Oh. Oh, I get you. Well, it's worth an hour's asking around," said Palliser.

Unfortunately, of course, they had no photograph of the elusive Trumbull, but the high-beaked nose was a great help in describing the man. The boat attendant at Echo Park Lake just shook his head—"I don't remember nobody like that, no. You fellows cops? You know, we had a murder here, just last year it was—"

Both Palliser and Grace remembered it vividly.

"He wouldn't have wasted money on boat rides anyway," said Grace thoughtfully.

But at the hamburger stand, inside the little building

built onto the jetty for the boats, the description and the suggestion by Grace that the man might have ordered milk frequently rang an instant bell in the mind of the genial fat man behind the counter.

"I think I place him, yeah. He was pretty regular Tuesdays and Thursdays, sometimes on a weekend. Kind of a thin guy, in the forties. Yeah, yeah. I don't think I ever heard his name—well, why should I?—but I remember the milk, and seems to me he said one time he had an ulcer. Is that the guy you mean?"

They thought it probably was. Trumbull's job had occupied him on Mondays, Wednesdays and Fridays. "Did he ever talk about himself much?" asked Palliser. "Aside from mentioning the ulcer?"

"No, can't recollect he ever said much. Quiet sort of guy. What you asking about him for, he done something?"

"We're trying to find him," said Grace truthfully.

"Oh. Oh, he's missing, huh? He acted O.K. far as I could see. No cracks showing. I tell you who you might talk to, though. One person comes here a lot, this guy did talk to, I know for a fack, I seen him sitting with her a lot o' times right out there on the bank. I don't know her name, but she's an old dame comes here and paints pictures."

"Pictures?"

"That's right. She's about a hundred by looks, but she's a spry old girl. Sets up her stuff—easel and all—and paints pictures. And this guy talked to her, I seen him. . . . Well, she comes a lot. Not exactly regular, but—"

It was a rather forlorn hope, but Palliser gave him a card with the number on it and asked if he'd call in when next the senior citizen artist appeared. "Sure," he said, tucking the card away. "It's no skin off my nose. Citizen's duty to help the cops. Be glad to. Acourse I can't see the whole park from here—but if I do see her—"

"You don't suppose we'd get anything new from her, do you?" asked Grace.

"Well, we never know. We've got to try everything. Is it any use nosing around MacArthur?"

"No. Not if he came here two or three days a week. Any man can take just so much of sitting in a park."

"That's just your reaction. We don't know how Trumbull felt."

"I am beginning," said Grace, "to feel that Trumbull is a will-o'-the-wisp. A straw man set up—just as I said. Nobody could be so ordinary. And it's ten past twelve, shall we go have some lunch?"

There wasn't exactly any press of business so they went back up to Federico's, and ran into Mendoza, Hackett, and Landers, and heard about Ray Webb.

"Well, that sort of ties up that one all nice and dovetailed, doesn't it?" said Grace. "Just retribution. And I do see what he means about the softhearted judges."

"But what a stupid damn thing," said Palliser.

"Most of the people we get to deal with," said Hackett dryly, "aren't exactly noted for their brilliance."

"Which I don't need telling. But— Has anybody checked the hospital?"

"I did. The usual runaround, doing as well as can be expected," said Mendoza.

In a depressed little silence, Hackett sighed and in a martyred tone ordered the low-calorie plate.

Piggott and Glasser had been about to start out on another dreary and probably quite unproductive round of questioning of all the proprietors of shops along that block where the unidentified corpse had been found, when a new flyer came in over the teletype and Sergeant Lake handed it to them.

"This just could be something to do with your corpse. I did read the description on the autopsy report."

"Don't tell me, a break at last," said Glasser. They read it together.

It was from the Royal Canadian Mounted Police, emanating from Vancouver, B.C. It offered particulars on one Rodney Shields, wanted in connection with a rape-murder and robbery. Shields had lived in California and it was thought he might have made his way back there. He was forty-two, five-feet-ten, a hundred and seventy, brown hair turning gray, medium complexion, blue eyes, no distinguishing marks. He had done white-collar work, drank ale and beer but seldom hard liquor, and was attractive to women.

"Well, we can't ask the corpse his preference in booze," said Glasser, "but you know, Matt, that description just could fit the body."

"It could indeed," said Piggott. "But if it was him, Henry, how did he come to get murdered down here?"

"One thing at a time," said Glasser. "They don't say if they've got his prints, but we'd better send up the corpse's. If they have, that'll settle it one way or the other right off."

"Suppose they haven't."

"One thing at a time," repeated Glasser. "The description sounds good. If it is him, we can sort out what happened later. With luck."

They sent the corpse's prints and description up to Vancouver. And whether the corpse was Shields or not, they still had to find out what had happened to him here; but Sergeant Lake, who was on the phone, told them to hold it just as they were going out the door. "New one. Call in from the squad car. Pawn shop over on Olive, the proprietor just found dead."

So they went out on that instead, and as usual found the little crowd around the place. The ambulance was there, and one of the uniformed men stationed at the door. The internes were just waiting for the Homicide men to say they could take the body.

"What's the word? asked Glasser, looking at the body—the body of a fat elderly man in shabby clothes, lying sprawled gracelessly behind the counter.

The taller interne shrugged. "Stroke," he said. "Massive stroke, maybe a heart attack, too. He wasn't so young, and he was overweight. Just paperwork for you boys—no mystery."

The other uniformed man from the squad car spoke up. "He was a nice fellow, sir," he said to Glasser. "Very well liked in the neighborhood, Papa Cabrini. Always doing things for people, and giving them extra credit. There's a big family—wife, sons and daughters and grandchildren—"

"Oh, shoot!" said Piggott crossly. "So we have to go and break the bad news. I don't like upsetting people that way. The nice people."

"It's just part of the job, Matt," said Glasser.

"Sometimes I wonder why I took the job, Henry, and that's a fact," said Piggott.

They all went back to the office together from Federico's. Hackett and Palliser to type up reports on their various doings. But Palliser had hardly rolled the triplicate forms into his typewriter when he was hailed by Lake.

"Outside call for you, John."

Palliser resignedly picked up the outside phone and said, "Sergeant Palliser."

"Kowaljic here."

"Who?"

"Me, me, the guy you was talkin' to in Echo Park."

"Oh. Yes?"

"You said to call. She's here. The old dame. She's just come, she's sittin' right down on the bank outside the boathouse. You can't miss her. She's got on the same as usual, black dress down to her ankles, black coat ditto, and a green scarf round her head. Clothes about as old as she is."

"Well, thanks," said Palliser. "Thanks very much." He hung up and looked around for Grace.

They couldn't have missed her, at that. She stood

183

out like a sore thumb. The hamburger-stand attendant had neglected to mention that she stood nearly six foot two and was gaunt as a skeleton. She was just setting up her easel when Palliser and Grace approached, and she maintained magnificent aplomb as they introduced themselves.

"Ah, police. I presume, plainclothes detectives." She did indeed look at least eighty, but her black eyes were bright as diamonds, and she gave them a gracious smile. "I am Hortense Dawson."

"How do you do," said Palliser. "What we wanted—"

"I assume you have some reason for accosting me. I have been painting here for some time, and no one has ever objected. In fact, since I first took it up—I am a great believer in the value of outside interests as one grows older, and I have taken up Latin, botany, the history of the early church, and the guitar, but recently I felt the need for more outdoor occupation, and while I considered bird-watching, I decided I don't really care much for them, messy creatures. Not that I consider myself to be much of a painter, but it passes the time. What *was* the reason?"

"Er—"

"For your accosting me? Am I breaking some minor law by—"

"Oh, no, no, it's nothing like that," said Palliser. "Er—"

Grace began to explain in his persuasive soft voice. "—Don't know if you ever heard the man's name, Miss Dawson, but we've heard that you talked to him here a bit." Or, both he and Palliser thought, the other way around. "A medium-sized man about forty-five, with a very high-arched nose—a quiet man with—"

"Mr. Trumbull," nodded Miss Dawson. "And why are the police interested in Mr. Trumbull? A very ordinary man. But are any of us ordinary, at that? Are we not all quite fascinating individuals, and each life such a totally separate thing— I find it crass to say, ordinary, of anything. Has he committed some crime?"

"Well, ma'am, we don't know about that. But we'd like to find him, and we'd also like to know more about him than we do. And anybody he talked to—"

"*I* see." She nodded sharply. There was nothing wrong with Miss Hortense Dawson's faculties. "He is missing? In any case, you are interested in him. His background, do I assume? It is perfectly true that we struck up an acquaintanceship here. Quite desultory, but we had much in common. Of course I am twice his age." Her gracious tone added, And therefore twice as intelligent. "You wanted to know about his background? He is rather a lonely man, you know, and I had encouraged him to talk. At one time I was quite interested in psychological therapy. That was after I had toyed with hypnotism and that colossal fraud Freud." Her diction was faultless. "I can tell you something, I believe. Mr. Trumbull came from a small town called Earlville, Illinois. He—"

"His birth certificate says Chicago," said Palliser respectfully.

"Ah, yes. I was about to say, his parents died in an accident when he was just a child and he was raised by an aunt in Earlville. He attended public schools there and later worked as a bookkeeper at a local department store, Fairfield's. After his aunt died, when he was thirty-one, he went to Chicago and there he worked, also as a bookkeeper, at an office-supply and stationers', Cameron's. He had never been married. Nor did he smoke. He—"

"Excuse me, Miss Dawson, but are you quite sure of all this? He told you this in all this detail—"

Miss Dawson regarded Grace severely. "I was sorry for the man, sir. I said I had encouraged him to talk. And I assure you I have an excellent memory. I am interested in individuals always, in the individual experience. And I must say I find it quite impossible to believe that Mr. Trumbull would be capable of any action which would excite the interest of the police. I am aware that we have an excellent police force here, and I should not dream of accusing you of—"

"She had it all at her fingers' ends," said Grace amusedly. "Spry old lady. Bright old lady. A very—" he paused and smiled—"gallant old lady. Poor as all get out—darns in her stockings, and her shoes need resoling, but—still liking life. Life and people."

"And," said Palliser, "she gives us all this—for whatever the hell it's worth—"

"It's what he told her," said Grace.

"Names and dates yet—he went to Chicago in 1951—"

"So we check it out," said Mendoza. "Earlville. There must be some police there. All we can do is ask. And at this place in Chicago—"

"Cameron's. Stationers' supply, on State Street. I noticed that in what he gave the State Employment Agency. But when it seemed he'd just been putting on an act, all that was probably phoney. But I ask you," said Hackett. "Where are we if it does check out?"

"It won't," said Grace. "He was feeding her a line. An act. I still say—"

"We now have," said Mendoza, "something from the Phoenix boys. That postcard on the pseudo-Trumbull. It seems that one Mr. Leonard Farbstein rented a small cottage at the rear of his own home to Trumbull from September of last year to April of this. Trumbull said he'd come west because of incipient TB, but he couldn't find a full-time job in Phoenix and didn't much like it anyway—said he was used to a bigger city now—and he left in April to come over here."

There was a silence. "I tell you," said Grace, "he was putting over an act. He was running from *something*, lying low, and—wait a minute, something's coming— No, he hadn't been planning any murder and substitution, but say he ran across somebody—the corpse—he saw could be a substitute for him. All the better. Q.E.D. and exit Trumbull. He's now in Acapulco or Buenos Aires. I tell you, if that rigmarole of Earlville, department store, Chicago, stationers', poor orphan and all checks out good as gold, I'll—I'll eat my badge. It's got to be—"

"Careful, Jase," said Mendoza. "Hunches are sometimes duds."

"Well, I haven't got any hunches," said Hackett, "but I'll go along with that. It's plain as—as the nose on Trumbull's face, Luis. If Trumbull wasn't responsible for the corpse passed off as Trumbull—who else could be? Who else had all Trumbull's ID? And if Trumbull is an injured innocent, where the hell is he?"

"I see that," said Mendoza irritably. *"Seguramente qué si.* I just have the irrational little feeling, Arturo, that we're not looking deep enough. . . . All right, all right, I said hunches don't always pay off! Anyway, we'll send a query to this Earlville, we'll ask Chicago to check this Cameron's, and see what shows up. We do have to be thorough. And I'm not taking any bets, boys, because—"

"Lieutenant!" said Lake. "George on the outside line."

Mendoza snatched up the phone. "What's the word, George?"

"Well, he'll be OK," said Higgins. He sounded very tired. "It was touch and go for a while, I gather, but they're saying now he'll make it. The—"

"Thank God for that," said Mendoza unthinkingly. Occasionally he did forget that he was the self-proclaimed agnostic.

"Yes. It'll be a long haul, though. The leg—there'll be therapy, and they aren't sure yet whether there'll be more surgery needed later—"

"*Dios*. But he'll be all right?"

"They say so. A lot of care needed and so on. I talked to Wilcox Street—"

"So did I."

"They've got nothing. No witnesses, no description."

"I heard. So," said Mendoza, "nobody's insurance company paying all the bills."

"That's about it. Well, I just thought I'd let you know. Know you're all—concerned."

"Yes," said Mendoza. "Thanks, George. Give Mrs. Dwyer our regards." He put the phone down and relayed that.

"Well, thank God for some mercies," said Grace seriously. "I suppose we can take up a little collection. She wouldn't be too proud to—"

"I don't think so, Jase. She knows how we all felt about Bert. She wouldn't let George—but a little collection from all of us—" *¡Por Dios!* thought Mendoza, annoyed. It would mean nothing—*nada absolutamente* —to his bank account. The whole bill. The crooked old miser, the canny gambler, ogre-on-the-hearth grandfather, leaving all the gilt-edged stock, the real estate. And Mendoza the dedicated cop staying on the thankless job regardless. The money meant little to him; he had done without it; he enjoyed it, but he could do without it again; it meant the nice things for Alison, the twins—Alison had a birthday coming up, and what should he buy for her? But he couldn't say to Mary Dwyer, take it.

There was such a thing as pride. He swore absently.

"Máiri called this afternoon," said Alison lazily. "She says Janet's coming along nicely and she's 'that homesick for the twins.' She thinks maybe only another month or six weeks, Luis. Thank heaven."

"That's good."

"Not that Dorothy's not efficient—but not like our

Máiri. And thank *heaven* about the little Dwyer boy. That poor woman. I ought to go and see her. Luis— I suppose we can't—"

"No, we can't. You think it hasn't been on my mind, too?"

Alison regarded him amusedly. *"¡Pues hombre!* No. You do work so hard to cover up that awful sentimentality—"

"I am *not*—"

"Oh, please, ma'am—sir," said Dorothy, hovering in the doorway of the living room. "I wanted to ask— if I may—it being to do with the police, I thought Mr. Mendoza, I mean Lieutenant—if I could ask—? You see, Mrs. Spain couldn't get the police officer to *listen*— and it's Carole—you see—"

"What?" said Alison. "Dorothy, what is it you're talking about?"

"The police were there—at the Newhouses'—and Mrs. Spain couldn't get the officer to listen, about Carole—"

"Just sit down and tell me what it's about," said Mendoza. He questioned her, got a few more coherent facts, and said, "Well, it's not my territory. I don't know anything about it, but we're all the same police force and we're supposed to be pretty good. If your friend's mixed up in this in any way, even innocently—"

"Oh, Carole wouldn't do anything wrong, sir! It's just that we don't know where she is—"

"They'll find out about it," said Mendoza soothingly. "If it'll make you any happier, I'll just give them a call in the morning."

"Oh, thank you, sir! Mrs. Spain said it was the one on a Wilcox Street—"

Wilcox Street. The Hollywood precinct. The boys looking at the hit-and-run on Stevie Dwyer. And getting no leads.

"It's just, where *is* she?" said Dorothy miserably.

189

Chapter 14

THURSDAY MORNING was just as clear and cold as Wednesday. Mendoza idly scanned the headlines, stopped for lights on the way downtown: WINTER RESORTS DIG OUT, POWER RESTORED TO MOUNTAIN COMMUNITIES.

He was late; there was a tie-up on the freeway. Hackett was in when he arrived, and Piggott, looking glum, hunched over a typewriter. It was Landers' day off. Palliser was typing a report. Higgins hadn't showed by a quarter of nine, and Hackett said it was all very well to be concerned but now they knew Stevie would be all right George ought to remember he had a job. Mendoza said indulgently that he was probably helping Mrs. Dwyer arrange things—there'd be a lot of details.

He had promised Dorothy to check with Wilcox Street on that business, and was talking to Barth at nine o'clock. "Not my affair, but as I told you this English girl—"

"Yeah," said Barth. "Well, it's a little tangle and we don't know there's anything much to it at all. This Felix Hill—owns a furniture store out on Vermont—comes in with a Mrs. Budd. She manages this apartment on Sunset Plaza. One of Hill's employees and his wife, a Mr. and Mrs. James Newhouse, live there. Or lived. Seems Mrs. Newhouse has recently inherited a lot of money. It's a rigmarole—Hill says Newhouse had told him there was arguing about the money, she wanted to blue it, Newhouse'd never have given into her. So when Hill gets a funny letter from Newhouse saying good-bye, we're going around the world, he smells a rat. Goes up to the apartment, to find out what's up. He says Newhouse'd never have done such a thing, couldn't have written the letter, etcetera. Upshot is, he can't get any answer at the door, so he persuades Mrs. Budd there's something funny, and she opens up for him. And it does look a little funny, there's a big section of carpeting cut out of the living-room rug and what looks like blood on the floor there. It is blood, by the way. Somebody'd tried to wash it, but enough was still there. But the doctor looked and said there wasn't enough there to say arbitrarily anybody'd been killed. Could have been just a fight or something. But no sign of Mr. and Mrs. Newhouse—or this maid they had."

"Funny indeed," said Mendoza.

"But as far as the maid goes, we don't think she comes into it, because all her things are gone. From what's obviously the servant's room. So probably she left, or got fired, before whatever happened did happen. Of course we'd like to locate the Newhouses— damage to the apartment and so on—but it's just a funny little tangle."

"So, thanks," said Mendoza. "Nothing on the hit-run?"

"Not a smell."

Mendoza talked to Alison briefly; she could pass that on to reassure Dorothy. As he put the phone down, Lake looked in. "You've got a new one. The Odeon Hotel on Hill."

"So here we go again." Mendoza got up resignedly. "I wish all the amateurs and pros would act more like the paperbacks, Jimmy, and let us clear up one thing all nice and neat before pulling another. Come on, Art, let's go look at it."

Everything was being handled very discreetly at the Odeon Hotel. No crowds, just the black-and-white police car in the yellow taxi zone outside, a uniformed man at the desk, presumably his partner with the body, and an irritated manager.

"Why do people have to come to hotels to commit suicide?" he asked Mendoza resentfully. "This is a good hotel. We don't like notoriety. It's the eighth floor—the maid found her when she went in to clean. The key was in the door, so she naturally thought—"

They went up and looked. They had gone together, over the years, to look at too many scenes like that. The neat hotel room, the suitcase, the clothes draped over chairs, and the woman in the bed, straight and very quiet—a young woman in a pretty blue nylon nightgown: a woman carefully made up with mascara and lipstick, for death. And propped on the dressing table, an envelope addressed "To Mom and Dad."

Mendoza took out the note and read it. It was a rambling, incoherent letter full of despondency. "Nobody loves me," he said, and put the note back in the envelope.

There was a handbag on the desk. They looked in it and found a woman's billfold, with plentiful identification for Jane Cummings of 241 Crowder Street, San Diego. The ambulance arrived about then, and Mendoza asked the internes, "Does it look to you the way it looks to me? The sleeping pills."

"Probably," said the older interne. "They will get hold of 'em. O.K. to take her?"

"Take her."

They went downstairs and looked at the register. She had registered as Jane Cummings yesterday afternoon.

It was all straightforward, just some more paper work. They went back to the office and Mendoza got on the phone to the San Diego force while Hackett typed up the initial report. He said to Palliser, rolling the forms in, "Suicide. Girl. A Jane Cummings."

"It really is?" asked Palliser, looking up.

"Down, boy," said Hackett. A while ago, Palliser had had a hunch and put in some dogged legwork to show a rigged suicide was really murder. "This one really is. Scouts' honor."

Piggott rolled his triplicate report out of the typewriter and said, "Nothing in from the R.C.M.P. yet. Do they use dog sleds? And look, if the body is this Shields, I can't figure how he came to get taken off down here. Of course, they said he had lived here— he might know some people here, I suppose."

"Grace would tell you not to argue ahead of your data," said Hackett.

"And where is our bright boy?" asked Palliser.

"Court. That Sam Keller's being arraigned."

"Oh, sure—I'd forgotten. I've had a kind of bright idea myself," said Palliser. "I'm going to check out. On Trumbull."

"Don't mention the name to me. Talk about will-o'-the-wisps," said Hackett.

There was no sign of Higgins yet.

Palliser's bright idea had to do with the U.S. mails, and possibly it had come to him in consequence of the doings in Echo Park yesterday. Last year's murder in Echo Park had been substantially unraveled by the chance memory of a mailman; so Palliser went down to the main post office, asked and was told which branch post office served the area where Trumbull's former apartment was, and went down there.

It took time, and patient explanation and showing of the badge, but by ten-thirty he had tracked down the mailman, who was walking his route, and persuaded him to take a few minutes off sitting in Palliser's car answering questions.

The mailman's name was Anthony Roubideaux and

he was conscientious. "I got to cover my route. You can see all the mail I still got to get rid of. Listen, who remembers all the names? Addresses we go by. And down here, people moving—"

"You can take a few minutes," said Palliser. "Your boss said so. This was kind of a funny name, Trumbull." He added the address. "Do you remember anything at all about him? What kind of mail he got? He was there nearly eight months. Did he get letters from back east?"

Being conscientious, the mailman cogitated. "Trumbull. I remember the name—it *is* a funny name, but there're plenty of those. I don't remember about any letters. Whether he got any or none. So probably he didn't get a lot, even if there were some. Wait a minute. I do remember—just last week—I'm pretty sure the name was Trumbull—I had a C.O.D."

"You did?" Palliser felt a little excited. "For Garvin Trumbull?"

"Yeah, I'm pretty sure it was that name and that apartment. Yeah. . . . Now, mister, how'd I remember where the C.O.D. was from? I collected the money and he signed the form and that was that. But I'm sure that was the name."

"Well, thanks," said Palliser. He was pleased. A little break at last? On the elusive Mr. Trumbull. He went back to the branch post office, exhibited authority and asked cooperation. The clerks were patient, and got interested in the hunt. After half an hour they turned it up for him—the carbon C.O.D. form signed by the consignee.

The C.O.D. had been for five-ninety-five, and the other address was the Sho-Mart Enterprises with an address out on Chandler Boulevard in North Hollywood.

Still hopeful of a break—at least a little new information about Trumbull—Palliser went back to the Rambler, got on the right freeway and drove out to North

Hollywood. Sho-Mart Enterprises was not a retail business; it was a big warehouse, and Palliser had a little time locating anybody in authority. He was passed from clerk to clerk—"L.A. *police*? What on earth you want here? Nothing wrong here—" until at last a harassed-looking little tubby man named Reynolds appeared.

"Police, hey? Well, I don't know what we can do for you, we're all too damn busy to be getting into police trouble, but whatever I can do. You ever have anything to do with the mail-order business?"

"No, sir."

"Don't," advised Reynolds. "Just don't. Bedlam—plain bedlam. Never a day when there isn't a snafu of some sort. But what do you want with us?"

"A C.O.D.," said Palliser. "A Mr. Garvin Trumbull ordered something from you—" The post office had refused to let him take the carbon, but he had copied down all the information from it.

Reynolds uttered a loud groan. "Oh, my God, you want to trace— My God. We sell *thousands* of things, Sergeant. All over. We advertise in hundreds of magazines— All right, all right, I'll see what I can do. It's local, that should help some. And not so far back. You wait here, have a cigarette, I'd offer you a drink except I've got nothing on the premises, if I had I'd likely be tying one on every day, the problems I got. I'll see what I can do for you."

Feeling pleased with himself, Palliser waited. Half an hour later Reynolds came back with the original order blank. It had been clipped from a rather high-brow men's magazine.

What Trumbull had purchased from Sho-Mart Enterprises was an abdominal belt guaranteed to relieve sacroiliac strain.

Piggott having stayed in the office to write the report and await, hopefully, some reply from the R.C.M.P.,

Glasser was methodically carrying on with the search. Armed with a photograph of the dead man, he was covering the area, block by block, all around the spot where the corpse had been found. Wolfe's clothing store was near the dead end of Wilshire there. Glasser and Piggott had covered that block, two blocks either way on Grand which crossed Wilshire there, and were now working farther afield up Grand and down Wilshire.

Glasser wandered in and out of all kinds of stores—drugstores, men's clothing, a secondhand furniture shop, a health-food store, Chinese imports, a liquor store, two women's dress shops (unlikely but you had to be thorough), a secondhand bookstore, a gifts and novelties shop with the most Godawful collection, he privately thought, of cheap ceramics and other junk he'd ever seen, a bar, a hole-in-the-wall malt shop, a record shop, a pawnshop, a hardware store. He was getting very tired of the repetitious questions and answers.

"Have you seen this man recently? Here, or around?"

"No, I can't say I have. Of course this isn't a very good photograph. He looks sort of dead."

Corpses seldom do take flattering photographs.

It was about eleven-thirty when he went into a shop on Grand Avenue, just past Tenth Street. It was a place called The Haunted House, and displayed in the little window was an arrangement of items which made Glasser feel even more tired. He didn't lay any claim to being a highbrow, but at about the age of twelve he had outgrown the notion that coercing somebody to sit on a cushion that emitted a loud vulgar raspberry, or inviting somebody to smell the boutonniere that squirted water, was sidesplittingly funny. And that was the kind of thing the shop sold. Hundreds of items like that. When Glasser went in, nobody appeared immediately to wait on him, and he had time to look around. There were rubber snakes in fancy gift boxes (Guaranteed to Startle the Ladies!) and plastic skull caps (See How You Will Look When It's All Gone—Startle Your

Wife!) and a pair of inflatable female legs (Put Under Sofa or Bed, Alarm Your Friends) and a fake hand to drape over a toilet bowl or somewhere—that was the illustrated suggestion—and fun-filled toilet paper printed with the suggestive quotations, and wind-up mice and rats and lizards, and a hundred other such jollities of adolescence, along with the cheap skull-and-crossbone rings, the plastic skull ash trays, and loaded dice, and Easy Magic Tricks to Startle Your Friends.

It occurred to Glasser that in all likelihood anyone who patronized the place much would soon have no more Friends to Startle; but that wasn't his business.

"Can I help you, sir?" The proprietor, appearing suddenly, was a genial little man with a naked-looking bald head.

"I hope so," said Glasser. He displayed his badge and hauled out the photograph. "Have you ever seen this man? Recently? In here, or somewhere else?"

The man took the photograph and held it close for study. "My goodness, I've never had the police in here before! I've been here nearly ten years, and never any trouble. There was a hold-up in the bar across the street once but it was after I'd closed for the day. This man? In here? Now let me take a good look and be sure. It's not such a good photograph, is it? He doesn't look alive, some way."

"He wasn't," said Glasser shortly.

"Oh, really? My goodness. Well, it's difficult—the expression—but there's something— Wait, now, let me think— Yes! Yes, it *is* the same man, yes, I'm quite sure it was, now I look closer."

"He *was* in here?" Glasser was surprised.

"He was." The little man was triumphant. "And I'll tell you how I remember as clearly as I do. It was last Saturday—no, Friday. Yes, Friday. I'd never seen him before. I have some regular customers, of course. And casuals who come in now and then. But this man was new. And I remember because it seemed he'd never

197

been in a place like this before, or seen anything like the little novelties I carry." The proprietor beamed on Glasser. "And I can tell you what he bought, too. He was quite fascinated with it—he laughed and laughed, just like a kid. It was one of those trick drinking glasses that dribble down your chin. He was terribly pleased with it. In fact, I was a bit surprised to see a man his age—"

Glasser stared at him. This was a twist. But he pulled himself together and took down the proprietor's name, asked more relevant questions.

He decided to go back to the office and consult with Matt about this, see if the R.C.M.P. had come through. But when he got back to his car, he found Piggott just walking up to it from the other direction.

"I figured you'd be heading back about now. It's noon," said Piggott. "The R.C.M.P. finally woke up and answered us. They haven't got Shields' prints. They're sending us the best available photograph of him."

"Oh," said Glasser. "Well, I just came up with something, Matt. But it's the funniest damn thing—" He told Piggott about The Haunted House and the drinking glass that dribbled.

Piggott's thin, normally morose face looked even glummer than usual. "That kind of thing," he said. "Very unfunny. The practical jokes. I don't like practical jokes, Henry."

"Neither do I," said Glasser. "I agree a hundred percent, Matt. But it does seem funny that he should have been in that place—" he paused. "Well, we don't know anything about him, of course. I suppose it's no funnier than if—"

"We know something about him now," Piggott pointed out. "We know he was the kind who thought it was a great big funny joke to give you a glass that dribbles down your chin when you drink out of it.

That we know, Henry. If the man was sure about the picture."

"That's right. And he was. But I ask you, Matt—" Glasser paused again.

"I know, I know," said Piggott. They both tried to visualize Rodney Shields, a rape-murderer and robber from the fairly civilized city of Vancouver, B.C., as an adolescent-minded innocent who thought dribbling drinking glasses were funny.

Well, he might be, at that. People did come all sorts.

"So we know now," said Palliser disgustedly, "that Trumbull has sacroiliac trouble! Big deal. I really thought for a while there—"

"*Así, así*," said Mendoza. "These things happen. We have to explore every avenue. As the old saw goes. It was an idea, John." He finished his steak sandwich and the waiter drifted up to refill his coffee cup.

"He must have been putting on an act," said Hackett. "Nobody could be so damned colorless. And besides—"

"Who but Trumbull could have presented the corpse with the nice ID? Yes," said Mendoza, "but I still have a funny little feeling, Arturo, that we're looking at it the wrong way round."

"What other way is there to look at it?" demanded Palliser.

Mendoza said, *"No se la respuesta.* I just feel—"

"*I* feel," said Palliser, "damn sorry I ever heard of Garvin Trumbull."

"Wait for the message from Chicago," counseled Hackett. "That'll tell the story."

They went back to the office from Federico's, and found that Jason Grace, returned from the arraignment of Sam Keller, had apparently been bitten by the same bug that notoriously attacks housewives in spring. He was on his knees in the midst of musty, dusty stacks of paper, before a file case tucked away in one corner of the sergeant's office.

"And what the hell are you doing?" asked Hackett, staring.

Grace looked over his shoulder. "Research. Just being thorough. We had a little while to wait while His Honor worked through all the divorce hearings, and a fairly bright idea came to me."

"They sometimes do," conceded Hackett. "What?"

"Well, we said that Trumbull is running from something. O.K. But by what we have found out, he's been on the run for at least a year ago in September, right? I just thought, suppose we have a look at all the old flyers and Wanteds, up to a couple of years back. In case we had something on him, once, from somewhere, a while back, and just forgot about it in the press of business since."

Hackett said thoughtfully that was quite an idea, and offered to help him look.

About then the San Diego police called Mendoza back to say that the Cummingses had been contacted; Jane Cummings had spent some time, on and off, in private sanatariums and was known to be a manic depressive. The father was coming up to claim the body.

And Hackett and Grace hadn't come up with any possible old Wanteds, half an hour after that when Mendoza summoned them all into his office. He was looking amused and irritated at once. "So, I said I had the funny feeling. And where do we go from here? Just look at these."

Chicago had got on the ball. That force was pretty good these days, since its reformation. They had checked. And sure enough, Garvin Trumbull—description adding up to just what L.A. gave them—had indeed worked at Cameron's, the big stationers' supply house, from 1951 to 1966. He'd been very highly thought of. A steady and valued employee. He had quit for reasons of health and gone West. And he'd originally had a recommendation from a department store, Fairfield's, in Earlville, Illinois.

"Oh, I don't believe it," said Grace. "I don't—"

"Don't believe it some more." Mendoza handed him another teletype.

Earlville, Illinois (population 1420) had evidently been agitated by the query from the big city. It had replied at length, through its Chief of Police, Dennis R. McCleary. Garvin Trumbull was indeed known in Earlville. He had grown up there, living with his aunt, the late Mrs. Hattie Spencer. He had attended the public schools, a fine boy, good record, and afterward been employed at a local store, Fairfield's, up until 1951 when on the death of his aunt he had gone to Chicago. Mrs. Spencer's estate had come to him, a small amount of savings and a house in Earlville, which he had retained and rented out. It was presently rented to Mr. and Mrs. Joseph Ayer, and they paid rent direct to Trumbull. Trumbull had kept up a correspondence with several old friends in Earlville, and the latest address they had for him was such-and-such—the apartment here. And why were the L.A. police interested in Trumbull? Was he in trouble? Had anything happened to him?

Earlville, Illinois, was concerned about Trumbull, still one of its own.

"I don't believe it," said Grace. "He couldn't be for real. He couldn't."

"I can't believe it," said Hackett. "It doesn't make sense, Luis! Who else but Trumbull could have provided the corpse with the ID? But this genuine Trumbull hadn't any reason to—"

"Any reason we know," said Grace doggedly.

"Don't cling to convictions that don't check," said Mendoza. "It's all very funny, but by this Trumbull is nothing but the respectable upright citizen. Even as your Miss Dawson said. But where the hell is he?"

"Oh, for God's sake!" said Hackett. "Nothing makes sense about this at all!"

Grace went home that night and told Virginia they had the damnedest funniest case ever since he'd been at Homicide.

"Even funnier than that thing with all the coffins?" asked Virginia interestedly.

"Well, in another kind of way—"

Palliser went home and told Roberta they had the *damnedest* queer case. "Nothing makes sense about it. It's—"

"So tell me about it," said Roberta, a wise bride, and listened absorbedly.

Hackett went home and said this was the damnedest thing he'd ever run across. There was no *shape* to it, as a crime.

"I expect you'll work it out," said Angel. *"Don't* wake the baby, Art! I just got her to sleep."

"I won't, I won't." Mark Christopher demanded attention, helpfully bringing Daddy the evening paper. "Thanks, son." Hackett glanced at the headlines— SNOWED-IN RESORTS DIG OUT—POWER RESTORED. It had been quite a storm. "It's just, it seems impossible that Trumbull—and on the other hand, all this evidence that he *is* a respectable citizen— What's for dinner?"

"I do try," said Angel. "All your low-calorie things —but it's so *dull*. Pot roast and wild rice for you, *au gratin* potatoes for the rest of us, and asparagus with Hollandaise sauce only you can't have that, of course, and—"

"Oh, hell," said Hackett.

"Don't swear in front of Mark. And a chocolate *mousse* only you can't—"

"Don't tell me, don't tell me," said Hackett.

202

Mendoza went home and told Alison it was the damnedest queer thing in the last year or so. Every now and then, of course, Homicide got the queer things. And had she any preference about what he got her for her birthday?

"Well," said Alison, "I've been thinking about having my ears pierced. You know I'm always terrified to wear the really good earrings, for fear of losing one. I really think I will. So I'll be needing a new wardrobe of earrings. *Costume* earrings, Luis. And you can have all the good ones—the diamonds and emeralds—changed for pierced ears."

"*Bueno.* Whatever you say." And at that moment Dorothy came running down the hall.

"Oh, ma'am—sir! Please come see! It's on the early news—the telly—about Carole! Just at the beginning they announced about it—they tried to *murder* her—it said—"

"What?"

"I *told* you Carole'd never have just gone off—"

They followed her down to the den. The early evening news had just begun, and the confident trained voice of the newscaster was rising.

"One of the strangest and most sensational stories of the recent five-day storm raging over Southern California was revealed today, as power was restored to many Forest Ranger stations and resort lodges in the Angeles National Forest and other mountain regions. A young English woman, Miss Carole Leslie, was rescued last Monday by Ranger John Wilkerson, as the blizzard started. As the area has been snowed in and all power off since then, only today was it revealed that Miss Leslie has averred that her life was attempted by an unidentified man and woman who abandoned her in the Jackson Lake area as the storm was beginning. It is understood that the police have been informed and enquiries begun. Here is Miss Leslie with

Ranger Wilkerson, who was interviewed this afternoon by your correspondent—"

"There she *is!*" said Dorothy. "Carole! Of all things—"

"—Darndest thing I ever did see," the big ranger was saying: a good-looking wide-shouldered young man, handsome in his uniform. "This buck, he'd evidently nosed around her where she'd fainted, and her head scarf caught on his antlers. When he showed up at the station, regular feeding time, with a lady's head scarf, I figured there might be somebody in trouble, and I took the dogs and went out looking, and found her. Must say she's been a nice guest to be snowed up with, the other boys and I all said."

"Miss Leslie's allegations are being investigated," said the newscaster earnestly. "We will be right back with more up to the minute news after this message." A commercial flashed on and Alison turned down the sound.

"Imagine!" said Dorothy. "I just knew something had happened. Trying to *murder* her—"

The English maid. Barth's funny case, thought Mendoza. Funny indeed, if they—what was the name, the Newhouses—tried to murder the maid. Murder? The maid? A very funny way to try it.

Barth would be busy. Almost as funny a case, thought Mendoza, as the little tangle about Trumbull.

Chapter 15

MENDOZA GOT to the office a little late on Friday morning. There was an overnight report from Galeano: a new one, woman beaten to death over on Ducommun, and the neighbors claimed the husband had done it, but he wasn't to be found. Grace was just going out to requestion the neighbors and look for him.

It was Palliser's day off, and also Sergeant Lake's. Sergeant Farrell was sitting at the desk in the ante-room, working a crossword. Landers was waiting for Jane Cummings' father, who had an appointment to be here at nine, to be escorted down to the morgue to go through the formalities.

Piggott was patiently waiting for the R.C.M.P. to come through again.

Of Higgins there was no sign at all. "Damn it," said Hackett to Mendoza, "what's he doing? What is there to do for her now we know the boy's going to be all right?"

"He's got a little leave coming," said Mendoza absently. He was trying to remember, from the insurance itemization, how many pairs of what Alison called good earrings there were. His grandmother hadn't gone in much for earrings. There was a diamond pair, and a sapphire pair, and an emerald pair, but that was all he could call to mind. He quite saw Alison's point: with pierced ears, no danger of losing earrings. He just might, for her birthday—

"What are you woolgathering about? Listen, Luis, I've had a little idea on Trumbull. He must be somewhere. That report from his home town said he'd kept in touch with people there. Could we ask that Chief of Police to ask *them,* who did he know here. Well? We haven't run across anybody who did, but he must have known *some* people better than he knew Daly or the waitress—"

"It's an idea," agreed Mendoza; and Sergeant Farrell buzzed him and said Wilcox Street was on the line. "O.K., Rory." He reached for the outside phone. "That's another funny one—did you pick up the early news on channel five last night?"

"No," said Hackett, and simultaneously Sergeant Barth spoke in Mendoza's ear.

"I heard your funny tangle has—mmh—escalated," said Mendoza. "The English maid rescued by the bold rangers."

"God, yes," said Barth. "What a tale. She claims they've murdered Newhouse, though there's no proof at all. Says they held her prisoner because she walked in unexpectedly and saw a lot of blood on the carpet."

"They being Mrs. Newhouse and a boyfriend?"

"Oh, yes. The husband's half-brother, incidentally. Well, whatever the truth of the matter is, she tells it straight enough how the man tried to brain her up there and finally just abandoned her hoping she'd freeze to death. Which I suppose she might well have, except for the rangers. So we'd like to talk to him about that, at least—but they've disappeared by now. God knows in what direction. And I don't think they'll be wandering around down on your beat, but we're getting some flyers made up and passing on the relevant descriptions all around. So. The female Newhouse—Evelyn—is about five-five, thin, thirty-five or so, bleached blonde, blue eyes, likes fluffy clothes and wears a good deal of jewelry. The man is five-eleven, about thirty-eight, medium build, brown hair, no make on eye color, clean-shaven, dresses fairly well. We don't know what he's driving—or was—but I've got a query in to the D.M.V. The Newhouses had a car—one used to drive the girl up to the mountains—a Caddy 1965, white, a four-door. That's all we've collected so far."

"Yes. What's the man's name?" Mendoza took it down as Barth gave it to him. "O.K. Yes. Did he have a job anywhere? Oh, really. Which state employment agency, not that it— Oh, really. Down here."

"Why?" asked Barth. "You think—"

"I don't know," said Mendoza. "Thanks, I'll spread the word in case. Try to cover the Union Station?"

"Oh, hell," said Barth, "the last anybody saw of them was last Monday."

"Mmh. Probably a waste of time. O.K." Mendoza hung up, swiveled around in his chair, and said meditatively, "Now why does that ring a little bell in my head, Arturo?"

"What?"

"One Harry Melvin, a civil servant at the state employment agency on—"

Hackett stared. "It rings a bell because I'd mentioned his name to you. His last name—I never heard his first. If that's him, and I don't suppose there'd be two Melvins in the place. I thought he'd been playing hookey from his job. Why is Wilcox Street interested in him?"

"Playing hookey," said Mendoza. "Oh, that you can say. Why did you—"

"What's he been up to?"

"Attempted murder at least." Mendoza lit a cigarette. "Why did you mention him to me?"

"Attempted— Because he was the clerk there who interviewed Trumbull," said Hackett. "He was the— what the hell, what's he done?"

Mendoza told him. "I suppose Barth has seen the

manager of that— *¡Diez millón demonios desde el infierno!* The clerk who—"

"But how—but what could— Wait a minute," said Hackett. "He saw Trumbull—but what's that got to do with—"

"*¡Carape!*" said Mendoza excitedly. "*¡Paso!* Now wait—almost it's coming to me—I *said* we were looking at it the wrong way round! *¡Como no!* He saw Trumbull—Trumbull coming in all innocent for a job —and he saw—"

Hackett stared at him. "If I'm following you right—"

"That says that he—or they—had murder on the mind already. Must have. And he spun Trumbull some tale—you know, Art, I'm afraid we'll never get to meet the elusive Mr. Trumbull. Now. I wonder if he tried the same game as he did with the English maid?"

"What was that? I didn't—"

"In a minute. I'm trying to see— Rory, get me Sergeant Barth at Wilcox Street. Tell him I think we've got a big piece of his case down here. . . . But the blood on the rug, I think, was unforeseen. Mr. Melvin seems to be astute only up to a point. He grasped one principle of safely committing homicide very well, but it was still a stupid effort altogether. *Está muy pagado de sí.* I think that was a little contretemps—he'd probably planned on actually killing the man away from home. And then the English maid— Mmh, very awkward."

"You're way ahead of me," said Hackett. "This is the husband? Divorce is simpler."

"That's where the stupidity comes in," said Mendoza raptly. "And how stupid he was—all this litter of leads behind him, and I expect we'll come across more— once we've made the right connection. And even without the English maid, the connection would have been made. Sooner or later. What with the Newhouses vanishing from all ken—and some people undoubtedly know of the relationship between Melvin and Newhouse—"

"Just who is this Newhouse?"

"The husband. The— And, *Dios,* of course, the first thing to do—"

"Wilcox Street, Lieutenant."

Mendoza picked up the phone. "Barth? Come to Papa. We've—"

"I'm *busy*," said Barth. "What the hell you want?"

"We're going to be busier," said Mendoza. "Due thought and rumination tells us that your funny little case fits right into a funny little case we've been trying to unravel. 'And he told a tale.' Kipling. I would a tale unfold. Here is a corpse with a lot of nice identification on it, beautiful genuine identification, for one Garvin Trumbull. At first we thought he was tied in with the B-girls, but we dropped that idea. And he was identified, Barth—by a casual acquaintance, but identified. Then when—"

"Look, I'm busy."

"Just listen. When we got the autopsy report, it was all wrong for Trumbull. By his past history. So we leaped to the natural suspicion that Trumbull was the villain, because who else could have supplied the genuine identification? And then it comes to light only yesterday that Trumbull is a genuine upright first-class respectable citizen, only the harmless bookkeeper he seemed to be. Naturally we have gone around on the legwork on Trumbull, and—"

"Look—"

"So now you come up with Melvin. Mr. Harry Melvin, who worked at the state employment agency and was the clerk who interviewed Trumbull when he went there to look for a job. A week ago last Wednesday."

"Oh," said Barth. "But what does that—"

"So I jump to more suspicions. Such as that Mr. Melvin is smart just so far. When you get a murder, Barth—a private kill, all cozy, in a house or apartment—who do you look at first and closest?"

"The relations, naturally. Wives and—"

"*Es verdad.* That, Mr. Melvin saw. I think. I also think I will admit coincidence only so far, and say that there was murder on Mr. Melvin's mind before he laid eyes on Trumbull. But when he did— Have you got a description of Newhouse?"

"Why, sure. Why? It's just the girl keeps saying they must have done something to Newhouse—he could have—"

"Tell me," said Mendoza, "by any chance, does Newhouse happen to be about forty-five, brown hair turning gray, five-ten or thereabouts, thin, with a great big beak of a Roman nose?"

"What th*e hell?*" said Barth. "How'd you know that? That's just what he—"

"Yes. I thought so," said Mendoza. "I really did. I think we'd better get together for a conference. And I also think you had better bring Newhouse's employer —what was his name—down here to the morgue *pronto.*"

"You think you've got—"

"I'm taking bets on it," said Mendoza. "Come and see."

Felix Hill looked at the body in the morgue tray and said quietly, grimly, "That's James Newhouse. I knew him for twenty years, and that's him. Jake Artz could say, too. So that fool bitch of a wife did for him at last, if she didn't kill him herself—or drive him into a heart attack like I always said she would. Not that he complained—he opened up a little to me, to Jake—silly damn woman, selfish as all get-out. James was a quiet fellow—sensible. When she inherited all that money, he was all for the safe investments, you know—and he'd have argued her around in the end. Only you say this other fellow was at her, too? James' half-brother." He nodded once, grimly. "And I'd heard this and that about him, too. James worked for me for twenty years.

We were friends. I remember about ten years back he was worried to death—this Harry Melvin'd got into trouble, stealing from the guy he was working for then, and I made James a loan so he could pay it back— the fellow agreed not to prosecute if he got his money. Melvin working for the state lately? I can't figure how he got that job, he'd been in trouble before, too, when he was a kid, James said."

"So," said Mendoza thoughtfully, "Newhouse could have made trouble for Harry on his job. If, say, he found Harry fooling around with Mrs. Newhouse—"

"*And* he would have. James was a quiet fellow but he wasn't weak. He'd told me he hoped Harry was straightened out, with a steady job—but it looks as if the money was just too much temptation for Harry. With that woman—well, of course I've met her. Know her. One of those weak-as-water please-don't-beat-me females. *Anybody* could manage her," said Hill. "I suppose Harry saw that as long as James was around he hadn't a hope of touching the money. The root of all evil, like it says."

"No, not money, Mr. Hill," said Mendoza. "The love of money. . . . If you'll come back to my office you can make a formal statement on all this."

Palliser called in about two-thirty. "I was just curious to know if anything else has shown on Trumbull. That *is* the—"

"Oh, my," said Sergeant Farrell, "what you're missing! Yes, it's broken. Very funny indeed. Witnesses right and left—we've just had the prettiest little English girl you ever saw—blonde. Cute. Luscious, I tell you. And the body's identified—not the latest one, but the one everybody thought was Trumbull at first—and he's probably dead, too. But I can't keep the line open to—"

"What? Listen, I might come in—"

"Oh, brother, is he the dedicated cop. With a bride of two months at home—"

The R.C.M.P. photograph of Rodney Shields arrived at noon by special delivery. It wasn't a very good photograph, but it was good enough to show that Rodney Shields definitely wasn't the man who had laughed so heartily over the dribbling drinking glass.

"You know, Henry," said Piggott, "this is sometimes a very discouraging job."

"I believe you, Matt," said Glasser. "Now where do we look?"

"It doesn't seem possible," said Piggott, "this year of our Lord when every petty bureaucratic agency on every side is collecting the personal information, the fingerprints and Social Security numbers and credit ratings and all, that anybody can still be so anonymous as to die and not get identified somehow. By some means. But it does still happen, now and then."

"And I guess this is one of the times," said Glasser.

"It looks that way, Henry. I wonder if we could get the papers to run his picture. Somebody might remember him. From somewhere."

"Over in Beverly Hills," said Glasser, "buying a rubber snake to startle his lady friends. I don't see what else we can do on it, Matt. . . . This is quite a thing about that Trumbull bit, isn't it? The Lieutenant's pleased as hell."

"Which makes it a good time," said Piggott, "to ask him to stash the corpse in the Pending file, Henry."

"You're right, Matt," said Glasser. But before he could do so, Grace came in busily and said he could use some help on this new one if they hadn't anything else to do, and what was all the excitement going on in Mendoza's office?

"Oh, my, what you missed," said Piggott, and started to tell him about it.

They had just taken a formal statement from Carole Leslie and Mendoza and Hackett had gone downstairs to shepherd her into the squad car which would take her back to her motel. They came back to the Homicide office to find two strangers waiting in the anteroom. Sergeant Farrell was looking excited. "Lieutenant—"

Mendoza looked at the smaller man and uttered a loud gasp. "*¡Caramba! ¡No puede ser!*"

The man looked at him doubtfully and then amusedly —a thin man about forty-five, dressed neatly in a gray suit which seemed to have been wet and roughly dried and pressed; a man with graying brown hair and a great beak of a high-arched Roman nose above a wide humorous mouth. "I've been reading my obituary," he said in a pleasant light tenor voice. "Was sort of disappointed I didn't rate more space. Couple of lines on a back page. It was, like Mark Twain said that time, kind of premature. I'm Garvin Trumbull."

"My God," said Hackett.

"This is Mr. Wall. He drove me down this morning, soon as they'd got the roads clear," said Mr. Trumbull cheerfully. "I've been snowed in, back in Illinois, but never quite so much snowed in as all that. Quite an experience. That fellow sure meant to do me in, all right, but he wasn't just so thorough."

"That seems to be an understatement," said Mendoza. "We're very glad to see you, Mr. Trumbull."

"Mr. Wall figured, and so did I, when we'd sorted it out some, you fellows'd want to hear my story."

"*That's* the understatement," said Hackett. "Come in and sit down. . . ."

"—Naturally I was pleased," said Trumbull, "when Mr. Melvin said he'd got a job for me. I didn't expect it so soon—I'd only been into the agency the day before. I wasn't too worried, I've always got the rent money from my house back in Earlville. He called me at the apartment, and it sounded just the sort of thing I'd like. It wasn't my regular work, but I guess you know I've been sick, wasn't quite up to par, and it sounded fine. He said this fellow he knew owned a nice resort home over on the desert, and wanted somebody to live in it, kind of a caretaker, when he wasn't there—there'd been some vandals around. He'd pay a hundred a month, Melvin said, and if I'd be ready on Saturday morning, give up my place and all, he'd be glad to drive me over there. Well, it sounded fine. I still don't know why Melvin picked *me*. Innocent bystander. Is the fellow crazy, or what?"

"He wanted," said Mendoza, "your nose, Mr. Trumbull. And of course all your nice identification."

"My *nose?* Well, the identification—what did that have to do with it? When Mr. Wall showed me the papers— You see, Mr. and Mrs. Wall own that cabin up there in the mountains, but they don't come up every weekend. Just came up last night, and they were mighty surprised to find me there, and I was mighty glad to see them. But I'm getting ahead of myself. I packed up, and told Daly I was leaving, and met Melvin Saturday where he said—the Union Station."

"Yes. Nice and crowded where nobody would notice," said Mendoza. Hackett and Landers were listening, fascinated.

"He had a car, and we started out. He explained we had to cross over the mountains, to get to the desert— well, I knew that, I'd seen maps. He was friendly as pie—I thought he was a nice fellow. Helpful and all that. Till we got up there. I've just got to figure he's crazy. There'd been a snowfall already—it was real pretty, on the trees, and I was interested in the scenery —I hadn't been up in the mountains here before. Lonely up there, too. Well, he made out he was having trouble with the car, and finally he stopped and got out and raised the hood. Got some tools out. And pretty soon he called out could I come help him, so naturally I got out." Trumbull was enjoying himself, an important person for the first and probably last time in his life. "About the last I remember is getting out of the car. I guess he hit me with something right then— I had quite a lump on the back of my head for a few

214

days. Anyway, the next thing I know I come to lying in the snow back from the road a way, maybe four or five rods, and cold as billy-be-damned. I don't know if he thought I was dead, or just figured I'd lie there till I froze to death. Anyway, he wasn't any place in sight. I managed to stagger up to the road, but there wasn't a car anywhere, and it was starting to snow pretty hard. I tell you, about then I was just feeling flabbergasted. I couldn't make out *what* had happened —why he'd want to do such a thing to me, but I figured, first things first, and I'd better take steps to get out of the little predicament I was in." Trumbull grinned. "I wasn't feeling so good, with that crack on the head, but I managed to start down the road some-how—figured the road had to go somewhere—and when I was just about all in, I come up against this house. The cabin. Along the road there. I had to get under cover somehow, it was really snowing then, so I broke a window—door was locked—and climbed in. And there I've been ever since, till this morning when the Walls showed up. It's their cabin, and thanks to the Lord they keep it stocked with the canned stuff and even water. And firewood. I sat there all snug and tight through that blizzard, and I've never seen such a storm back east, I tell you. It was something. And all the while I kept puzzling about why in the name of goodness that nice fellow Melvin would want to—"

"You were very damned lucky, Mr. Trumbull," said Mendoza. "Very damned lucky indeed. You and Carole Leslie. Yes, Mr. Melvin isn't a very successful murderer, is he? He got one out of three, that's all."

"I would dearly love to know why he wanted to murder *me,*" said Trumbull plaintively. "I'd only seen him once before."

"Well, I'll tell you. He was smart up to a point. He wanted your nose and your nice genuine ID. You see, he had a half-brother with a nose just like yours— and you'd told him you didn't have any relations or

215

close friends out here. He isn't very smart, and he never thought to ask if you had close friends anywhere else. And as for his half-brother—well, that's another part of the story. . . . You see—"

Trumbull listened and said thoughtfully, "Well, I will be damned. He wasn't just so awful efficient, was he? Have you caught him yet? And the woman?"

"We'll catch him," said Mendoza. "Mr. Melvin is not a very big brain. We'll catch him, Mr. Trumbull."

About five-thirty on Friday afternoon, with witnesses still coming and going to make formal statements, Higgins drifted into the office.

"Well, our wandering boy!" said Hackett. "And where have you been? You knew Stevie'd be OK two days ago. How is he?"

"Coming along fine," said Higgins. His craggy unhandsome face wore a vaguely complacent look. "Of course it'll be a long haul. Therapy, maybe more surgery on the leg, a lot of care."

"How's Mrs. Dwyer?" asked Mendoza; hearing Higgins' voice he had looked into the sergeants' office.

"Oh, fine," said Higgins. "Just fine. I'm taking a week off."

They stared at him. "You're—just like that," said Hackett. "A week off." Higgins had not asked about any of the current cases.

"That's right. We're going over to Vegas to get married the easiest way. Only she says in a church. That's O.K. Laura can stay with this girl friend a couple of days," said Higgins. They say Stevie can come home in about ten days, and there'll be a lot to arrange."

Hackett couldn't get his mouth to close. He said finally, "That's— Married? Mrs. Dwyer? You? I mean —well, that's—that's fine, George, but how did you— how the hell did—"

216

"Why, I just *told* her," said Higgins. "I *told* her, that's all. The only practical thing to do, so I can take care of them all. She couldn't go on working, Stevie needing all the care, and she can't live on the pension. It's the only practical thing to do. *As* I told her. So I can take care of them. That's all."

Mendoza began to laugh.

"I don't know what you're laughing at," said Higgins. "It is the only sensible thing to do. Mary saw that. She's a very sensible girl, after all. So I'm taking a week off. I just dropped in to tell you."

Mendoza leaned on Palliser's desk weakly. "*Gracias*, George. We appreciate it. We'll miss you. Congratulations and good luck."

"Well, thanks very much," said Higgins seriously. "I guess it just needed something like this for me to use some sense and *tell* her. I'll be seeing you, boys." He wandered out, and Mendoza exploded in another fit of laughter.

"I will be damned," said Hackett.

"George comes through in a crisis," gasped Mendoza.

"No, but listen, Luis—if he's just sort of browbeaten her into it, because she's worried about the boy—"

"I have met Mary Dwyer," said Mendoza, feeling for his handkerchief. "George didn't browbeat her. He only thinks so. She's a very smart female, Arturo. Even if she was worried about Stevie."

He told Alison about it amusedly over dinner, with the twins shouting in their baths down the hall and the cats parading under their feet. "I *am* glad," said Alison. "It'll be a good thing—if she really wants to marry him."

"She wouldn't if she didn't," said Mendoza succinctly.

"I hope they'll be happy. . . . Máiri called this afternoon, and she says she'll definitely be home next

217

month. . . . But you were going to tell me about Mr. Trumbull's nose."

"Well, it was like this—"

Dot was feeling definitely annoyed with Carole. The little idiot. She hadn't learned a thing about judging people or thinking twice. Talking dreamily about those nice Forest Rangers, and she'd decided to stay here after all—for a while, anyway. "Did I *tell* you, Dot, some man rang up and said he could get me a TV test —he'd seen my picture in the paper, and he said—"

Dot could have slapped her. After all the worry she'd caused. And try to tell her to be careful!

"He said I was very photogenic," said Carole.

On thinking it over, Dot was surprised she *hadn't* slapped her.

On Saturday they located both Harry Melvin's Chevy and Evelyn Newhouse's white Caddy, sold at the same time, last Tuesday, to a used-car lot in Hollywood. The salesman who had bought the cars had overheard them saying something about New York.

On Sunday morning Harry Melvin and Evelyn Newhouse were picked up by the New York police as they were about to board a jet flight to Paris. And Mendoza said sadly, predictable. They were fetched back to L.A. on Monday, and Mendoza got them to question just after lunch.

"So all right, we had bad luck," said Melvin sullenly. Evelyn Newhouse just sat and cried. The weak-as-water female.

"It wasn't bad luck, Melvin," said Mendoza. "It was your stupidity. Your damned stupidity. Amateur or pro, all of you are forever so damn stupid. Because *you* thought James Newhouse was a nonentity, it never crossed your mind that he had friends who were concerned about him. My God, you didn't know enough about him—in your utter self-centeredness—to know he was on first-name terms with his employer! You thought he could just drop out of his daily life, and nobody would notice or investigate. Just send the forged letter to Hill and everybody would airily dismiss the Newhouses as traveling, how nice for them. Just leave the body with Trumbull's ID down here fixed up to look as if he'd been rolled by a B-girl, and nobody would think twice about it. And sure as hell, you didn't know much about *us*, Melvin. You reasoned just fine, up to a point—if you could get the corpse identified as definitely somebody else, you'd never be connected. But you didn't have any notion how thorough an autopsy surgeon is. The corpse only matched Trumbull superficially, on the outside. You'd had murder on your mind before, and when you saw Trumbull walk in that day—with the big nose just like Newhouse's, and roughly the same build—it made a fine plan, didn't it? On the surface. You didn't intend to kill Newhouse at the apartment, did you? Why did you?" He sounded merely interested. Sergeant Lake was taking notes, Hackett and Palliser listening silently.

"I had bad luck," said Melvin, sullen and unwilling. Still bewildered. Still shaken at the retribution arriving, when he'd thought all his clever little planning—Stupid, stupid people, thought Mendoza. Cut out the rug with the blood on it, clumsily try to wash the floor where the blood had come through—didn't they know the police had scientific laboratories? "He came home early, damn it. I was going to persuade him into the car some way, and drive somewhere—we weren't expecting him then. He said he had indigestion, and—"

The heavy meal of Mexican food. Of course.

"I'd just got back from taking Trumbull up there—Saturday afternoon—"

"Lieutenant," said Grace anxiously, "have you warned him?" Grace had just come in. "All the damn rights and privileges—because this won't be admissible if—"

"I've warned him. I've informed him."

"I just thought—"

"So go on, Melvin!"

"He heard Evelyn and me talking, I didn't know he was there, I'd just come in, he was in the kitchen taking some bicarbonate—Evelyn, the damn fool, never said he was there—"

"I didn't have *time,* Harry!"

"—And he came out— It was all the damn bad *luck!*" said Melvin. "I had it all figured out just fine—"

"Not allowing for the innocent witnesses," said Mendoza. "You are a very stupid man, Mr. Melvin. Leaving this plain trail of evidence behind— What, by the way, did you do with the suitcases? Mr. Trumbull's and Miss Leslie's? Just for the record."

"Oh, we couldn't think *what* to do," quavered Evelyn Newhouse. "It was awful—I didn't want to hurt them—I didn't know what Harry meant to do, honestly I didn't—he just said leave it to him and everything'd be fine. I didn't know—"

"You knew he meant to kill your husband, didn't you?"

"Oh—well—we'd talked about it—some, yes, I suppose I knew—James was so *tiresome* about everything—so stodgy! He didn't want me to have *any* fun, but the money was left to *me,* wasn't it? And Harry said—"

"The suitcases," said Mendoza.

"But I didn't want to hurt the others—I didn't know what he was going to do, really—that nice girl, and— Oh, well, we almost forgot they were there in the back of the car—the suitcases, I mean—and *I* suggested— we put them in a couple of those lockers at the bus station in Hollywood—but I never knew Harry was going to—"

Stupid little people, thought Mendoza.

The amateurs and the pros.

And that was it. Hackett took them away.

"You know, Jase," said Mendoza, "it's like that story of Kipling's, isn't it? 'The Wrong Thing.' In Rewards and Fairies. The little lesson that has to tell. The moral of that being—"

Grace grinned, also a devotee of Kipling if not as fanatic as Mendoza, and paraphrased the moral. " 'Anything worth doing is worth doing well.' . . . You taking off early, Lieutenant?"—as Mendoza reached for his hat.

"I guess," said Mendoza, "you can handle whatever comes up in the next couple of hours. . . . I've got a date with a jeweler. Alison wants some new earrings."

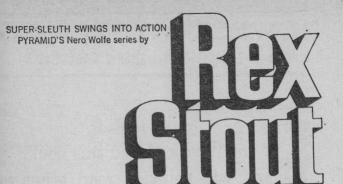